THE RETIREMENT PARTY

THE
RETIREMENT
PARTY

GRAHAM H MILLER

Graham H Miller Cyf

Published by Graham H Miller Cyf

ISBN 978-1-9161307-0-8

Typesetting services by BOOKOW.COM

PART 1

CHAPTER ONE

The beginning of the end, DCI Rob Haines thought. He held two pieces of paper in his hands. One was his notice of promotion to the rank of superintendent, the other was the notice that a new DC, Emma Angel, would be joining his team.

Of course, he knew it wasn't the end. It was the beginning of a role that would see him based in the office. Gone were the days of chasing and arresting villains; now he'd be behind a desk and attending committee meetings and strategy briefings. It was just the end of his life as an active officer.

He picked up a slim personnel file and wandered to the window. By virtue of his rank, he had a proper office, with a window out onto the open-plan area. Even though it was only eight twenty, he saw the figure of Glen Hargreaves, his DI and second in command, making his way across the open-plan office. With a slight nod of his head, he invited him in.

He was settled back behind his desk, leaning back in his chair, when Hargreaves entered. They were as different in looks as they were in personality. Hargreaves was neat and tidy, always looking more like an accountant than a police officer. Haines on the other hand, had run to fat a little and leaning back in his chair accentuated his bulk. He was aware that soon he'd be back in a role where he'd have to wear uniform more often and was taking advantage of the opportunity to look scruffy now.

Hargreaves glanced at the folder Haines was still holding. 'Second thoughts?'

'No, not really. Wait 'til you're this side of the desk.' He rubbed his temples. 'You'll get targets and budgets that you have to meet. Look out there.' He gestured wearily towards the window.

'What about them?' DI Hargreaves twisted round to glance through the window. 'They're a good team, you know that.'

'Yeah, but look at it through HR's eyes. All white and all male.'

'And that's why they've bonded. Anyway policing should reflect the community. Have you been out from behind that desk recently?' Glen asked. 'This is a white town, hell it's more or less a white county. You'd have to go to Bristol for diversity.'

'You won't be able to say stuff like that when you take over.' Haines knew there was diversity in Bradwick if you looked for it. But Hargreaves wouldn't listen. 'You probably won't even be able to think it in five years' time. Anyway, until they manage to get some racial diversity up through the system to CID, this is what we've got.' He held up the personnel file.

'Don't see why we need anyone else. It might just ruin the team dynamic, the ethos.'

'Because,' Haines said slowly, 'we've been given the budget. Soon, I'll be up to superintendent and you'll be running the team. You'll be able to bring up a new sergeant, which'll leave a gap for a detective constable. Be thankful they're giving you the budget for that.' The unspoken hung between them. Hargreaves hadn't been given a promotion. It was fair – CID should be run by an inspector, but it was still a bit of a sting.

'Yeah, I know all that.' Hargreaves turned back to face his boss. 'But what do we really know about her? We don't want to rock the boat.'

Haines steepled his fingers and considered. DC Angel had interviewed very well and the references from her sergeant were good. She'd done well at Hendon and got good marks on all her training courses.

'You know we've both asked around,' Haines said. 'She's a good cop. Everyone says she's a good officer – conscientious, good at crisis management and calming people down. Have you seen her? She's tiny, nothing to her, but the word is that she's the one you want to have your back in a tight spot.'

'Yeah, but what's she actually like? Will she fit in?'

'Well, she's not local – comes from the Midlands, some-where around Nottingham. It's annoying that we can't tap into the Bradwick grapevine like we could with a local, but maybe it'll be a good thing. Breath of fresh air.' What else had he learned? In the years that she'd been here, she'd bought a house, rented rooms to fellow shift workers, mostly colleagues and nurses, and kept to herself. No one knew much about her family, relationships, anything personal.

'So.' Hargreaves pointed to the personnel file. 'How do you want me to play it, boss?'

'What do you mean?'

'Well, we've got a tight-knit team here. How are we going to work this out? We'll need to sound her out. Or do we make sure she leaves?'

'No, no.' Haines shook his head. 'Everything is very politi-cal at the moment. One hint of difficult treatment and there'll be a claim of constructive dismissal. Don't give her the shitty end of the stick but also don't roll out the red carpet. Play it straight up the middle, treat her like one of the team.'

'Totally like one of the team?' Hargreaves gave Haines a knowing look.

'Don't worry about that side of things. I'll take her under my wing for the remainder of my time in charge. By the time I formally hand over to you, we should know where she stands.'

DI Hargreaves nodded. Haines had always planned to han-dle the new recruit personally. Whether or not she worked out, he could act to isolate Hargreaves from any fallout. It would mean that he could start his time in charge with a clean slate.

CHAPTER TWO

Despite nearly five years in the police, DC Emma Angel still couldn't shake the lessons learned in childhood – the police were the enemy. Worse than that, she now had to walk past all the uniformed officers and start her first day in CID. The same plain clothes officers that she'd been taught never to trust since she was a child.

When she was in uniform, she had, paradoxically, felt a freedom in what to wear as she just had to arrive at work and then everything was provided for her. Now, the week before starting her new role, she'd had to abandon her quirky, ethnic style and dress in what felt frumpy and staid to her. But on the plus side, it wouldn't raise any eyebrows and was comfortable enough if she ended up chasing and catching suspects.

She was used to moving around and starting fresh so she wasn't nervous about working with a new team and settling in. But she hated those first few days where she was spinning her wheels and not really contributing.

She was also aware of the ability for an established team to play tricks or haze new recruits. She'd asked around and apparently DCI Rob Haines' team were very tight. They were all friends and hardly any gossip left their office.

She mentally squared her shoulders and prepared to enter the lion's den. She had made her own best guess as to what to wear for her first day in plain clothes. She wore comfortable but smart clothes. Something she could run in but looked good, yet not so good that she would be accused of using her looks to get ahead. The last thing she needed was criticism from either men or women on that front.

Instead of heading to the locker room to start her shift, she made her way to the CID office. It was a large open-plan area with desks interspersed with the usual cabinets, printers, and water coolers.

There was a small office that opened on to one side of the area and in there were two men, who rose to greet her as she walked in. One was tall and broad with curly hair, while his counterpart was average height and looked neat and tidy.

The taller one approached her confidently, hand held out to shake. 'Hi, you must be Emma Angel. I'm DCI Rob Haines, welcome to the team.' He indicated the man standing a pace behind him to the left. 'This is DI Glen Hargreaves. He has the unenviable job of taking over the management of this team when my promotion goes through.'

Hargreaves nodded briefly at her before going back to his desk, a screened-off area in the corner of the open-plan office. DC Angel wondered why he looked so stony-faced – hopefully, it was just that he couldn't wait to take over the reins. She hoped she wouldn't have a boss who had a problem with her from the off.

Soon Haines had installed her at her own desk with a computer and all the usual accoutrements of office work. Finally, he went to a cabinet and returned holding a stack of files.

'Right, here's something to get you started.' He lifted the stack of files slightly, as if she hadn't already seen them. 'This is our main focus at the moment. There's been a spate of violence throughout the poorer areas of town. Look through the files and you'll see that our victims aren't exactly throwing themselves forward and volunteering information. And as for witnesses, well, don't hold your breath!' He let the files drop onto her desk.

She settled down with a strong coffee and a map of the local area. She was fortunate that she'd been posted here as a uniformed officer so she knew the territory. She methodically worked her way through the stack of buff files. After the first five cases, she could see a pattern emerging.

Most of the victims were more used to being on the other side of the law. At first, DC Angel was shocked that the arresting officers had run the victims through the computer, though it did seem like a good precaution as they were all guilty of minor offences. There were cautions for drug possession, breach of the peace, disorderly conduct. It gave a very clear picture and explained why none of those attacked gave statements.

The most comprehensive parts of the files had been completed by the medical professionals who'd treated the victims. She flicked through the sixth file. The victim, Ryan Edwards, was first brought to the attention of the police when concerned members of the public reported him sleeping off his drink in the park off the promenade. When officers attended to move him on, it became obvious that he was seriously injured.

When he woke up in A&E, he was aggressive and abusive. Nonetheless, a report had already been started and more details were added to it. It was obvious that Mr Edwards had taken a kicking. He had several broken ribs and needed a cracked cheekbone reset. However he wouldn't talk to police and discharged himself as soon as he got a good supply of painkillers.

His address was given as a house in Coopers End – one of the dodgier estates on the outskirts of town. DC Angel firmly believed that there shouldn't be any no-go areas for police but she made a mark on the map and decided that it was an area where the police should take caution. They certainly wouldn't go in single-crewed and would make sure they had good reason to be there.

She gamely ploughed on through the reports. She was able to read between the lines and see that all the victims were criminals, however, they all seemed to be on the minor end of the scale. Most of the offences were breach of the peace and possession and nearly every one ended in a caution. Added to this, each of them was marked as known to the police – in other words, they were probably guilty of far more than the records suggested.

She went to get a coffee and think over the implications of what she had just read. The attacks had all the hallmarks of an escalating turf war between drug gangs. Back at her desk, she called up the monthly crime figures, going back over a year. To her surprise, there had been no significant change over the past twelve months.

She frowned and went through the figures carefully. Every month had a good number of seizures of both drugs and the paraphernalia that went with them – weapons and money. But nothing had changed significantly since the attacks started. Usually, a battle over territory would show up as an increase in assaults and seizures of drugs. But the figures were at the same level as they had been for the months before the attacks started.

She shook her head. Her first thought was that maybe vigilantes were trying to clean up the town – a whole group of concerned citizens working to rid Bradwick of its drug problem. Again, the figures didn't bear this out.

She went back to the files of the attacks and looked at the list of victims. None of them had been convicted of dealing or possession with intent to supply, so most likely they were just unfortunate users.

Despite her interest, DC Angel did her best to remember that she'd been put in here as a trainee detective constable. Her job was to process cases, arrest suspects, learn the territory and above all, follow orders. She had moved around a lot as a child and had learned the hard way that no one liked the smart kid coming in and checking everything. She wouldn't win any friends by suggesting a whole new approach based on analysing patterns on her first day in the job. No, the best way to fit into her new team would be to keep her head down and do what she was told.

CHAPTER THREE

DCs Angel and Hobbs sat in the car drinking their coffees, parked up with a good view of the high street. 'Spend the day with DC Steve Hobbs,' Haines had said that morning, her second day in CID. 'Learn the ropes, get a feel for the town, let him fill you in on the current situation.'

She sighed. It was true that Steve Hobbs knew the area well. But he had been a DC for over ten years and had no real interest in moving up, or moving forward. He was, for whatever reason, marking time.

So, DC Angel wasn't really listening to what he was trying to tell her about forming links and cultivating sources. He was being patronising – DC Angel already knew the basics. And she knew that the only way to form relationships with informants was to build personal connections, and that couldn't be taught.

Instead of listening, she was watching the people on the busy high street. Her eyes flicked past people as soon as she understood what they were doing. Two mothers chatting while walking with their children in pushchairs – next. A couple of office workers heading straight to the sandwich shop on their lunch break – next. Teenage, maybe early twenties girl focused on her phone – next. A young man, shaven head, baggy tracksuit trousers and a vest. He wasn't doing anything. DC Angel corrected herself as she studied him – he was doing the same thing that she was, watching the crowd. Scanning them, almost. He might have been looking for someone, but something felt off to DC Angel.

'Hold my coffee,' she said distractedly. Steve turned round to look at his colleague. He frowned at her, looking annoyed. 'Please,' she added. He looked at the cup held in front of him and took hold of it automatically.

DC Angel turned back to Skinny Guy. He was on the move. He was focused, dodging his way past the two mothers, around the end of the queue for sandwiches. DC Angel was looking at the high street and now visualised the street map in her mind. There was the shopping centre further on, a large pedestrian area covered with CCTV and private security. His best escape route was the housing estate behind them and that meant going straight past their car.

'Tall skinny guy, vest and tracksuit trousers. Keep an eye on him,' she said to Steve Hobbs.

'Why?' Steve snapped at her. She didn't blame him. He obviously hadn't wanted to show her the ropes today and she knew how bossy she'd sounded. But, if she was right, she didn't have time right now to answer him.

DC Angel got out of the car and casually leant against it. She didn't wait for Hobbs' reaction, instead she got her mobile phone out and pretended to look at it while watching the skinny man approach the teen who was also on a phone. DC Angel had seen that the teen's handbag was slung over her shoulder and out of sight behind her.

The man was a professional, he walked up behind her, there was a flash of silver in his hand, then the strap was cut and he was starting to move. Angel had to think fast. The weapon was a short craft knife in his right hand, blade inwards, the handbag was tucked under his left. He suddenly put on a burst of speed, and his sporty clothes meant he moved easily.

As he came past DC Angel, she reached out and grabbed the back of his right wrist. He was moving fast and his momentum swung him round into the car. In a second he was face down on the bonnet with his arm stretched out.

DC Angel flexed his elbow back, against the natural direction of the joint. 'Drop the knife now!' He had little choice and the knife clattered to the floor. In one practised move, she swept his arm around, clipped on a handcuff, then gathered up the second and had him restrained.

'Well that was stupid!' DC Hobbs was out of the car and thumped the bonnet in frustration.

'What do you mean?' DC Angel pushed down on her suspect who'd flinched when Steve hit the bonnet. 'You saw him swipe that handbag. Casual muggings like that have been one of our targets on crime reports for weeks.'

'He was armed and you tackled him alone, without your baton.' DC Hobbs spread his arms in exasperation. 'You didn't even caution him or identify yourself as police.'

DC Angel was fed up with his attitude. She was sure she'd been through all the courses more recently than him. In a sing-song, learned by rote voice she said, 'He had a knife out in a crowded public area. I feared for the safety of the public so acted swiftly to contain the threat. As he was running, there was not time to call out or warn him before I acted.'

DC Hobbs frowned at her. She knew she'd gone out on a bit of limb waiting for him to steal a handbag but the result justified the risk.

* * *

Back at the station all hell broke loose. Detective Sergeant Dave Parry was shouting at DC Hobbs. 'Why didn't you recognise him. He's my informant and he should have a degree of protection. That's the deal.'

'By the time I recognised him, she already had him in cuffs over the bonnet. Not much I could do by then.'

DC Angel stood slightly back from the argument. As the new person on the team she didn't want to dive in until she'd figured out the situation.

A dangerous silence fell as everyone in the office realised that the boss was there. He was not just the boss, but DCI Haines, at least two ranks above everyone else there. DC Angel felt her stomach drop. Had she messed up on only her second day?

'Angel.' He barked. She turned to focus on him. 'You saw him lift the handbag. Were you undercover?'

'Undercover? What do you mean, boss?' She wondered what he was playing at.

'Well, what car were you in, how were you dressed?'

'Me and DC Hobbs were in a pool car, sir. Dressed as you see us now.' Their dress code might be best described as office casual.

'Just sat there, in full view?'

'Yes, sir.'

Haines nodded. He turned to DS Parry and DC Angel relaxed slightly. She still hadn't figured out the dynamics so she watched the exchange carefully.

'You'd better have a quiet word with your CI,' Haines said to Parry. 'If he thinks he can go around lifting handbags in full view of two CID officers in a pool car, then he's an idiot. They might as well have been in uniform. Every scrote from here to Bristol can spot one of our unmarked cars, especially with two of our finest officers sat in the front.'

'Yes, sir.' DS Parry paused for a second. 'Sir, what shall I do with him? Caution or charge?'

'It's DC Angel's collar, so it's up to her.'

'Well,' DC Angel played for time. She looked straight at DS Parry. He looked thoroughly pissed off, although she wasn't sure if it was at his informant, at her, or even at his boss. And now Haines had put her in a tricky situation. Should she be a good copper or a team player? 'He is your informant but I didn't know that when I nicked him.' There was an undercurrent to her voice. She would have nicked him anyway, had she known, but she wanted to at least sound apologetic. 'Thanks, sir, but I'll defer to rank and experience. He's your prisoner.' She gave a curt nod to DS Parry. This was the safest course, she thought, chuck the ball straight back to Parry and let him sort out his own mess.

DS Parry said, 'Thank you. I'll go and caution him and tell him to keep his bloody eyes open!' He still looked thunderously angry and the door slammed behind him as he went down to the custody suite to sort it out.

Haines walked back to his office, his mind turning over what had just happened. He was still undecided as to how DC Angel would fit into his team so had tested her. He was pleased that she had chosen to be a team player rather than hanging on to a collar. Lots of rookie detectives would have dug in and demanded that they charge the mugger. She was also canny. Ostensibly she had deferred to DS Parry as her superior, but she'd actually chucked a live grenade back to him. As he walked back to his office, he smiled to himself. DC Angel could play the long game.

He also liked the way she had held up under close questioning and the fact she had given quick straight answers to his questions. He knew however that she would ruffle feathers and upset his other detectives. On the other hand, maybe it was time to go back to basics. Maybe it was time to have a detective who would see a crime being committed and arrest the villain. Sometimes you could overthink and be too political.

This was part of his long-term plan – he didn't want to just leave his team behind to fall apart. He'd seen that too much in the past. It seemed that each time a good group got together then management would step in and break it up.

So, he wanted to move on, move up, as he had done his whole career. He knew that he was taking a big step – superintendent was a senior rank. He would be moving into the realm of strategic command with hundreds of officers under him. And within striking distance of assistant chief constable. Those were proper roles. He was about to say to himself that it was an ACPO role, but that had all changed, now it was the National Police Chiefs Council.

Anyway, he thought to himself, he wouldn't leave a mess behind when he went. He had already chosen his successor but that would mean that everyone lower down would shuffle up one, leaving a gap. The question he now asked himself was – was DC Angel right to fill that gap?

He thought back to all he'd learned from his mentor and superior officer, now retired ACC Reg Patterson. Regardless of rank, even when they'd become friends, he'd always been Patterson to him. Even when he'd been given permission to address him as Reg, he'd still been Patterson. He had taught him that he needed to mould a team, look at strengths and weaknesses, find ways for people to get along, work together.

In that respect at least, Patterson had been a very modern policeman.

Chapter Four

Tuesday evening was the time that Haines had set aside for meeting with Billy King. The two men had known each other for years and moved their meetings around the town to avoid attracting suspicion.

This time they were sat in the luxury leather seats of Billy's Jaguar, parked on the promenade, nose out to the sea. As it had been all summer, the weather was overcast. Not cold, not rainy but certainly not sunny either.

'I'm dying out there, Rob,' Billy said when they'd exchanged greetings and small talk. 'There's only so long I hold on to people if they're getting beatings and having their money and product taken.'

'We're doing what we can. But it's tricky because a lot of them come from out of town, yet they seem quite savvy when it comes to CCTV.' He thought of the battles he'd had recently over improving the quality of the cameras surrounding the train station. He decided that King wouldn't be interested in the fights over budgets. 'And those we do identify are usually on their way back home by the time we know who they are.'

'Tell me about it – even the papers are talking about county lines now. Can't you disrupt them back in the city centres?'

'That's not how it works – we all have our territories and divisions, much the same as you have your own turf.'

'Except no one's coming onto your turf and beating up your officers, are they?' When Haines didn't reply, he continued. 'This is all on me to fix. I'm the one they look to.'

'Even if we do manage to arrest a kid in the city, there are ten more stepping up to fill their shoes.'

'It's not like you to give up.' King turned to look at his passenger.

'I'm not giving up,' Haines explained. 'We need to keep doing what we're doing.'

An uneasy silence fell between them. Finally, King spoke reluctantly, as if the words were being dragged out of him. 'There are rumours, vague, some are only hints.'

'Rumours? Of what?' Haines wished he could make King talk, but he knew King would never be rushed.

'We might be getting a visit from some of the senior members of a Birmingham gang down here.' King spoke while looking straight ahead, out at the sea. 'One of the bigger gangs wants to move in wholesale. That's what all the beatings are about. They're not satisfied with running a few lines but instead they want to take over the whole trade, the whole town.'

Haines nodded. It was what he feared. Not just dealers coming in intermittently but an established presence. He had a thought and considered what to say.

King said, 'What? You're thinking something.'

'Just considering options.'

'Deciding who you can trust, more like,' King said with a smile. 'I know what you're thinking anyway, and I can help. They're not just handing out beatings, they're offering membership of the city gang if any of my men want to defect.' He smiled slowly. 'I could order some of them to accept the offer.'

'Run an undercover operation you mean?' Haines couldn't believe he'd be so reckless. 'Do you have any idea how much training and experience that takes?'

King laughed, a low chuckle. 'That's for your lot. We're already criminals so we don't need no training courses on how to blend in. And I don't need authorisation. I'll pick some of my men who don't have deep links with the town. Tell them to check in when they can, not to take risks. It'll be a piece of cake.'

Haines shot him a sideways glance. 'You know I can't authorise—'

King laughed, a short bark this time. 'None of this is going in your official notes, is it?'

'Well no, but you'll have no backup from me if this goes tits-up.' When, Haines thought; when it goes tits-up. He knew from hard experience that an operation like that could only go wrong. He thought it through for a moment while they sat in the car and watched the waves crashing on the beach. 'You know, I always wanted something big to go out on. If you do manage to get some men in undercover, could you find out the details of the meeting? If the rumours are true that is?'

'What, about the Latvian gang from Birmingham?' King asked. 'I see what you're getting at. First we see if the rumours are true, then you can take them down. Especially if they're here on your turf.'

'It'll buy you a lot of time.' Haines nodded. 'If we round up the top people in the gang, that could trigger a power struggle back in the city. It might be years before they come back down here. Also, it'll give me a big send off from the job.'

'You're not leaving, are you?'

'Not altogether, no. But I've got over the final hurdle,' Haines announced. 'I've got a bit of time to tidy up loose ends, and then I'll be leaving CID and getting my promotion. This time next month I'll be superintendent.'

'What does this mean for us then?'

'It'll be business as usual. We have the system and it works.' Haines tried to sound encouraging. 'I won't be as operational, but DI Hargreaves will be heading up the CID.'

'But you'll still be involved, won't you? I'll be able to come to you to iron out problems?'

'Not really. If I interfere with CID business after my promotion it will be noticed.' Haines considered telling him about the hierarchy. How it was detective sergeants and constables who really made the difference on the ground and how if he kept interfering as a superintendent then he would never get another promotion.

'We work well together. I want that to continue. I don't want our arrangement to end. It's been beneficial for both of us.'

'And it won't end.' Haines knew he had to be firm with Billy King. 'Like I said, it's just a natural progression. I get promoted, Hargreaves steps up. It'll be fine. You've met him, and I'll make sure that you have a proper handover.'

'Hargreaves? Are you sure?'

'What? Don't you trust him? He's been my second in command for over five years. It's just natural that he'd follow me. And he can do it as an inspector.' He paused, realising that the other man didn't care about police politics.

'It's not that I don't trust him, as such.' King rubbed at an imaginary spot on the steering wheel. 'I certainly trust you and if you trust him then so do I. It's just, I dunno, we've been working together for years. It'll be a change, that's all. Is there any way we could keep working together? After your promotion?'

'I don't see what the point would be,' Haines said shortly.

'We need each other. We've both risen to the top of our fields because we helped each other.' Haines registered the subtle threat – they both knew too much to be cut loose.

'Risen. That's the key point. Past tense. Not we're rising. We've done it, it's time to move on.'

'Not if I don't want to.' Billy King sounded almost truculent.

The silence hung between them, as palpable as a third person in the car. Both of them worked out how much they had to lose.

Finally, staring out of the side window, Haines said, 'I guess we could, you know, meet up. Once I've got my feet under the table.' He hurriedly added, 'But nothing like now. Not regular like. Just now and then.'

'So you could keep me updated on progress? What I need to know?' Billy tried and failed to keep the eagerness out of his voice.

Haines nodded, thinking that most of his life would be sitting in committee meetings and forwarding reports about logistics and procurement. 'And I'd need information flowing back the other way.'

'Of course, of course. It's what we do best. Keep this town safe. I can't tell you how helpful it's been over the years.' Now he'd got the concession he wanted, Billy King was expansive and generous.

'And to us. Keeps the statistics looking good.' There was another loaded pause from Haines. 'So, Hargreaves? You'll be okay working with him?'

'I guess. I don't know.' King stared out of the window for a moment. 'He's a bit... what am I looking for? An incomer?'

'So am I. I wasn't born here like you. I used to come here on holidays when I was a kid.'

'You know that doesn't count. You have your aunt just up the road who's been here forever. Family connection matters, you know.'

'Well yes, I stayed with her in Highcliffe for my holidays.'

'So you see. And you've been here for at least twenty years. Hargreaves came in from the city. He doesn't care about this place like you and me. If he got a promotion to another force, he'd take it, wouldn't he?'

What does that say about me, Haines thought. Chained to this place, trying to preserve a past that only existed in childhood memories. On the other hand, he thought of all the good he had done. The dealers and thugs he'd run out of town. Every successful caravan park and retirement home was, in a small way, a testament to his dedication in keeping the town free of trouble.

'That's as maybe,' Haines said. 'But don't forget Hargreaves has spent the last five years as my second in command. He might not be here for the long haul but he knows what's important.'

King nodded to himself. Haines realised with a jolt that King was someone who'd never accept someone else's opinion. Well this was one change that the other man would have to accept. He was moving up and away from all this and Billy King wouldn't hold him back.

'So, Billy,' Haines said. 'I know it's a risk, but you'll put people into the Latvian gang from Birmingham?' The other man nodded. 'I don't have long before I leave CID, so could that happen quickly?'

'As I said, I'm not all tied up by bureaucracy. I'll have a word with them tonight. Should be fairly quick to set things in motion. The people I've in mind have already been approached.'

'And the usual arrangements would apply, obviously.' Haines paused for effect. 'Except of course that if the meeting is bigger, then well, the arrangement would be bigger. On both sides.'

'I hear what you're saying. I hear you loud and clear.' Billy nodded enthusiastically. 'I didn't need any convincing. As soon as I know, I'll pass it on to you.'

'That's really helpful,' Haines said. He was still thinking about the promotion and was glad that things could move quickly enough. 'And I'll see what I can do about the beatings. I'll stir up the immigrants in Bradwick, see if I can find any with links back to Birmingham, try to break up their network.'

Both men nodded and let the silence fall between them. When it was clear that neither of them had anything more to say, Haines slipped out of the car and walked back to his own vehicle.

Chapter Five

DC Angel cradled her coffee and tried to keep warm. There was something desolate and cold about five thirty in the morning no matter what the season. This particular morning was even bleaker than usual because of the reason for her being there.

Already there was police tape over the end of the alley which led between two shops and down to a small square yard where the big industrial bins were kept. It was a grim place, surrounded by brick walls topped with razor wire.

A uniform met her and waited while she put on a white forensic suit and overshoes. She went through the motions mechanically, wondering grimly what lay ahead. It wasn't her first body but the nervousness didn't lessen until she'd seen the body. When she was all ready, she went down and met DCI Haines.

'Thought you'd like to be in at the sharp end. Get to know the ropes,' he said by way of greeting.

'Thanks, sir,' she answered. Why was she here, she wondered, on her first week in the job.

Haines nodded and led her to the scene. He was still thinking over everything both Hargreaves and King had said to him. Hargreaves clearly didn't trust DC Angel, while judging by last night's meeting, King didn't trust Hargreaves. He was aware that he'd made promises to King to take some pressure off so the last thing he needed was a long drawn out murder investigation.

He had decided to bring DC Angel in at the beginning, to keep her close and see if she'd fit in. In the meantime, he could let Hargreaves run the operation to catch and prosecute the out of town drug dealers trying to muscle in.

DC Angel got her first sight of the victim. She was sprawled out on her back. One foot had been left exposed beneath a pile of black rubbish sacks. The scene of crime photographer had no choice but to clip numbers to each bag that he could see. He then photographed the pile and removed the first layer, before repeating the process.

It was a job for the truly patient as now parts of her body and long auburn hair were starting to become visible. Although the temptation was to pull the last few bags off her body, DC Angel knew that the evidence gathered now might be invaluable in solving the case.

While scene of crimes took photos and labelled and moved bags, DC Angel considered the victim. She had the pale waxy look of the recently dead. DC Angel had to suppress a feeling of deep sadness that this girl had been dumped here like this. She wasn't sure, but she thought there was bruising on the left side of her face, disappearing into the hairline. Her headphones, tiny white buds were still in, with the cable looped over the back of the ear before it disappeared beneath her. DC Angel made a mental note to keep an eye out for the mobile phone that should be on the other end of that wire.

The victim was young, probably late teens. With a shock DC Angel realised that meant she was probably around ten years younger than her. But those ten years spanned a lifetime in most people's lives – from carefree teenager to professional woman. And, thought DC Angel, it was a path that this girl would never take.

Trying to be more professional, she had a proper look at the scene. Tiny clutch bag on a gold chain, short skirt and glittery top together with discarded high heels all indicated that she'd been going out for the evening. The owner of the sportswear shop confirmed that he'd locked up and checked the yard at six last night and there had been no body.

Haines watched her taking everything in, then said, 'What are your first thoughts then?'

'First thoughts? It's a bit early for that, isn't it?'

'Never too early for a first pass at the crime scene. We've got techs and a pathologist and a whole host of experts to come along later with the evidence. So you can be wrong, but I'd like to know what you think immediately.'

'Preliminary hypothesis then,' DC Angel said as she walked back to the main road. She was glad of the distraction, the chance to be logical amid such an emotional scene. 'Most of the pubs and clubs are that way.' She pointed right. 'And there's a big residential area to the left. We'll have to wait for the pathologist to give us a time of death, but based on where she was found and what she was wearing, my best guess would be between ten pm and two am. She'd be walking home from a good night out and the streets would be quiet, especially around here in a more commercial area. With a bit of luck, once we've got an identity, we can put together an itinerary of her last movements and see if I'm right or not.'

'Sounds about right to me. Most murders are fairly straight forward. Our first job will be to see if she turned down any of the hot-blooded young males of Bradwick.' They walked back down the short alley to have another look at the victim. 'Judging by the way she was dressed, I'd say that finding a rejected boyfriend would be top of our priority list.'

'You can't say that, sir!' She spun to face Haines. Any thought that he was her boss was eclipsed by her outrage that he'd say such a thing. 'Haven't you done any courses on sensitivity and victim blaming?'

'First off, I'm not blaming the victim.' He stood his ground, turning to face her. 'There's no way on earth that anyone, young or old, male or female deserved to die in this way. But the fact remains she was young and pretty and dressed as if she was out on the town. It follows logically that she would have attracted some attention. All my comment really shows is that I have a low opinion of the young men of Bradwick. Unfortunately that's the product of many years of experience.' He paused for breath. 'As for the sensitivity, well, again, if you put the years in, you'll find your own way to cope. I prefer to say things as I see them.'

'I suppose you might have a point,' she said grudgingly. She knew she had already made assumptions based on her clothing. She still hoped she wouldn't develop such a thick skin.

Their argument ended when another black sack was removed and Angel had to subdue a gasp. Right across the victim's neck was a straight red mark, so dark it was almost purple. All her attempts to remain dispassionate were futile. Who would do such a thing to a teenage girl? She knew the perils of second guessing the pathologist but it did look like they had a clear cause of death.

She turned to look at the pathologist, Dani Price, who gave a brief nod, but there was a warning look in her eyes. Yes, she'd seen the mark but she was reserving judgement.

'Right then, body's all clear. Over to you.' The SOCO who'd had the painstaking job of removing the bags had finished. DC Angel knew that somewhere in a lab, every one of those rubbish sacks would be analysed.

She watched the pathologist examine the body. I've known GPs who were less gentle with the living, she thought wryly. She was taking her time, manipulating the body, checking for vital signs and rigor mortis. When she had the hair swept back, she called for close-ups of the left side of the face. DC Angel was nearly overwhelmed with pity for the poor girl.

There was a shout from a corner of the yard, followed by a flutter of flash photography and then one of the techs brought

DC Angel a clear plastic bag. Inside was a Samsung mobile phone with the screen smashed. She peered through the plastic and saw that it wasn't just smashed, it was destroyed. This wasn't one of those cases where there was a crack but you could continue using it, there was actually a hole in the screen. She turned it over and saw that there was a slight bulge on the back opposite the hole. Turning it sideways, she saw the frame was bent as well.

She started to fill in the evidence form. Hopefully the technical boys would be able to get some data back from it although she didn't hold out much hope. Although it was only a phone, it had suffered violence. She didn't ascribe to ideas of psychic residue, but the yard suddenly seemed close and oppressive. In the last few hours someone had come here and acted out their anger, their rage, and destroyed a young life and their phone. She knew that her main job now was to work out why and who. And to put the horrible feelings far from her mind.

A shadow fell across her and she turned to see her boss, DCI Haines. 'What have you got there?'

'Presumably it's the victim's mobile phone.' She held it up to show him. 'Although it doesn't look like we'll get much back.'

'Wow.' Haines took the phone and held it up to the light. 'Someone really did a number on this.'

'Presumably our attacker.'

'Yes.' He passed the phone back. 'Enter that into evidence.' He had a quick look around the scene, all the technicians still working away. 'Right, I've had a quick look at the scene, so I'll head back to the office.' He caught the questioning look that DC Angel shot him. 'Listen, I'm not one of those mysterious TV detectives who needs to be on the scene to pick up some feeling of the crime. I don't put myself in the mind of the killer. Anything I need to know from the scene will be reported to me by the SOCOs and the pathologist.' He walked up the alley, then stopped and peered at the pavement. He waved over a uniform. 'I want this pavement cordoned off, twenty yards each side of the alley, then a fingertip search. I reckon she was overpowered here on the pavement, then dragged into the alley. She died somewhere between here and the yard most likely.'

A sudden wave of sadness swept over DC Angel. No matter how hardened she had become during her time in the police, she still had feelings. Last night this girl had been walking home, either listening to music or chatting to friends when she had been swept into a nightmare she didn't escape from. It was as sudden and unfeeling as a car accident.

As the morning wore on, the machinery of sudden death moved into motion. The hospital mortuary van arrived with a couple of orderlies to remove the body. Something changed, lifted slightly in the atmosphere once the body was removed. Whoever she was, she had been a silent accusatory presence demanding answers, justice.

Now, the whole yard belonged to scene of crimes officers. Haines had already gone back to the office to start the investigation. DC Angel knew all about the first twenty-four hours and how it was a vital period to gather evidence over. On the other hand, she needed time to process and decompress. On instinct she decided to walk back to the station, then return at lunch or after work for her car.

She was walking down a terraced street when she heard a door open behind her. It was still early morning and the area was deserted. She tensed for a moment and spun around. Her hand found her baton. She recognised the figure approaching and breathed a sigh of relief.

'Lukas!'

Lukas Mills was the only person in Bradwick that had known her when she was growing up. He was a link to her past and it made her nervous. But she was very fond of him so she tolerated him.

Somehow, he'd got wind of where she was living and made his way down here. She'd known him since school where they'd both been outsiders. He was still beautiful in a wasted, rock star way. High cheek bones, blue eyes, natural blond hair. But she knew how dangerous he was. A childhood of low boundaries and easy success had set him up for an adulthood descent into drugs and mental illness. Now he drifted around from squat to sofa, busking and scrounging for the money he needed.

'Angel! I thought it was you.' He moved closer, saw her frown at his words and corrected himself. 'Sorry, sorry, it's Emma isn't it?'

She nodded her thanks, taking in his appearance. He was only slightly dishevelled so was probably staying somewhere with a working shower, she thought, though he'd obviously been up all night.

'What you doing up so early?' he asked.

'Work. Crime happens at all hours. Have you eaten?' When he shook his head, she continued. 'Walk with me then, I'll sort you out something.' They walked on into the main part of Bradwick. She marvelled at the ease of his life. He might not have money or security, but that gave him freedom. He could stumble out of his house at half seven in the morning and just walk off. No one to explain to or to worry about him.

She also found it slightly uncomfortable that he was only wearing a loose vest over tracksuit bottoms and trainers. As he walked, she caught glimpses of a shoulder blade or the curve of his shoulder as the garment moved. He had random, swirling tattoos which only enhanced the intimate nature of the experience. He stepped into the light and she saw blond stubble on his chin, just visible in the bright light. He had that early morning feel to him that she found attractive, whether it was from waking with a man in her bed or from staying up all night.

She lengthened her stride until she was just ahead, but still able to talk to him. Soon she had installed him in a cafe on the high street that did a decent vegetarian breakfast. She left some money with the owner and promised to pop back later to collect her change. It was one of the old-fashioned perks of being a police officer.

As she walked back to the station, she thought about Lukas. She had a genuine fondness for him and was also attracted to him. But she also knew that he was a dead weight. If she got into a relationship with him, he would drag her down. She had clarity about this – if she was with him, then within months she'd have descended to his level without any hope of elevating him to hers.

As she climbed the steps up to the Victorian frontage of the police station, she banished all thoughts of Lukas from her mind. The team had a major enquiry now and she needed to be ready to start the long job of finding out who the victim was and who had wanted her dead.

CHAPTER SIX

Haines bustled his way importantly into CID. The official guidelines were full of the golden twenty-four hours. Was he using his as best he could?

He knew what the protocol was. They had already found a missing person that was reported in first thing this morning. If this was right, then they had a seventeen-year-old victim. In reality, whoever it was, he had to call together a Major Investigation Team. Without waiting for the formal report from the pathologist; it would be a miracle if it wasn't a murder.

There was only one thing that he wanted to do now and that was to get on the phone and find a contact in West Midlands Police. Someone who he could get on with and who would work with him. He could see the shape of the problem now. Despite his initial misgivings, he liked the idea of Billy sending in one of his own to work undercover. It simplified his operation and removed him one step from the risk. But he was aware that he needed to get up to speed on the current intelligence. If a name was reported back to him, he had to know who they were and where they fit into the current organisation.

This was what he wanted to be doing. Intelligence-led policing. Keeping the lid on the drug menace. He was almost unique among his colleagues in that he enjoyed collating the monthly crime figures. These numbers showed how well he was serving his community. The more he kept things under control, the better the stats.

His firm belief was that the drug trade had to be controlled. From the use of illegal narcotics a tide of other problems flowed. Users were responsible for all sorts of crime from muggings all the way through to vehicle theft. As well as that, they were the fuel that kept the brothels and the trade in illegal immigrants going. Drugs caused anti-social behaviour and drove down property prices.

So, he knew he had to control the drug gangs. But he couldn't ignore the murder of a seventeen-year-old girl on his patch. He hoped fervently that in the next few days they'd round up a likely suspect – probably a boy who was mooning over her or had been otherwise jilted. Then he'd be able to get back to solving Billy King's problems and keeping Bradwick safe.

With a heavy heart, he placed a call through to Diane, the station admin manager to start establishing an MIT. She had already heard on the grapevine that a body had been found and the emergency suite on the fourth floor was being readied. He could move his office up there, with his laptop, and the phone could be redirected.

It would be a good chance to see if DI Hargreaves was ready to step up to the job of being in charge. The next chance he got, Haines decided to brief his DI and tell him he'd have day to day control of CID while he was running the MIT.

He went back to his desk to trawl through the computer system. He soon found the missing person report for seventeen-year-old Mazey Taylor – Haines shook his head when he saw the spelling. She had gone out yesterday evening and never returned home. The on-duty officer had assured the parents that she was probably out at a party or something and assured them that if she wasn't in touch by the morning then they would start a search.

Rob Haines shook his head. This was bad news to hand to any parent anywhere. He knew he had a phone call to make even if he didn't want to.

'Hi Jem, it's Rob,' he said. He hadn't even convinced himself he sounded bright and breezy.

'Rob, what's up?' His wife's voice was tight with tension.

'Not the kids, it's fine.' He understood her concerns immediately. He took a breath. 'We have a body, a murder.'

'Okay then. I know the drill by now. Lots of long nights and a distracted husband.' She paused again. 'But there's something else isn't there Rob?'

'Yeah, our victim looks like she's a seventeen-year-old girl.'

'How are you holding up?'

Rob wanted to assure her that he was a seasoned police officer. It didn't matter that his own daughters were only a few years past seventeen or that he could see the parallels between them and his victim dispassionately.

But he also knew how perceptive his wife was. And what he couldn't get away with. 'Yeah, not too bad. I keep telling myself to be rational. I know Abby and Charlie are both safe and there's no way that even if this was the beginning of a serial that they'd be in the right area.' Both his daughters had left home, one to Cornwall, the other to Bristol. He was glad they weren't in Bradwick where he'd worry over every report but he sometimes wished they were closer so that he could keep an eye.

'Even so, I'll get in touch, just to make sure.'

'And when you do...'

'I'll drop you a text.' Jem paused for a moment. 'Is there any point in asking when you'll be home?'

'You can ask, but this isn't the only case to land on my desk this week.'

'Thought so.' Her words sounded resigned but there was a lightness in her voice. After over twenty years as a policeman's wife, she knew better than to complain about the hours. Besides, he was only weeks away from a desk job, so she could wait.

When the call was over, he sat back in his chair and rubbed his eyes. He thought about resources. Something like this was likely to be a boyfriend or ex-boyfriend. Probably listened to too much gangster rap and was all about his woman disrespecting him. What the investigation needed was a way to get into her social circle. Getting her friends talking could unlock this case.

He frowned over the top of his monitor at the open-plan area beyond. He saw the blonde hair of DC Angel. Something tickled in the far reaches of his memory so he called up her file. He was right, she could add definite value to this investigation. He made up his mind. He'd lead the MIT and take DC Angel with him. She could talk to any witnesses, deal with sobbing relatives. He'd request as many officers from other parts of the force as he could. He'd need family liaison and exhibits officers if nothing else. He'd also use a lot of civilian staff to update the computer and uniforms for the footwork.

If he was careful, he could keep his team intact under Hargreaves, sorting out the details ready for when Billy King came across with the information. And, he thought to himself, justifying his decision, DC Angel was meant to be on a fast track so this would give her experience of a major investigation. It didn't matter that she was young, he was doing what he should. He also made a note to talk to all of CID. Emphasise the benefits of tying up the drug deal. He knew he had ambitious detectives who would love to get onto a murder investigation.

Well, he'd tell them that they could do that next year. There'd always be another case. Murder cases were double-edged swords – a positive result wasn't always guaranteed and you could be forever remembered as a member of the team that failed to catch a killer.

And, as an overriding concern, he owed it to Hargreaves to work closely with DC Angel and sound her out. He couldn't be handing her over as an unknown quantity. With all this is mind, he crossed the open space. 'DC Angel, with me.'

She got up from her desk and followed her boss. As he walked, he said, 'We've got a preliminary ID on our body from this morning. Mazey Taylor. She was only seventeen. You did some school liaison work back in uniform, didn't you?'

'Yes, sir. It was a few years back though. Why?'

'All the better. Whether or not the body is Taylor, she's a young woman. We need someone to talk to her friends and more importantly find out who her enemies were. Any jilted boyfriends, or even better, rejected suitors.'

'Suitors? Sir, I think you're a bit out of date. Hook-ups maybe.'

'You see, that's why I need you. With a bit of luck, some of her circle of friends might be the same kids you spoke to when they were in school.'

DC Angel nodded. 'It's certainly possible. I spoke to hundreds of kids across a whole range of ages. I'll do my best to get them to talk to me.'

* * *

DC Angel was intimidated by her experience of the MIT. She was at the front for the first briefing having been led up there by the boss, DCI Haines. She wasn't yet sure why she'd been chosen for the MIT but it made her nervous. CID was a tight-knit team, she was the new girl, and yet she'd appeared to leapfrog over all of them onto a murder team. She suspected that there were other factors at play.

She paid close attention as Haines outlined the case so far. They had a dead body and a missing girl – Mazey Taylor. Initial photos of the body and Ms Taylor suggested very strongly that they were the same. Formal identification would take place later on.

Haines outlined the procedures for data capture and assigned uniforms to the house-to-house and civilians to the data entry. Tasks were assigned to check the few houses that were in the vicinity and the CCTV for the night in question.

DC Angel was starting to wonder why she'd been brought in at all when she heard her name mentioned. 'DC Angel and I will be talking to Mazey's social circle. First indications are that this was not a planned attack. We expect the pathologist to confirm that death was by strangulation and the body appeared to have been dragged down the alley and dumped where we found it. We might well be looking at someone she knew. So that's what we'll be focusing on. Boyfriends, girlfriends, jilted exes, all that area. I'm sure you know that most murders are committed by someone known to the victim. We have recovered a broken phone from the scene which is currently with the technical people. Obviously, there's a reason why it was broken. Hopefully we'll soon have a list of contacts and be able to start building up some idea of her social network.'

The rest of the meeting was a long series of handing off tasks to various other teams. Liaison roles were assigned to the forensic teams, to the family, and with the many uniformed branches assigned to the team. DC Angel only really listened with half an ear. She was instead wondering about the life and death of Mazey Taylor. DC Angel had yet to be hardened to life by her time in the police – she still wondered at how everything could change from one minute to the next.

When the meeting broke up, she went over to the white board. A photo was pinned there – a group shot with a red circle around Mazey's face. DC Angel felt like an alien or a sociologist studying humans from afar. She could see that Mazey Taylor was one of the lucky ones. She was in the centre of the shot, happy, with her arms around two friends, one each side. Down the front were two girls who weren't quite as beautiful as the trio in the middle. And off to one side was a girl whose hair was just too short, who's attitude was just too spiky. She wasn't even looking at the camera – she had been caught in profile.

DC Angel had done psychology at A-level which led her to ponder the question, were the trio at the centre of the photo because they were beautiful, or was the situation reversed? Were they born into good families, well treated and expected to be successful, so they were? Or, were they gifted with even features and taller, thinner builds so they were praised as children and grew up to be successful?

She knew from her own experience that the question was not worth asking – nature and nurture were tangled together. On the nature side of the equation, she had been told since she was tiny that she was beautiful or pretty or lovely that she supposed it must be true. But on the other side of the coin, nurture, she'd had such a weird upbringing that any conventional social situation had her feeling like a foreigner who didn't speak the language.

She looked back at the photo and considered those that she'd starred in from her sixth form days. She definitely wouldn't be one of the alpha-girls in the centre, arms around each other. More likely she'd be stood at the back, but not as aloof as the girl in this photo. In most of them, she'd been watching the camera, paying attention while being on the edge.

DC Angel replaced the photo on the board. She knew her musings had little bearing on the case. Whatever her outward trappings of success, Mazey Taylor had not enjoyed a long and happy life.

On her way back to CID, she thought over what to do next. She was pleased to have been chosen to be a key part of the MIT but she didn't want to lose her chance to become a member of the team. She would rather pass up this opportunity than be alienated from her colleagues.

She pushed her way into the open area, still trying to decide how to proceed. She didn't want to challenge one of Haines' decisions. On her way to her desk, she saw that DI Hargreaves was sat alone at his desk. He hadn't yet graduated to a full office, but his desk was in a corner and shielded by partitions. When Haines got his promotion, Hargreaves would be running the team. Getting on his good side now would be a good step forward.

She slid into the chair opposite him and waited for him to finish typing.

'Ah, yes, Angel, what can I do for you?'

'Well, sir, I just wanted to make sure there wasn't any bad feeling.' Hargreaves looked confused, so she continued. 'I'm the newest member of the team, and I'm on the MIT. I didn't want people to think that I've pushed to the front of the queue or anything.'

He leaned back in his chair and studied her from under heavy eyelids. 'I know there's a certain mystique to solving murders, but at the moment we have bigger fish to fry. We're just setting up a long-term drug operation. It makes sense to put you on the murder, because all the lads have the in-depth, local knowledge to make sense of the information that might come in while we're setting up this operation. You'd have to spend a week just getting up to speed. Not to mention the fact that we've all built up relationships.' He shook his head. 'No, none of them want a murder. It might sound glamorous but either you'll catch the killer, in which case Haines will get the glory, or if it doesn't lead to a conviction then you'll be part of the team that messed up.'

DC Angel nodded, trying to gather her thoughts. Had she really been given this role as a poisoned chalice? She was annoyed that Hargreaves had burst her bubble. 'Actually, I just thought that Mazey Taylor deserved justice and I didn't want to upset the team. But if no one else is bothered, I'll happily help to find her killer.'

Without waiting for a response, she pushed back from his desk and stalked back to her own.

Chapter Seven

The Bradwick Club was an institution that had changed to keep in line with current rules on private members clubs. The fact that a lot of councillors were listed as members meant that it was always under the radar and compliant with the letter, if not the spirit, of the law.

For example, women were perfectly free to join, pay the fees, and drink with the men on an equal footing. All they had to do was find three existing members to propose them and they would be in. Of course, very few women knew that the club even existed and it had yet to come under sustained attack from the forces of fairness and equality.

It was here that Rob Haines chose to meet his mentor, Reg Patterson. From the outside, it looked like a normal house on a nice street within half a mile of the seafront. It was well proportioned, detached, and stood in its own considerable gardens. Inside however, all traces of a residential house had been erased. Instead there were all the trappings of an old-fashioned club, from cloakrooms to reading rooms and a bar and kitchen.

Rob Haines warmly shook the hand of Reg Patterson, his old friend. Until three years ago, he had been Assistant Chief Constable Patterson. Now, he was retired and looked like a grandfather from a saccharine children's TV program. He had neatly parted grey hair, a paintbrush moustache and round wire glasses.

However, Haines knew he cultivated the image so that people underestimated him. He was not remotely overweight and boasted about still running six miles a day and going to the gym.

'How are you doing, Rob? Looking forward to moving up to superintendent?'

'Yes. There aren't many days when I want to get away from the sharp end, but today I could really do with a desk job.'

'Well, it's the way of the world. Move onwards and upwards. Soon you'll be influencing the direction of the whole division, not just one department in Bradwick.' He paused and studied his companion. 'What's troubling you?'

'I've got a murder, right in the middle of my patch. A seventeen-year-old girl on her way home. While I'm trying to get any traction on this, Billy King is making demands. Of me! As if he's my only problem!'

Patterson subtly slid Haines' whisky tumbler closer to him. They were sat around a table in a wood panelled booth off the main bar. It was understood that no one would eavesdrop. 'He's not your only problem, but it's what I've been teaching you ever since you joined as a wet behind the ears DC and I was your DI. Drugs are the main problem. They generate money that's funnelled into the pockets of the worst of society. With drugs comes violence, property crime, prostitution, corruption of children.'

'So, I should listen to Billy King?' Haines was keen to head off another lecture. 'And prioritise that over the murder?'

'He's scared, that's all. He's had the trade all wrapped up for years. Being at the top of the tree as a drug dealer is a scary place to be, and a lonely one. It's your job to keep him there and keep him calm.' A big part of Patterson's strategy when he'd been in the job had been to keep the least-worst drug dealers onside and use them to run the real problems out of Bradwick. 'Listen, his early warning system means we're one of the very few towns in this area not to have significant county lines problems.'

County lines was a whole new problem for police forces. Big drug gangs from cities would ship dealers in wholesale from their centres of control to outlying towns. Coastal and rural towns were their main target and Bradwick had to be close to the top of their list. So far, however, Billy King had put the word out to his network of dealers to report any county lines activity straight to him. As he was working with rather than against the police, they could run the outside dealers straight out of town, scoring some good statistics in the process.

'The tide might be turning on that one. They're not just coming here with mobile phones and holdalls full of drugs. They're handing out punishment beatings to some of King's crew. I'm also hearing that while one hand is wielding a stick, the other is offering work and money.'

'I've seen the reports,' Patterson said. 'There is some serious pressure being applied to King's network. He needs some protection, he deserves it. I'd focus on that – the rest will sort itself out.'

'What about Mazey Taylor?'

'Who?'

'It's not like you to have your finger off the pulse, sir. She's our seventeen-year-old murder victim.'

'Have you found a boyfriend yet? Or a stepfather? You know what these cases are like. Mostly the victims know their attacker. You've got lots of experience and you know Bradwick really well. You'll find the bugger sooner or later.'

'Yeah, you're probably right on that one.' Haines paused to consider how best to phrase his next comment. 'She was quite a looker too, dressed up nice. Chances are that there's some young lad out there with his nose out of joint because she turned him down.'

Patterson nodded. 'There you go. Some young lad somewhere will be to blame.' He paused again and took a deep breath. 'You'll be okay though, two operations running at once?'

'Yeah, should be all right. Like you say we'll wrap up Mazey Taylor fairly quickly. I'll rope in some uniforms to do the donkey work and civilians for the data capture and keeping it all on computers.'

'It's not an old man's game, I tell you that.' Patterson shook his head. 'All this forming official teams and having computer databases and what have you. I was happier when we knew all the local villains and could just round them up and lock them away.'

'That's true.' Privately Haines was glad that Patterson had retired. Having a boss and mentor who thought the old way in the age of PACE was difficult to manage.

'Have you thought about combining the two enquiries? You know a murder case will have access to a bigger budget – you could use that on the county lines.'

Haines shook his head. 'Maybe back in your day we could swipe funds from one budget and use it for another. Get your people to assign their hours and expenses to the wrong code? Fudge time sheets and overtime? It's all logged now. One hint of something fishy and Professional Standards will be all over it like a rash.' He gave a meaningful look to his mentor. 'You and I both know that's the one thing we need to avoid.'

'You always did lack imagination, Rob.' Although the words were stinging, they were delivered with humour. Not for the first time Haines was glad that Patterson was only a friend, without any command over him. 'All you need is an outside chance this girl could've been killed by a visiting drug dealer. Chase up her background, find any hint of drugs. You know what this town's like. You turn over anyone's life and you'll find someone who sniffs, smokes or injects something they shouldn't. Might be a friend or a cousin, but you'll find someone. Then you can get someone to go through the CCTV from the time of the murder, see who's coming in and out of the station. The forces in the big cities will be only too grateful to send over some pictures. You could build up a picture of who's operating in Bradwick at the moment.' Now he did become slightly condescending. 'And, you'd be able to fill in your spreadsheets and time allocation forms so they're all completely correct.'

'You can bust my balls over it all you like,' Haines said amiably. 'But we both know that the paperwork made us as successful as we were for as long as we were.'

'Hm. Well, we'll see. But there's always a way to fiddle records – you just have to be dedicated.'

'Yeah, I suppose you're right. We have both made a career out of it.' He theatrically looked at his watch, then finished his glass. 'Listen, I was looking at a dead body at five thirty this morning, then establishing an MIT and allocating tasks. I'd better head off so I can do it all again tomorrow.'

CHAPTER EIGHT

DC Angel was starting to build up a coherent picture of Mazey Taylor's last few hours. The killer had either planned well or been lucky. There was no CCTV around the area where her body was found so her last few minutes were a mystery. Her final evening had been spent round a friend's house, chatting and sharing videos on their phones. At about midnight she had made her way home, never to arrive. DC Angel had tried to trace her through the CCTV system. However, she had left a residential area and died in a black spot. So far there was one sighting when she crossed the high street diagonally. It was heartbreaking to see her walking along, without a care in the world, headphones in, looking at her phone and bobbing her head in time to music.

DC Angel had spoken to several of Mazey's friends and built up something of a picture. She was one of the middle of the road students. She wasn't in the excessively rich and pretty crowd and she wasn't at the other end with the free school meals and charity shop clothes. Even in appearance she was of average height, long auburn hair, moderately pretty. There was an ex-boyfriend but the split seemed amicable and Mazey had wanted to concentrate on her schoolwork until the exams were over so there were no boys in the picture.

She pushed back from her desk a little and let her eyes stare at the screen without focusing. In some ways Mazey's life was an ordinary one, a small one. But there was no telling what she could have become and now there never would be. She ran her fingers through her hair. No point in moping. All she could do now was to banish emotion and do her job to the best of her ability. Maybe that way she could get justice for Mazey.

All in all, there were no leads in her social life. That made it more likely this was a random attack which in turn made it harder to solve. She was also aware that the time was ticking away. The first twenty-four hours were crucial and they were all gone.

'Angel, get in here.' Haines sounded excited but controlled. 'The tech guys have played a blinder. I've just been given a CD with all the data off her phone.'

DC Angel went through to his office and pulled up a chair next to her boss. 'How the hell did they do that? It was wrecked.'

'Well,' DCI Haines picked up a document. 'The damage was primarily to the screen and the battery. It missed any vital organs.' He scanned further down. 'It, in this case being the victim's stiletto heel. It's an opportunistic attack on a defence-less phone but it failed. They replaced the screen and battery from a good phone, plugged it into their computer and this was the result.' He held up a writeable CD before inserting it into his laptop. They both leant forward. Nothing happened at first and then a list of folders came up on the screen.

'This is your ballpark. Where do we start?'

DC Angel squinted at the screen. 'If you give me a copy of the data, I'll pull out the contacts and cross-reference it with the texts, WhatsApp, Messenger, and calls. I should be able to dump it into a spreadsheet and correlate it all to give us a top ten of who she spent most time chatting with.'

'How long will all that take?' Haines didn't like to admit that he had understood little of what she'd just said.

'A couple of hours, maybe all afternoon. Depends how much is there.'

'Is there anything that can give us a quick overview?'

'Well we could try that folder.' She jabbed at the screen. 'Photos and videos. We should get a rough idea of what kind of teenager she was.'

Haines navigated to the folder and a huge list with thumbnails filled the screen. DC Angel leaned forward and pointed. 'Bingo! That was taken at fourteen minutes past midnight on the day we found her. We know she left her friend's house around midnight. That must have been when she was attacked.'

Haines double-clicked and a vague blob filled the screen. They both squinted but it was fuzzy and indistinct.

'Could be a hand? Those bits at the top could be fingers and these darker bits the gaps in between.'

'Yeah, maybe.' Haines didn't sound convinced.

'I don't suppose there's much clean-up can be done on it?' DC Angel wasn't hopeful either.

'Even if they could, which I doubt, then it wouldn't be admissible in court. What do you think it means?'

'Well, the time of the photo matches with her last known location. So we can suppose she was walking home, some creep attacks her, she whips out her phone to take a picture of him and...' DC Angel paused for a moment, staring into space lost in a thought of how desperate that last moment must have been. 'Well I suppose that escalated things. You know, if the creep was only planning a rape or an assault but then he worries that his photo might be out there. Could be an opportunistic killing.'

'Yeah, that figures.' DCI Haines sounded resigned. 'The crushing to the windpipe could be the result of a forearm being pressed down with full body weight.' He started ticking points off on his fingers. 'So, no weapon brought to the scene, no body dump, she was on her route home. Certainly keeps it all simple enough.'

DC Angel nodded. Simple, depressing, and hard to solve. She went back to the list of files.

'That one is a video and only about a week old.'

He double-clicked and the video filled the screen. Confusingly, it was a film of a mobile phone.

'Now, I'm filming, accept the message.' The disembodied voice of a teenager came out of the computer.

On the screen a finger came in and accepted a message from a sender called "WankyBoi". Now watching a video inside a video, Haines and Angel were horrified to see it was a close up of a male crotch in loose jogging trousers. A hand down the trousers was jiggling up and down in a distinctive motion.

Suddenly the other hand tugged on the waistband and the head of the penis made a sudden appearance, already spurting semen.

'Ewww!' DC Angel leaned back instinctively from the screen. The camera panned up and showed that they were in cafe. All around them people were drinking coffee and eating.

'That's it, I got it.' The voice that floated out of the speakers had to be Mazey Taylor, from beyond the grave. The video on the screen ended.

'That's just gross!' DC Angel covered her mouth.

'That's probable cause, that's what it is.' Haines' voice was tight. 'Why were they videoing it from one phone to another like that? I can't imagine they wanted to share it and if they did, couldn't they just send it from one phone to another?'

'No,' DC Angel shook her head. 'The other phone was running an app called TimeBomb. It means you can send messages, pictures or videos and set a time when they'll delete themselves off the recipient's phone. It's the sort of thing that encourages bullying and the papers are whipping the parents up to have it banned. Mind you something else will replace it. That was probably their only chance, a video like that would have been set to delete once it was viewed. So whoever the boy is he thinks he can't be caught.'

Haines frowned. 'This video was on Mazey's phone? So she had a friend who was sent this message, and before she clicked on it, she got Mazey to record it. It's a good idea to collect evidence, but it might have put her in danger.' DC Angel nodded, noticing the strain as Haines tried to keep up with the new technology. 'So, what we need to do, as well as tracing the man in this video is to find that friend. Again, we'll need to get into Mazey's network of friends. See if anyone else has been sent videos from this joker.'

The last thing DC Angel wanted to do was to see the video again, but she shut her eyes and went back through it in her mind's eye. Something was troubling her. Something other than the content, that was. Her eyes flicked open. 'Play that again.' Haines looked at her questioningly. 'I want to check something.'

They watched the video again in silence. 'Pause it there.' Haines stopped the video just before the waistband was pulled down. 'Look, the left hand pulls down the waistband, the other one is obviously, errm, well, busy. So who's holding the camera? The pan up to the cafe is shaky so it's not on a tripod or anything.'

'Two perverts then. Two suspects.' Haines was grimly satisfied. DC Angel nodded. 'So, I'll make sure you aren't given any work or interruptions for the rest of the afternoon.' He handed over the CD ceremoniously. 'I want that spreadsheet sent over as soon as you can. We need to find these jokers. Off you go.'

DC Angel fetched herself a coffee and settled down with the CD and her computer. She methodically started from the most recent files and worked her way backwards. She restricted herself to the last year as she knew how fast teenagers changed.

Everything she uncovered reinforced her initial appraisal. Mazey Taylor lived an unexceptional life. If she had a problem with a creepy stepdad, jealous ex-boyfriend or stalker, she wasn't talking to her friends about it. While she sorted through the data, she did what had been promised and input all the details on a spreadsheet. Soon she had a picture of who Mazey had spent most of her time talking to. Unfortunately it correlated quite closely with the list that was given to the police by Mazey's mother. No secrets were uncovered but they did know who to interview when they went to school.

CHAPTER NINE

The situation couldn't have been more awkward for getting the truth out of teenagers. They had been allocated a small work room off a busy corridor. There weren't even sofas and low tables. Haines and Angel were sat behind a table while the students sat in a chair opposite.

The first of Mazey's friends came in. DC Angel checked her list and saw that this was Alice Freeman. She had long dark hair, not tied back but held on either side by combs.

After they'd made small talk for a bit and Alice had started dabbing at her eyes with a handkerchief, DC Angel decided to get straight to the point. She looked sideways at Haines and he nodded slightly.

'We've analysed the contents of Mazey's phone and we found a disturbing video. I just wondered if you knew anything about it?'

'Oh, you mean the WankyBoi.' She had, despite the situation, a cheerful voice with round West Country vowels.

'Have you received one too?'

'No, not me. I'm not silly enough to leave all my settings open. But the girls here all get them. When one comes in, we all crowd round and have a look and a laugh at them.' Alice shook her head. 'Sad cases really, doing that in public and sending it to girls. Always figured out you'd catch up to them sooner or later.'

DC Angel was struck by how much Alice viewed the whole situation as normal. Boys sending round videos of themselves masturbating wasn't a big deal in her world. That fact alone made DC Angel angry at how wrong the world had gone.

'Well, we need to find out who they are now.' DCI Haines was stern.

Alice furrowed her brow. 'I never found out. Must be someone around here though, they seem to know all the girls. I reckon they left this place with a few GCSEs, didn't find a job and just hang around doing this.' She stopped to think. 'You know what this place is like though. Someone will know.'

The third person to come in after Alice Freeman was Lisa Short. She revealed that she was the friend who had originally received the video that had been recorded on Mazey's phone.

'So, did you or Mazey show that video to anyone?' DC Angel asked.

'No, I don't think so. She didn't even send it back to me once she'd recorded it.'

'So, what was the point then?' Haines asked.

'She said she wanted a bit of time to think. To work out what to do next. And then...' Lisa dissolved into tears.

DC Angel waited for the sobs to die down. As carefully as she could, she approached the subject. 'Would she have shown it to a teacher maybe? Or someone else who could help?'

'I'm not being nasty, because you seem like someone nice.' Lisa was talking directly to DC Angel now. 'But really, who could help? It's just what happens, you know. It's only a small step up from dick pics isn't it? And nothing ever gets done about that.' Depressingly, DC Angel couldn't think of anything to say to that so the teenager carried on. 'I mean what would you do if there was a man, a sad case at the back of the bus who was knocking one out? You'd probably just sit at the front.'

'You should report it. To the bus driver at least.' DC Angel tried to hold on to her professionalism even though as a woman she felt inclined to agree with Alice.

'What difference would that make? The guy would see you talking to the driver, he'd know who got him thrown off the bus. Unless of course the driver doesn't believe you. Trust me, you just shrug it off and carry on.'

Unable to contend with the teenager's cynicism, Angel decided to change tack. 'So, you don't think Mazey showed anyone the video?'

'I dunno. If she did, she didn't tell me about it.'

'And do you have any idea who was in it, who's responsible?'

'Nah. I know some of my friends want to figure it out. I think that's what Mazey was going to do. Ask around and see if she could find the cafe, work out who they were. But I can't see the point, even if you locked them up, some other saddos will replace them.'

DC Angel just nodded. Then she asked the usual questions about where Lisa had been on Tuesday night and if she knew of anyone who might have had a problem with Mazey. As she had done before, she drew a complete blank.

'Shall we take a break, boss?' They had interviewed seven of Mazey's friends and had learned nothing new. No one was showing a special interest, no one knew who WankyBoi really was. It was a dead end so far.

'We could even knock it on the head,' Haines said. Even he sounded defeated. 'You listed the friends in order of closeness. If we haven't got anything this far down the list, it's unlikely that there's going to be anything to find.'

DC Angel nodded. This murder wasn't turning out to be as quick and easy as it had looked on the surface.

CHAPTER TEN

Emma had just finished her chores at a large out-of-town shopping centre. She'd visited a huge supermarket and a DIY store and was making her way back to the car. She passed a McDonald's and even while she was off duty, she was always checking out the area, in case there was any threat or something that needed dealing with.

Outside the McDonald's there was a group of teenagers, just hanging around, not causing trouble. She was about to pass by when she recognised a couple of the girls she'd interviewed the day before about Mazey. She had a sudden thought and veered off to chat to them. The last time she'd seen them it had been in the stiffly formal setting of the school. Maybe now, they would be a bit more relaxed, more forthcoming.

'Hey! It's PC Emma!' She would obviously never get over doing the round of PSE lessons that she'd had to do as part of her probation.

'Hi, girls!' She briefly checked them out – there were five of them, mostly sixth formers from the school. She was amazed by how far they were from her with only ten years age difference. 'I know we've talked before about Mazey. But that was a bit formal, you know in school, with my boss there. Is there anything else you want to say now?'

'Yeah, but you're still police though, aren't you?'

'That's true.' Emma nodded. It was written clearly that there was a gap between them, both in age and status. She needed to break the ice. 'Tell you what though.' She got her notebook out and held it out them. 'This what I'll do.' She wrote "Information Received" at the top and underlined it. 'No names, I'm not even going to ask you who you are.'

The girls all looked at each other. One of the five was slightly taller, high cheekbones, straight black hair and bright blue eyes. She was obviously better groomed and dressed than her companions. Subconsciously, the others looked at her and she gave a slight nod, almost imperceptible.

'Okay then,' asked a smaller girl with mousy brown hair, who hadn't been interviewed yesterday. 'What do you want to know?'

'Well, one thing that would really help would be tracking down WankyBoi.' The word felt odd in her mouth and she couldn't hide her disgust.

'One of my friends, didn't come over to sixth form with us,' the mousy girl said. 'She reckons it's her cousin and a couple of his mates.'

'How do you know that?' Emma was making notes.

'Well, it's basic psychology, innit?' This came from a girl with curly blonde hair. 'Why do you think they do it? I mean they could just be, you know, doing this and not sending it to girls. So it's obvious – they want people to know. They probably want to be caught. They probably each boast about it to a couple of mates about what they're doing, and then it spreads. Everyone feels better if they know a secret.'

'Psychology A-level,' one of the other girls said with a knowing look. Emma nodded and resolved to listen to what she had to say.

'So, does this friend's cousin have a name?'

'Errr, it was Katie Smithson who left school in year II. Her cousin was called Justin or something like that? Sorry I can't be more help.'

'No, it's fine. I can get her details through the school, follow the trail. This really helps. We need to find these boys. You said there were three of them?'

'That's what people say. We all get these messages and compare notes.'

'Anyway, it's probably not them. They're just sad little boys.' There were nods around the group.

'Besides which if they had killed Mazey, they'd have put a video up by now.'

'No! It would be too much. They'd get arrested straight away.'

There were general nods and agreement around the group.

'Well if it's not them, who else could it be?' Emma asked.

Again there was that look over to the lead girl with the straight black hair and again there was a quick nod.

'What about DCM? He gives all of us the creeps.'

'DCM? What's that?'

'Dark Car Man.' Emma gave another blank look so they carried on talking. 'There's this guy in a dark car, drives around at night. Slows down when he goes past a girl. You can never see who it is. It's a bit spooky.'

'Yeah, my brother always thought it was an urban myth, you know, something to scare people. But one night he was walking home and a car slowed down right next to him. It only drove off when they realised he was a boy.' Emma frowned so the girl continued. 'He's got long hair in a ponytail, so from the back...'

'Right.' Emma was still making notes, but she was using her professional duties to hide her unease. It was a universal fear of women, being targeted when alone and at night. Just because she was trained and a police officer, it didn't make her immune. She was still scared, even in the middle of the day in a public place, talking about it. 'So do you know what make or model this car might be?'

'It's always a family hatchback.'

'Astra.'

'Fiesta.'

'One of those Japanese ones?'

'Hold on, I'll ask my brother. He knows his cars.' There was a pause as the girl whipped out her phone and tapped away. After a moment, she looked up and announced. 'It was a Ford. Like I said, either Focus or Fiesta. Black, dark grey or dark blue.'

'That's not very clear,' Emma said making notes. 'Can he be any more definite on the colour?'

More tapping followed then the girl said. 'No, it was those funny orange street lights. But it was him. Dark Car Man. No doubt.' The other girls nodded. He seemed to be a well-known part of their lives.

Emma realised that her Saturday of sorting out chores was over. She needed to get this information into the office and see if she could track down the mysterious cousin and find the Dark Car Man. Two people to trace.

Haines was sat at his desk on a Saturday. Nothing was going right on this case. Forensics had come back as a blank. The victim wasn't stabbed or cut anywhere so there was little chance of evidence transfer to the perpetrator. Her body had been dragged and dumped in a yard and covered with rubbish bags that had all been taken from the bin next to her. Plenty of opening for a defence lawyer to argue that any transfer was accidental or non-probative.

Some progress had been made, however. The body definitely was that of Mazey Taylor and she had died at some point between eleven pm and two am. She had been killed by strangulation – something had been pressed hard enough across her throat to crush her windpipe.

Preliminary theory was that she was walking home from a friend's house and never got back home. There were surface bruises across her back as if she'd been pinned against a wall or the floor. Presumably she had been killed on the pavement and dragged into the alley.

Thankfully there was another negative in the forensics. There was no sign of sexual assault. Her clothes were disturbed, but no more than you'd expect after a struggle and being dragged down an alley. However reassuring it might be to her parents, this information did mean that another forensic route had been closed down.

Next he'd moved on to the video from WankyBoi. Nothing turned up anywhere on a Google search and because it was a video of a video it was impossible to find the original time or date that it had either been made or sent.

The photo taken around the time of death had been sent off for analysis and this had borne out their initial findings. It was probably a close up of a hand. Which, Haines, thought would explain the viciousness of the attack on the phone. He could imagine a teenager of today being attacked and reaching for their phone to take a picture of her attacker. It was a shame, he thought, that she hadn't chosen to run away or call 999 instead.

DC Angel walked in and took a look around the office. 'It's quiet in here. I thought we were running a murder enquiry. First week should be buzzing.'

Rob Haines stood up from his desk and came over. 'Trouble is the case is all negatives. No forensics, no CCTV, no sexual assault.'

'Surely that's a good thing?'

'Well, yes, it is. But it does mean that we can't round up all the nonces who live in our area and lean on them.'

'Come on! This isn't an episode of Life on Mars. You can't say that any more.'

'Sorry. We are unable to go through the sex offenders register and find anyone on there who might be relapsing on their rehabilitation.' He paused for a second. 'Doesn't matter what you call it, we don't have many leads.'

'Ex-boyfriend?'

'The delightful Kyle? Yeah, turns out he started seeing someone while he was still with Mazey. She found out and dumped him. He's a bit of a spotty teenager. The only real mystery is how he got two girls to go out with him.'

'And Mazey wasn't bad-mouthing him around the area? Nothing like that?'

'No, she just moved on.'

'So, what is happening?'

'Well, I've got people out trying to track down this Wanky-Boi. And we're also going through anyone who likes strangling girls and has just got out of prison. Going nationwide too, you know, in case it's not a local.'

'Probably is a local though,' DC Angel countered. 'Or someone really lucky to pick a blind spot on CCTV to carry out their attack.'

'Hmmm, there's not much else that we can do at the moment.'

'I might be able to help there. I ran into some of the girls who knew Mazey, hanging around McDonald's.' Haines' eyebrows shot up but DC Angel continued. She briefly outlined what she'd learnt about a possible route to the identity of WankyBoi.

'Well,' Haines grinned. 'This is a bit more like it. Did you get names and details?'

'No, it's all information received. It was the best way to keep them talking.'

He nodded. 'If you're confident in this it's something I can get started on.' He made notes as he spoke. 'Katie Smithson left year 11 last summer, from Bradwick Comprehensive.'

'I think you'll find it's Bradwick High School now.'

'I'll tell you one thing that hasn't changed.' He reached for the phone. 'The school secretary. She knows everyone who goes through that place.'

'Will she take a call on a Saturday?'

'I have her home number. You'd be surprised how often you need to trace someone from school. One I've spoken to her, I'll also try the recently retired headmistress.'

'You really have access to her as well?' DC Angel couldn't hide her surprise.

'Well, she is my aunt and only lives up the road. But if these lads are being naughty as grown-ups then it's likely they weren't behaving themselves in school.'

DC Angel tried, and failed, to work out how many data protection laws and police procedures were about to be broken.

'First of all I'll see if either of them can remember Katie Smithson and her family.' Haines was in his element now. 'This is excellent, it's a step towards finding who's behind the videos. And Mazey was already halfway to reporting them.'

DC Angel debated with herself whether or not to challenge the exact nature of the shortcuts. But she could also see that the sooner they could apprehend the makers of the video, the quicker they'd find Mazey's killer. And they could write off the shortcuts as information received if they were careful with their wording when questioning the suspects. 'You're right. You work your magic on the phones.'

She left him to plug into the Bradwick grapevine while she found a terminal to put her findings into the system. It was only when she went through her notes that she realised that she hadn't mentioned Dark Car Man to Haines. On reflection, she realised that looking for a dark coloured family car made by Ford was a fool's errand. She put the details into the computer and tried to forget about them.

It was already late afternoon by then so she switched off and went to see if Haines needed anything before she went home.

'No, you're all right. I'll stay for a bit. This is what I like about this town, everyone knows everyone and they're all willing to help. Sue, the secretary is heading into the office now to look up some records. I think we'll have a name by tomorrow morning.'

'Well good luck, sir, and don't work too hard!' DC Angel left the office wondering if Haines had even noticed that tomorrow would be Sunday.

Chapter Eleven

Emma sat in her car in the station car park and tried to plan what was left of her evening. She'd woken in the morning intending to sort out a few errands and generally catch up on the work of looking after the house. But she was too used to the job and its demands to be upset about the change of direction.

What she really wanted was to sink a bottle of wine and watch some rubbish on late night TV. But then she'd seen the look in Haines' eyes when she'd passed over the information she'd gained from the gang outside McDonald's.

Going home, getting drunk and staying up 'til the small hours was a bad plan. She suspected that by tomorrow he'd have everything he needed to go and make some arrests. The last thing she wanted was to be either still drunk or hung over when the call came through. This was her big chance and she wanted to be in on the action with a clear head.

She started the engine and headed for home. She lived in a smart four bed semi in one of the nicer areas of Bradwick. She'd had a simple plan – she got the mortgage and rented out rooms to cover the bills. She had the nicest room and had re-sisted the urge to turn all the downstairs rooms into bedrooms, although she had converted the garage into one. She always rented out to other shift workers – primarily nurses and police officers and always to women. There was something comforting about knowing that everyone around you was in the same boat with long shifts and erratic sleeping patterns.

She let herself in and Florence the cat immediately wound itself around her legs. She used to be a huge animal, but a few years ago the vet had insisted that she be put on a diet. Emma had chatted to her housemates and realised that the wily animal was getting far more than her required two meals a day. This had led to a very simple system being implemented. When Emma was led into the kitchen by the cat, she glanced at the cat food on the counter. On top was a piece of cardboard which said "evening" and the other side said "morning". Whoever was around fed the cat, flipped the cardboard to show when she was last fed, and her days of being corpulent were over. Now she knew that Florence had been fed Emma ignored her, no matter how often she miaowed or sat by her empty plate looking pathetic.

Emma settled on the sofa with her single glass of wine and got her mobile phone out. She'd met a traffic officer called David Marks through a specialist dating site for workers in blue-light jobs. They'd had a fairly informal relationship for several months. It was her perfect relationship – she didn't have the time for someone who'd make a lot of demands of her. With David, they had an agreement that they could text each other for a bit of no strings attached fun whenever they felt like it. And it was definitely what she needed right now.

She texted and asked him to come over for a glass of wine. When he responded and asked if that was all, she told him to bring his toothbrush and added some flirty emojis.

As she expected, that created the right response and he said he could be there in twenty minutes. She had a quick shower, moving quietly around the shared house as she wasn't sure who was asleep. When she was done, she stayed in her bathrobe and waited in the lounge. She was glad of a few quiet minutes to herself, sipping her wine and taking in the peace of the house around her.

She heard David's arrival before she saw him. He was a motorcycle police officer and had arrived by his personal bike tonight. She moved to the front door to avoid him having to ring the bell and wake people up.

He stood there and took in the bathrobe with a slow grin. 'I feel a bit overdressed now,' he said, indicating his leathers.

'Well, why don't we take the wine up to my room and we'll see what we can do about that?'

'You are forward, aren't you?'

'Is that a problem?'

'No, no, not at all. Nice to know where you stand.'

* * *

The next morning she was woken by a text message from Haines. "It's nice and early on Sunday morning. Fancy waking up a naughty teenager who's been making videos?"

She had been expecting this. She quickly replied and agreed to meet at the station. Glancing across the bed she saw the sleeping form of David. His hair was tousled and he was spread out over his side of the bed. She needed to get moving and hoped he'd stay asleep.

Returning from her shower and morning routine she found David sat up in bed. She kept the bathrobe on and slipped into fresh underwear without undoing the robe.

'Why are you being so coy? I think I saw everything last night!'

'I'm not being coy.' Emma wasn't prepared to get into this with David right now. 'I just have to go to work today.'

'No! It's Sunday. We could spend the day in bed together before grabbing some brunch.' Seeing the look on Emma's face, he faltered slightly before ploughing on. 'Or, or, how about going out for a proper Sunday lunch? My treat. After coming back to bed, of course.'

'No! I did tell you last night what the deal was. You knew then there was a chance I'd have to go in to work early today.'

'I thought you were just joking. Flirting.' He looked genuinely hurt.

'No. You're in the job. You know what it's like.' Despite her harsh words, she did feel an urge, a basic need to go back to bed. David was sat up in bed with the duvet pooled around his waist. She took in the sight of his bare shoulders and chest, muscles at rest, the stubble on his cheek. She was tired of being the career woman. She wished she could go back to bed, could have the warmth of human contact and the companionship of a day shared.

But balancing out that basic need, she had her career. She knew that being there when the arrests were made was critical. She might get into the interviews, contribute to the report to CPS. All of that was what would help her career. And, on a personal level, she felt she needed to be there at the arrest. To be a woman when the men were arrested. She shed her robe and clipped a bra on with her back to him.

'Well, in Traffic we tend to have shifts. And if you're not on the rota, your time's your own.'

Emma took a deep breath. 'Look. I don't have the time to do this now. I need to be in work.' She felt uncomfortable so she slipped a teal top on and started looking for trousers.

'So, you can just call me up, have your fun, then boot me out in the morning?'

'Hey! As I remember it wasn't all one sided. You got your fun last night as well. And I did say in my text that it was just for the night.'

'Like I said, I thought you were messing.' He looked hopeful and patted the bed next to him. Again Emma felt that tug.

She could smell him, imagine the sleepy early morning, languid feel that sex would have. 'We could have one more go. No, brunch or spending the whole day. Just some quick fun?'

'No, we can't. I'm already showered and dressed. I have a job and a career.' She found her jeans and pulled them on.

'Okay. Well I'll leave then. I know when I'm not wanted.' He pulled a T-shirt on, messing his hair up even further and started looking around for more of his clothes.

'You don't have to leave straight away.' She put on her shoes. 'Stay if you want. Have a shower and a coffee before you go home.' She attempted to be conciliatory. 'I could give you a ring later, when I get home?'

'You think I'm going to go home and stare at the phone waiting for you to be ready?' Anger was rising in his voice. 'Actually I have more pride than that. You can't just pick me up and put me down when you feel like it. You go to work if you want, but don't expect me to be available when you get back.'

Emma glanced at the clock and at David Marks who was now lying on his front, trying to snag his clothes without exposing himself. She knew she needed to get into work. They had a mountain of work to do to prepare for the interviews if the arrest went off okay. And then they'd have to work on tracking down the other two WankyBois as well. She realised that she was focused on work and still hadn't answered David. She just couldn't deal with this argument and her work at the same time. 'Just don't slam the door on the way out. Everyone here is on shifts so they need their sleep.'

With that she slipped out of her room and went to work.

CHAPTER TWELVE

Haines and Angel pulled up on a very ordinary suburban street. Grass and trees separated the road from the pavement. Haines always looked at the cars to judge an area. Here it was all smart family cars, mostly three to five years old and mostly good makes. The houses were all solidly built 1930s semi-detached and looked well kept. It was early on a Sunday morning and the street was quiet.

DC Angel saw Haines frowning at the sat nav and checking his notes. 'What were you expecting? Somewhere run down? A council estate?'

'No, but this looks like a nice area.'

'Precisely.' DC Angel nodded. 'They can afford to give their kids smartphones and computers and they probably just leave them alone and unsupervised for hours on end.'

'Now who's being prejudiced?'

'I'm not,' DC Angel argued. 'It's just that if you have a big house then the kids can hide in the bedroom and edit and send dodgy videos. If they're growing up with a big family in a small house then they're more likely to go out and cause trouble on the streets. Stands to reason.'

'I suppose you're right.' Haines turned to look at DC Angel. 'Are you all right with being in early on a Sunday?' He had picked up something in her attitude when she'd arrived at the station.

'Yeah, it's fine.' She hoped that she hadn't brought her argument with David into work with her. She was aggrieved that her planning hadn't accounted for his ego. 'To be honest I was kind of expecting it when I saw how hard you were going after the information yesterday afternoon.' She was keen to move away from analysing the past day. 'Anyway, who are we here to see?'

'One Julian Lockwood, age nineteen, left school with no real qualifications, still lives at home, unemployed.' Haines read from his notes.

'He sounds like a fine example of manhood. Let's see what he has to say for himself.'

'Take it easy though, Angel.' For once Haines sounded slightly vulnerable. 'We're on shaky ground with the identification. You have information received and I used my contacts to get his name and address. Let's let him dig himself into a hole, otherwise a defence lawyer will be screaming "entrapment".'

'Okay then. We'll take it easy and let him incriminate himself.'

The door was opened by a middle-aged woman they soon ascertained was Julian Lockwood's mother. As soon as she knew what they wanted, she called for her son. A teenage boy sloped down the stairs while the mother looked concerned.

'What have you been up to, Julian?' she asked.

'I told you, it's Jules!' He sounded sulky.

Haines glanced over at DC Angel with a slight nod. She took the hint and said, 'Is there somewhere we can talk in private?' She left the slightest of pauses as his eyes widened in panic. 'We need your help with some videos we've found the internet.'

Instantly he went from slouching to on the move. He wheeled past his mother and ran for the kitchen.

'Is there any way out of the back garden?' Haines barked at the startled mother.

'No, only his shed is out there.'

'Right.' He barged past the startled woman and through the kitchen. Angel made a snap decision and went round the outside to the gate that she'd seen when they approached.

The gate opened onto a narrow passageway that led from the front, down the side of the house towards the rear garden. She waited just at the end of it, listening to her boss cursing as he chased the teenager around the garden. Her instincts were spot on as Julian appeared at the other end of the passageway.

He thought for a fraction of a second then charged straight for DC Angel. She deliberately shifted her weight to one side and he went for the opening. He made contact with her shoulder as he barged past. She caught hold of his wrist as he passed her and spun on her foot.

He wasn't expecting it and spun right around the corner. His own weight and speed had worked against him and he smacked into the wall. DC Angel hadn't let go of the wrist and now twisted it expertly so that he was pinned in place.

Behind her Haines nodded in satisfaction at two things. Firstly the skill of his new DC in subduing a suspect and secondly that Julian's phone skittered out of his pocket, unseen by either of them.

'Julian Lockwood, I am arresting you for assaulting a police officer. You do not have to say anything, but it may harm your defence if you do not mention when questioned something which you later rely on in court. Anything you do say may be given in evidence.' DC Angel had him cuffed and frogmarched up the front garden before he knew what happened. Haines slipped Julian's mobile into an evidence bag just before his own phone started buzzing. They bundled Julian into the back of the unmarked car.

'Wait there a minute,' Haines said to Angel. 'I'd better take this. It's DI Hargreaves.'

He walked a short distance away and then came back with a face like thunder. 'Damn it! I need to get back to the station.

73

No, I can't do that. I've got to meet someone. Smooth things out.'

'What? Now? In case you haven't noticed, we've just made our first arrest in the Taylor case.' DC Angel realised she might be overstepping her bounds and added, 'Sir.'

'I know. But DI Hargreaves has someone I need to meet. He actually used the phrase "organ grinder not the monkey".' There was a significant pause. 'To me.'

'Right. What do we need to do now?' Angel stopped dead and held up a hand. To his credit Rob Haines just waited. He could see the concentration on her face as she rewound what had just happened. In a matter of seconds, she smiled. 'It's the shed. That's what the mother said. "His shed" not "the shed". That must be where he spends his time, not in his bedroom at all. We need to get that secure before we do anything else. We know there is more than one of them. For all we know one of his co-conspirators will be on his way over now to delete everything. Did you secure his phone? We don't want him texting his creepy friends.'

'The phone is here.' He held up the evidence bag. Then he looked at his watch. 'Crap! Okay. Five minutes to sort this out. You whistle up uniforms to secure the scene and we'll need whoever's on weekend call-out at the technical team to start right away with whatever we find both in the shed and his bedroom.'

'Okay, boss. I'll get on the radio and keep an eye on Julian here.'

DCI Haines looked up at the house. Julian's mother was striding down the driveway with a face like thunder.

'What are you doing? Where are you taking him? Don't you go hurting my boy!'

'It's Okay.' Haines held his hands out to calm her and stop her getting any closer to the car. 'He assaulted my colleague so we've arrested him and we're taking him to Bradwick Police Station.'

'He wouldn't assault anyone. He's a good boy.'

'He pushed her out of the way. I saw it. That's enough.' There was an uneasy silence between them. 'Does he live here? With you?' The mother nodded. 'Right and the shed you mentioned?'

'That's where he spends most of his time. He's very good with computers.' A hint of pride crept into her voice.

'Right. Okay. We'll send a couple of uniformed officers to search the shed and his bedroom for any computers. We might have to remove some items, but you'll get a receipt.'

'All this for brushing past an officer?' The fire had started to go out of her attack and now she was edging towards exasperated. 'It's a bit much isn't it?'

'We came here to ask him about some videos that were uploaded to the internet and he ran.' Haines tried his hardest to sound reasonable. 'We need to know why he didn't want to talk to us.'

'Well, he's my boy. Can I at least be the responsible adult? Sit in on the interview?'

Haines frowned. 'I understood he was nineteen?'

'Well, he is. But...' She trailed off, suddenly uncertain of her ground.

'Listen, the uniformed officers will be here soon. Is there anyone you want to call? Someone to come and sit with you while all this is sorted out?'

'I'll have to tell his father. He'll be livid.'

'Is there anyone in the shed at the moment?' Haines was worried that things were being deleted as he spoke.

'No, his friends usually come over in the evenings. They'll spend hours in there, playing video games and chatting. You know what boys are like.' Haines thought rather grimly that he had a far better idea of what her boy was like than she did.

'And these friends...?' he left the question deliberately half formed. With a bit of luck he could write this up as Julian's mother volunteering information.

'Oh, that'd be Ceiran and Tom most nights.'

'Right. Who are they exactly?'

'Ceiran Knight and Tom Small. Ceiran's been friends with Julian since primary school and Tom came along as he was friends with Ceiran's younger brother but kind of latched on to the older two.'

'Thank you, Mrs Lockwood, you've been most helpful.' He wanted to keep her there until he could get hold of the other two suspects. The last thing he wanted was a concerned mother talking to the other parents involved. But on the other hand he had a problem to fix with his other operation. He was saved when he looked around and saw the familiar colours of a marked police car driving up the road. 'Look, here they are now. I'll just show them where we are and we can be on our way.' With this Haines went to guide the police in and warn them to notify DC Angel if the mother made any attempt to contact the families of either Ceiran Knight or Tom Small.

When he finally got back to the car, he started giving orders. 'Right, Angel, you drive.'

While she navigated the car back to the station he phoned back to DI Hargreaves.

'I know, I know. I am in the middle of a murder enquiry here. Maybe you could tell him that?'

'It's just that I know how much effort we've all put in to make this work. No one wants to see it go tits-up because you missed a meeting.'

'I'm still your commanding officer, don't tell me off.' Haines paused to draw breath. 'I know you're not working on the murder case but if I'm going to this meeting you'll need to pitch in with the MIT. I'm on my way back to the station with a suspect for the Taylor murder. There are two further suspects – Ceiran Knight and Tom Small. I need them brought in as soon as possible. Take two people for each of them. There's a chance that Small is under eighteen so be careful and make sure there's a responsible adult. Just hold them at the station and I'll interview them as soon as I'm back.'

DC Angel kept stealing sideways glances at her boss as she drove back to the station. Eventually her curiosity won out. 'So, what's this important meeting then?'

'It's an operation that's been months in the planning and now one of my contacts is getting jumpy. If I don't go and pat him into shape then we might lose everything. That's all I can say.'

'Okay, boss.' DC Angel couldn't believe it. They were in the process of arresting their main suspects in a murder case and he was going off reassuring people on another case.

They drove in silence until they got onto the high street when Haines spoke. 'Pull up over here on the left.' DC Angel swung the car in to the kerb and looked questioningly at her DCI. 'I'm getting out here, I'm already late for a meeting.'

'Sir, we have a suspect on board. We should have two of us present at all times.' She spoke in a tight, quiet voice.

'The station is right up there. He's handcuffed and you'll be parking in under a minute.' With that he got out and shut the door. Swearing under her breath she glanced in the rear-view mirror. Lockwood was staring sulkily out of the window, apparently oblivious to the argument in the front.

The final two hundred yards to the police station passed without incident. The custody sergeant gave DC Angel a look that meant he'd noticed that she was bringing in a suspect on her own. But he didn't say anything and Julian Lockwood mumbled his way through the whole procedure.

When he was safely locked in the cells, she went back to the MIT room and made some calls. She found out that an impressive collection of laptop, desktop and tablet computers was in the process of being bagged up and logged in to evidence ready for technical analysis.

She tried DCI Haines number and it went straight to voice-mail so she felt a bit lost. She made some notes and tried to plan her interview strategy but her mind kept wandering to where her boss was and what he was up to. It must be something important to keep him from the first breakthrough of the case.

Her planning was disrupted by the phone. The desk sergeant called to ask for someone from the MIT to come down as there was a situation in custody. The background noise certainly sounded as if there was a problem.

Chapter Thirteen

DC Angel heard the noise from three fire doors away. When she came in, she found the source of the noise to be a small woman with long dark hair and sharp features. She was berating DS Stonor while DC Ed Mitchell tried to fade into the background.

'You can't just come round to my house and arrest my son and then not tell me!'

'We did tell–'

'You said it's part of an ongoing investigation and something about uploading videos. That doesn't really explain anything!'

'Look, here's DC Angel now. She's on the case and can help you.' He shot her a look beseeching her to step in. 'Why don't you take her to one of our relatives' rooms and get her some tea?'

'I don't want your bloody tea! I want some answers!'

'Okay, come on then. Let's just talk in normal voices for a start.' DC Angel was deploying all her training to calm her down even though she was seething. DS Stonor was an experienced officer, why couldn't he defuse the situation? She suspected it was because she was a woman.

'Who exactly are you?' The woman's voice was calmer now.

'I'm DC Angel and I'm working on the case connected with the arrest of your son.' She kept her voice calm and even. 'And you are?'

'Tabitha Small. You've arrested my boy Tom.'

'Right. This is probably not the best place to deal with this. Why don't you come over to one of our rooms and we can chat?'

With a mutinous look, Tabitha Small agreed to follow DC Angel into a small side room. This wasn't an interview room, instead it was a softer space. It had low sofas and tables with boxes of tissues.

Soon they were seated and ignoring cups of tea. Tabitha peered suspiciously at DC Angel who felt uncomfortable and wished that she looked more mature. Her fears were realised when Tabitha asked, 'What was your name and rank again?'

'I'm DC Angel and I'm investigating the Mazey Taylor case.'

'DC? That's a constable isn't it? I've seen enough TV shows. I want to see the inspector or the superintendent or whoever's in charge.'

'There is DCI Haines but you have to understand that this is a large and complex investigation–'

'I don't care! You've arrested my sixteen-year-old son. You've said it's something to do with obscene videos on the internet and now you're telling me it's something to do with that poor lass who got killed.' She folded her arms. 'I want to speak to someone in charge.'

There was an ominous silence as DC Angel assessed her chances of changing Ms Small's mind. Internally fuming that Haines had dropped her completely in it, she spoke in a curt voice. 'Fine. I'll just go and see where he is and when we can expect him back.'

In the corridor outside she tried Haines' mobile again. And once again, it went straight to voicemail. She didn't trust herself to leave a polite message so she broke the connection. She leant against a wall and mentally took stock. They had Julian Lockwood and Tom Small in custody. Ms Small was in a waiting room and didn't look like she would move until she found out what fate awaited her son. DCI Haines, her boss, had disappeared in the high street, presumably switching off his mobile as soon as he left the car.

Before she could decide what to do next, she caught sight of movement in the custody suite. She pushed herself off the wall and went to see what was happening now.

Ceiran Knight was being brought in. DS Parry and DC Osborne were looking slightly scruffy and very pissed off. 'Bastard tried to leg it,' a slightly out of breath DS Parry said. 'We had to chase him halfway down the street.'

DC Angel looked at Ceiran Knight. He was not only short, but also small boned. She could imagine that once he decided to run he'd be tricky to hold on to. Now, with his hands cuffed behind his back, he was docile and sullen.

'He must have had a tip-off from somewhere,' DC Osborne said pointedly, looking at DC Angel.

'We've just arrested three suspects who are very clued up on technology with families who all know each other. It's a Sunday but we've still thrown uniforms at it to search the Lockwood house and shed. Most likely a family member or neighbour tipped them off.' In turn she glared at DS Stonor. 'Of course, if our DCI was actually here, he could have got the resources allocated to make sure that we had everything locked down.'

'What? Haines isn't here?' DC Osborne obviously wasn't in the loop.

'He had a meeting.' DI Hargreaves had just arrived back at the station. He glanced uneasily at Osborne. 'You know how hard we've been working on the other operation. Well the wheels are nearly coming off and Haines is needed somewhere else to keep things together.' He looked round at all the assembled officers. No one dared challenge him, so he rounded on DC Angel. 'Angel, you're on the MIT and we're here to help. What else do we need to do?'

'We've got the three suspects in custody. The uniforms are bringing in a van full of computers. Haines won't thank us if we start interviews without him.' And he's burning through the available twenty-four hours with his phone switched off, she thought. 'If you could use your rank to put the rush on the technicians that would certainly help. We really need at the very least a summary of what files they have. How many videos are there? When they started making them? And, if possible, how many people they sent them to? That should be enough for either an extension or a charge so we can fill in the details later.'

Hargreaves nodded, glad that DC Angel hadn't pressed him on where the boss had gone. 'I can do that.'

'Well, I'd better go and search for any previous offences on our suspects, work on an interview strategy and wait for DCI Haines to come back.' She left a pause for anyone to explain to her what was going on. When she was met with silence she turned on her heel and left for the CID office.

CHAPTER FOURTEEN

DCI Haines watched DC Angel's pool car driving up the high street and turning into the police station. He had deep misgivings but he had to do what needed to be done.

He walked up the high street and turned into an arcade. He noticed a car parked on double yellows with two guys in the front and a clear view of the arcade entrance. The man he was going to meet was obviously nervous.

He went into the wine bar and sought out Billy King. He saw him in a corner, facing the room. He was, as always, dressed as a successful business man. Haines knew the truth about how he earned his money, so always thought of it in those terms – he was dressing up, pretending to be legitimate. He went to get a bottle of designer lager from the bar before approaching the table.

'Finally! I have to say there's not many people would have the nerve to stand me up.' Billy King stood up and leant his fists on the table.

'Come on! You know if it was up to me, I'd have come straight here. But I'm heading the MIT for the Mazey Taylor killing. We've had a breakthrough and it'll raise eyebrows that I'm not at the station.'

'That poor girl who was killed and left in the rubbish? Terrible thing, terrible!' He shook his head and left Haines wondering how much was genuine and what was put on for show. 'But listen to me. For all that she's pretty and going to be in the papers, I have people too. People that are being stabbed and beaten and shot. And I know the papers will look down on them as thugs but they're my people, damn it.'

'I know that. I'm doing what I can. Come on, let's sit down and be reasonable.' Haines sat in his seat, leaned back and waited for King to follow suit. Eventually the other man settled down.

'I've been up all bloody night.' He ran a hand through his hair and sipped his coffee. 'Down at the A&E. It's definite now. The war is on.'

When it was clear that King wasn't going to be forthcoming, Haines asked, 'Why were you at the hospital?'

'Four of my men were in there. All of them took a right beating. And do you know why? Because they were given a number to call, to set up with a new supplier, from Birmingham. All four of them told the new guys to fuck off, and now look where we are. Thing is, I don't know how many other people took the number. Don't know who I can trust.'

Haines thought of the two men in the car outside and now realised why King was so nervous.

'And now, I hear on the grapevine that one of my boys was arrested this week. I can't turn a profit if my people are either cooling their heels in a police cell or sitting in A&E waiting to be seen. I thought we had an agreement.'

'We do.' Haines could sense the frustration coming off Billy King and knew he had to tread carefully. On the other hand he'd taken as much grief as he could today. 'Firstly that was just a caution for bag snatching, which to be honest we should've done him properly for.' King looked sulky. 'Listen, it won't happen again. It's the new girl, she's just come in as a DC.' He stopped to look hard at Billy King, to make sure he made his point. 'But you should have a word as well. They were sat in a pool car drinking coffee in broad daylight. Bloody obvious. And if they see someone commit a crime under their noses...'

King looked mutinous but didn't offer any comment.

'Listen, we've had a good thing going for years,' Haines continued. 'We have common ground – whatever's best for Bradwick. But nothing good lasts for ever. I'm moving up to a desk job, all strategy and meetings. That means you'll have to deal with DI Hargreaves and it also means that everyone will shuffle up one and new blood will come in at the bottom.'

'So, this new girl.' King had a knack of homing in on the one part of the conversation that mattered to him. 'What's she like? Stickler for the rules? Or is it possible she could, you know?'

Haines considered the question. Not just the answer, but whether he'd be prepared to expose DC Angel to this world, the other part of the job. She was an incomer, would probably not understand what the town meant to him and Billy. On the other hand she had shown that she could play the political game. 'I don't know. You know we cut you some slack, scratch each other's backs. But I hope that if any of my officers see someone steal a bag then they would act. You can't hold that against her. It's what the job is.' Haines could tell from Billy King's expression that he'd pushed as hard as he could. 'Leave her to me. Maybe when I bow out with a spectacular raid then she'll come around. How's the intelligence on that shaping up?'

'Before I give you the update, I need your help. You need to do something about those bloody Latvians. I don't know how many more weekends like this one I've got left in me.' He paused, registered that Haines wanted an answer. 'I've got a couple of people undercover. They took the phone number and now they're in Birmingham, meeting new suppliers. That's the last I heard.'

Haines shut his eyes and tried to think. He knew he was already cutting corners with the Taylor murder enquiry. And now he needed to do more here. He opened his eyes as he reached a decision. He would stop chasing the Latvians piece-meal. 'Okay, Billy. I can sort it. Give me a couple of days to put all the pieces in place but we can get the Latvians to back off.'

'You said that last time. Will it really happen this time?'

'Yes. I give you my word. I noticed the goons in the car outside. Are they yours?'

'These are dangerous times. And we were right about the big meeting coming up. All this – the beatings and the cheaper product – that's just phase one. Phase two, they'll bring in a huge amount of product and flood the market with cheap drugs.' He shrugged. 'It's basic capitalism. Once they've edged me out of the market then the prices will go back up again.'

'So we need to survive phase one and disrupt phase two.'

'And when you do, there'll be lots of cash and lots of drugs all in one place.'

Haines nodded. 'That's what I need.'

'As soon as I know you'll know.'

A pause fell between the two men. Haines drank some of his beer. 'You know that this is my swansong? It's my retirement party. I'd much rather leave by heading up a big raid than sitting around in a function room out the back of a pub with warm wine and tired crisps." King nodded. 'I need this to work. To put the seal on my career in CID. When the dust has settled, we'll have a meeting with DI Hargreaves. You need to rely on him.' King looked mutinously at Haines but didn't say anything. 'But in the meantime, I'll try to take the pressure off you.'

CHAPTER FIFTEEN

It didn't matter how much the regulations changed, how many new devices like video capture were introduced, interview rooms remained fundamentally unchanged. They were places where desperate people were questioned and somehow that despair seeped into the fabric of the room itself.

DC Angel suspected that her boss, DCI Haines had deliberately paired her up with DS Stonor in an effort to mend bridges after the debacle with her arresting his informant. For his part, Julian Lockwood was surly and unresponsive after spending most of the day in the cells.

She had given her boss a quick rundown of her opening strategy and knew that he'd be watching. That was a problem with the modern video interview suites. You never knew how many people were watching. And you never knew what would be seen when the tapes were reviewed.

When the formalities were over, Stonor let her open the questioning. 'So, Julian,' she emphasised the word, letting him know that he wouldn't be called Jules. 'You are here because you assaulted me.' He looked up at her from under his eyebrows, furious that he'd been tricked by her standing in his way. 'But what we're really interested in is Mazey Taylor.'

'That girl who was killed? What's that got to do with me?'

'Well, she had a video on her phone that showed a friend's phone receiving a video from an account called WankyBoi and we wondered if you might know anything about that?'

'Mazey? Nah.' He shook his head. 'We never sent her a video. I'm fairly sure of that.'

'But you do admit to sending videos using the name Wanky-Boi?' Gently does it, she thought. Just build the confession one piece at a time.

'Yeah, so what?' Julian shrugged. 'Everyone does it, don't they? The whole world's on YouTube. It's not a crime.'

'And you do this, in your shed, with Ceiran Knight and Tom Small?' Angel pressed.

'I suppose so.' His eyes narrowed as he realised he might get his friends in trouble.

'You do realise,' DS Stonor leant forward and started speaking, 'that our technical team is already taking your shed apart? Preliminary reports are that they've found a list of who you sent it to along with the unedited videos.'

DC Angel looked sharply at DS Stonor. According to her strategy she was about three questions away from getting Julian to admit to a whole string of offences. From what the schoolgirls had said to her and what the police search had revealed, she was fairly certain that Tom had been under sixteen when the videos started. If that fact could be confirmed, new offences would be on the table for the older two – creating and distributing child pornography. If she could just get Julian Lockwood to admit to it, then they could charge them there and then which would take the pressure off the technical teams to get the data quickly.

Now DS Stonor had spooked their suspect and he looked dangerously close to going silent and getting a lawyer.

'My shed? You can't go in there!' Julian looked around as if he could escape. 'I've got a new padlock and everything.'

'We arrested you at your home address. Under PACE we can search your premises and that includes any outbuildings.'

Julian Lockwood went silent, the colour draining from his face. 'You've been in my shed?'

'Yep.' Stonor nodded. 'Even now the technical team are examining all the computers they found in there. We've asked TimeBomb to check your account and if we find even one girl who got a video the day before her sixteenth birthday, we'll come for you.'

'Right. You can't pin this on me. I need my lawyer.'

'Is that a formal request for legal representation?' As Stonor said the words, Angel groaned inwardly while maintaining a calm expression. Now the interview was over, depending on the advice of Lockwood's solicitor. Given the time of day and the weekend, she was doubtful if they'd get much further until Monday morning.

* * *

DC Angel went back upstairs to CID where she found a harassed looking DCI Haines.

'Any thoughts about our strategy for interviewing Small?' Haines asked. 'And have we got a responsible adult?'

'I do have a plan. And Mrs Small isn't going anywhere.'

She outlined her strategy to DCI Haines and he agreed. DS Stonor was still around so they sent him to manage the video suite while Haines and Angel handled the interview itself.

Tom Small was unremarkable – average height and build – and had a mop of curly dirty blond hair that was shaved round the back and sides. His mother was showing the strain with bags under her eyes and a drawn expression. Her face was angular, with a pointed nose and sharp cheekbones under a severe fringe.

When they walked into the interview room, she laid a protective hand on her son's arm. After all the formalities were completed, Tom Small spoke first.

'I've been talking with my mum. It's probably best I don't answer any questions. You can only hold me twenty-four hours so I'll just wait it out.' Although his words sounded brave, his voice wavered, as if he was testing waters, asking for permission.

'That is of course, your right,' DC Angel explained smoothly. 'But maybe you'll listen to us first. We only need to ask you a few questions, we could have all this cleared up really quickly.'

She deliberately let the pause stretch out until Small took the bait. 'What sort of questions?' he asked grudgingly.

'We've already seized your phone, and your friends' phones and all the computers we could find at your addresses. But if we could just clarify a few details with you now, well it would save us waiting for the computer technicians to tell us the details.' This time he kept quiet over the pause, so she continued. 'When did you start making videos with Jules and Ceiran?'

He looked at his mother, who gave a small shrug, as if to say you might as well answer. 'I dunno. Quite a few months back, I guess. Less than a year.'

'Would you say it was before Christmas or after it?'

He frowned and looked at the table top. 'It was just before Christmas. Ceiran got a new hard disk with his Christmas money and we copied everything over to there.'

'Okay. And was it always you and Julian Lockwood and Ceiran Knight?'

'What do you mean?' He started to look suspicious.

'Well, you seem to have been a little group, the three of you. Was there anyone else who joined or left? Or did the three of you start making videos together with no one else involved?'

Tom Small looked mutinous and shook his head.

'For the record, Mr Small is refusing to answer.' DC Angel then softened her tone slightly. 'Listen, we have your phones. Within a few days we'll have a record of where and when they were switched on. I think it's highly likely that it'll show that your phone was often with Ceiran's at Julian's house. Most evenings. Is that right?'

'Yes,' he said resignedly. 'It was just the three of us. We used to go round, hang out in his shed. Mess about with computers and stuff.'

'And the videos? Who's idea was that?'

He shrugged. 'I dunno. We were all just talking and stuff. About what goes viral what's not been done before, what would be funny, you know. What you could do with TimeBomb if you couldn't be traced. That kind of stuff.'

'So, the three of you came up with the idea and made the videos together?' Angel tried to keep the excitement out of her voice. 'No one else?'

'I suppose so.' He paused as if he realised this wasn't enough. 'Yes. What of it?'

'Thank you. You've been very helpful.' DC Angel turned and nodded at DCI Haines who was looking smug.

'Wait a minute,' Tom Small nearly shouted. 'What have I done? Why are you looking so happy about it?'

'Tom.' DC Angel tried to be friendly. 'We have technical support looking through all the hard drives. By the end of the week we will have found out who made the videos, when they started, who they were sent to. You haven't done anything, just confirmed what we were going to find out anyway.'

He looked confused so DCI Haines took the opportunity to close things up. 'Interview suspended at sixteen fifty-three,' he said officially as he started switching off equipment and gathering up his notes.

'Thank you, Tom, you'll be taken back to your cell for a bit.'

'What? I can't go?' Tom started to panic. 'How long for?'

'We're not sure. We've got to go over what you've said, discuss things with the CPS and find a magistrate. Don't worry, it won't take long.' DC Angel caught DCI Haines shooting her a warning look so she stopped talking.

Haines and Angel reconvened in the MIT room.

'So, what did we get out of that?' Haines asked mainly to get complete clarity on where they stood.

'Well, we know Tom Small had his sixteenth birthday in March.' DC Angel indicated his file. 'And he's admitted that the three of them were in it together since before Christmas. He's just given us his two friends on a plate. We can charge them right now with producing and distributing child pornography.'

'Are you sure that will fly?' DCI Haines paused while he picked his words carefully. 'You heard him just now. It was the three of them. They planned and executed the whole thing between the three of them. Surely in terms of consent, and his age...?' DCI Haines tailed off as he realised he was entering murky waters.

'In terms of consent and age,' DC Angel said firmly, 'legally he was incapable of consenting to sexual activity until his sixteenth birthday. It's all in how we present it to the magistrate. Two older boys, no, not boys, men. One eighteen, one nineteen, preying on a fifteen-year-old to make videos and send them out to unsuspecting girls.'

DCI Haines nodded. 'And when we get the records back from TimeBomb, if one of those girls was under sixteen...'

'...then we can add that on as well.' She stopped to think. 'They probably were, but there are a lot of hurdles to get over in that case. Firstly, we have to wait for TimeBomb to comply and they're demanding a warrant. Then we'll have to match up the numbers they give us with names. When we have the names, we have to then check how old they were when they received the videos.'

'But what we got this morning is much more concrete,' DCI Haines said, nodding. 'And the fact they were sending these videos out to unsuspecting women or girls is good too. We can sell it to the magistrate that these are sex offenders in the making. Who knows what they would go on to if they're not stopped now?'

'Just because it all happens over the internet using phones doesn't change anything. They're not going to go on to become sex offenders – that's what they are right now. It's no different than if they sat next to these girls on the bus and did this or jumped out at them in the park. The only difference is that they think they can hide behind the technology.'

DCI Haines nodded. 'Once we've got all that squared away, we can put the pressure on them over the Mazey Taylor killing.'

'Do you think that'll work?'

'Yeah. At the moment Lockwood and Knight are laughing at us. They've had an uncomfortable night in the cells, expecting to go home in a couple of hours. They think that even if the videos are obscene, they'll probably get a slap on the wrist.'

'No worse than if they'd been sending dick pics I suppose,' DC Angel said morosely.

'Exactly. Now we can sit them down with their solicitors and their parents and lay it out for them. Sex offenders register, time on remand, special conditions, all of that. I reckon they'll suddenly get a lot more co-operative. Especially if it's only one of them who's the killer. We'll have them turning on each other before the end of the week.'

'What about Tom Small? Shall we release him?'

'No. Just because he was underage, it doesn't exempt him from charges of child pornography at all.'

'Well, technically. But they hardly ever prosecute if it's just a child sending dodgy photos of themselves.'

'I think we can push the CPS to lay charges as this case is far more serious.' Haines' face was set in a hard expression. 'And we'll go for remand as well. They're just middle-class kids messing about with their computers. A few days on remand should wake them up. I reckon we'll have our confession soon enough.'

DC Angel wasn't convinced that her boss was right. She knew the three of them were perverts. But she also knew they were solid middle-class boys. For sure they were a horrible product of the same culture that had made #MeToo a necessity.

But they were not really, in her opinion, capable of murder. But she saw the look in Haines' eyes and couldn't see a way to shake her boss's conviction that one of the trio was guilty. Best not to say anything. 'We'd better get to work then.'

Between them they contacted the CPS, formally charged their suspects and kept them in the cells for a court hearing.

Chapter Sixteen

'Right, everyone, listen up.' For the first time, all of CID were crammed into the MIT room, along with the assorted uniforms and civilians who made up the bulk of the team. 'First of all the good news. We've got three strong suspects and we've been granted a full extension to hold them for further questioning. That should give the technical team enough time to present us with the details from their computers. Even better,' he nodded towards DC Angel, 'it looks as if the youngest of the three was making obscene videos before he was sixteen. So we can put pressure on the other two with charges of making and distributing child pornography. I'm sure that with some diligent questioning that'll lead one of them to flip on the other and we should have a confession for the killing of Mazey Taylor by the end of the week.' There were nods and congratulatory glances around the room.

'What do we do if they don't confess?' This was DS Stonor who was obviously feeling brave.

'It shouldn't be a problem. They had a motive – to keep their secret. We have proof on Mazey's phone. And they had opportunity, they're all each other's alibi. It'll still go to court.'

DC Angel had a niggle of fear at the back of her mind. There was no physical evidence against the three boys. Given their predilections for masturbating and making videos she would have expected to find either semen at the scene or a private video of Mazey.

She was sure that they were nasty pieces of work who enjoyed sending out upsetting videos to teenage girls but she wasn't convinced they were killers. What was worse was that she'd investigated Mazey's social network and concluded that there was no real link between her and the WankyBois. She didn't know who they really were and there didn't seem to be a credible route for the boys to find out that she had one of their videos saved. In fact, she didn't appear to have told anyone that she had copied one of their videos. So, she couldn't see how the boys had motive to kill Mazey.

She knew she was new in the department and so she really didn't want to question the boss. She did have to admit that they had motive and their only alibi was that they'd spent all evening in the shed together. Their shed was only a short walk to where Mazey was killed. DC Angel shoved these thoughts aside as she listened to the rest of what DCI Haines was saying.

'Given that we're confident of a result we need to address the other problem plaguing Bradwick. With that in mind, this week will see the start of a multi-disciplinary crackdown on immigration. We'll be spearheading a campaign to target all the immigrants who come here from across Europe and beyond. We'll have full co-operation from the DSS to check for benefit infringements, and we'll be working with national agencies to check for both domestic and international arrest warrants. On top of that we'll work with border force to make sure all visas are in order for people from outside Europe.

'Obviously this'll mean a lot of leg work. My team especially, I expect to spend a lot of time outside the office. I want you talking to farmers, gang masters – they need their licences checking too, taxi drivers, community centres. And I want this done as a zero-tolerance operation. You find one weapon, one sniff of drugs, one outstanding parking ticket, and you process the case.'

There was a stunned silence. What he'd just outlined took very little time to say but added up to a mountain of work.

DC Angel glanced around the room. She could see the officers split between those who were mentally adding up the overtime payments and those who were working out how to break it to their families that they wouldn't be around so much in the following weeks.

As no one else was going to say anything, DC Angel decided to speak up. 'Sir, why has this decision been taken now? There's still a lot of work to do to close out the Taylor killing and there's still this spate of drug related violence across the whole area. Won't we be stretched too thin?'

DCI Haines looked around the room, trying to decide if he should include uniforms and civilians in what he was going to say next. 'Could I ask those not in my CID team to go for a coffee? Just five minutes?' DC Angel's heart sank at those words although she was grateful for a smaller audience when she was carpeted by her boss. Once everyone had left, the room resettled to expectant silence. However, her expectations weren't met. 'Right, what I'm going to say next is for our ears only. It could easily be misinterpreted, especially by the press. I have received intelligence that the latest spate of violence has its origins in a turf war over drugs. Latvians are trying to establish a base in Bradwick and in doing so are intimidating the local dealers.' There were nods around the room. Everyone there knew it was the lower members of Bradwick society who'd borne the brunt of the attacks. 'Now, we are working on identifying the structure of the Latvian gang that is behind this. But at the moment this is the best strategy. We'll put pressure on their foot soldiers. We'll pay special attention to people who have connections with or are from Latvia. Those who've either arrived in the last three months or who appear to have suddenly changed jobs and got more money.' He stopped to glance around the room. 'I don't need to tell you how sensitive this will be. To the public we're just carrying out a multi-disciplinary operation, across the board, all nationalities without favour. Behind the scenes we'll apply pressure and try to build a picture of this operation.

'We also think this is linked to a county lines operation. The Latvian gang we're interested in is based in Birmingham. So we'll have a rota of CID sitting outside the station. I'll give you all timetables so you can wait for the right trains. Anyone looks dodgy, give 'em a spin, look for knives, drugs, phones.' There were nervous looks around the room, so before the comments started, Haines continued, 'Yes, I know. It is profiling. And that's not what we'll say what we're doing. It's a multi-agency initiative. This part will be working with the BTP to reduce rail-related crime. Are we all clear on that?'

* * *

Over the next week, work was relentless. DC Angel had no time to worry about David Marks, who'd gone suspiciously silent. She was spending most of her time analysing the raw data that was being sent over daily as the technical team analysed the three suspects' many computers. Their charge list was growing as they found the unedited videos that confirmed who was definitely involved and where they were. So far, the date stamps on the videos corresponded with the apparent time of day so there was little doubt they'd be found guilty.

The only fly in the ointment was that so far none of them had accused any other of the murder. They all stuck to their alibi that on the night in question they'd been at Julian's shed until about midnight when they went home. Tom Small's parents had confirmed that he'd come in some time before one in the morning but couldn't be precise. Ceiran Knight's mother took sleeping pills so only knew that he was there when she woke up. Julian Lockwood confirmed that his friends had left down the side of the house and his mother thought he might have come in sometime between midnight and one.

In short, all three could easily have been walking around Bradwick at exactly the time Mazey Taylor was being attacked and killed. Although there was no forensic evidence, they had a motive, no alibi, and the opportunity. Things were looking bleak for them.

The workload in CID was added to because DCI Haines had stuck to his guns and launched a multi-disciplinary operation. International arrest warrants were enacted, gang masters were checked, all the various businesses that used immigrants, from hotels to fruit farms were checked.

Thursday morning, Haines asked Angel to come down to the custody suite with him. They were backed up because of a lack of interpreters and another six suspects had been brought in. This was enough for them to start diverting any future arrests to other stations.

'These new people we've arrested, they're all claiming they need an interpreter. I don't believe them.' The desk sergeant had his usual air of calm, but DC Angel could tell he was nearing the end of his tether.

DCI Haines turned to DC Angel and said, 'I need you to watch the suspects.'

'What for?'

'You'll know when you see it. Think of it as a lesson in practical policing.'

DC Angel could see that he was in good humour so she went along with it. Haines leant on the desk to talk to the custody sergeant. Angel turned around so she was facing the room.

'Say, Bob, we must be nearly full down here.' DCI Haines sounded almost carefully cheerful as if he were playing a part.

'Yes, I'd say that we were.' Desk Sergeant Bob Holmes had been here forever and was certainly used to Haines' tricks.

'So, with this many inmates, we'd better switch off the alarms for the cells.'

'Are you sure, what if there's a fire? Or if someone needs help, has a medical emergency?'

'They're just immigrants, it doesn't matter. Just check every hour, should be fine.'

DC Angel now saw the plan. Three of the new intake were suddenly animated. She saw the shock on their faces before they started pulling at their friends and talking in a fast babble of some eastern European language. Just as the outrage was building to a dangerous level, DCI Haines slowly turned to DC Angel with an expectant look on his face.

'Him, him and him.' She pointed to the three who had reacted. 'They speak English well enough to be interviewed right now.'

The three men who had been singled out visibly deflated. DCI Haines was pleased. 'Right, now we can get some of these processed and out of the door.'

CHAPTER SEVENTEEN

The atmosphere in the CID open-plan office was strange and tense. It was a Friday evening and DC Angel's turn to man the phones, always an interesting task at the beginning of the weekend.

This time, however, she was joined by the two DCs, Mitchell and Hobbs together with DS Stonor. DC Angel felt uncomfortable because she didn't know what the three men were up to. Their excuses were thin – they were finishing up paperwork, chasing down leads or typing up notes. In practice, she didn't have to be a detective to determine that they were waiting for something and they weren't going to tell her what that was.

So, she kept her head down and deliberately ignored everyone else in the office. This policy worked well until the phone rang and broke the atmosphere. Aware of the eyes of the other CID members on her, DC Angel picked up the call.

'DC Angel.'

'It's PC Steve Walsh, we've got a body. Is DI Hargreaves about? DCI Haines?'

'They're off shift. I could call them at home but I'd need a good reason. Can't you just find who's on call for the coroner and give them a bell?'

'It's probably nothing.'

'Well, you've got a body there. Definitely dead? Not just drunk?'

'No, she's definitely dead.'

She, DC Angel thought, with an instinctive sadness. So many times it was women who were the victims and men the aggressors. She also had the first inkling that something big was up. 'Okay so we have a dead body. Is there any reason why we can't just call the coroner and pathologist in? Let them investigate.'

'It might be another one.' An awkward pause, as if he was moving away from someone overhearing. 'Like, you know, I was one of the first on scene when Mazey Taylor was found. You know, dumped by the bins.'

There was a pause as DC Angel thought frantically. It was obvious that PC Walsh wanted to get out of uniform and into CID. Fancied himself as a detective. It was an occupational hazard in dealing with uniform.

'You do know that we have suspects in custody? We've laid charges and are preparing the case for the CPS.'

'Yes, I know that. It's just that...'

DC Angel took a moment to consider. She could tell that PC Walsh was going out on a limb and challenging CID. There must be a reason. She would see what he had and then decide. 'Talk me through it, what you got there?'

'Well, it's a young woman lying dead on her back. Just off a path through the woods. I don't want to say what the cause of death is but she's got a red mark over her throat.'

'Is it a straight red mark? Any other injuries?'

'Yeah, it's straight and kind of red or purple. Like a really dark bruise. Might be a mark on the left side of her face.'

Shit, DC Angel thought. This was bad. The only thing worse would be if they lost the opportunity to check it out properly. The sooner they secured the scene and interviewed witnesses, the better their chances of catching the killer.

'Right, give me a few minutes to hunt down a senior officer and then I'll call you back.' She took some basic details.

She hung up and looked round at the other people in the office who were all watching her closely. Aware that something weird was going on, she first tried Haines on his mobile, then Hargreaves. Neither even rang, it just went straight to voicemail. She slammed her phone down on the desk. 'Well, where the hell is either Hargreaves or Haines?'

There were awkward glances but no one spoke.

'What, is it a secret squirrel meeting that I'm not invited to? The first rule of secret squirrel is that you don't speak about it?' She saw the guilty looks and threw her hands up. 'Fuck! What are they actually doing? Has anyone actually tried to contact them?'

There were nervous glances around the room. Finally, Ed Mitchell decided to speak. 'Thing is, you see, they've gone to meet an informant. And these days, some of the informants, well, they've got all tech savvy. They think they're in some film or something. So, some of the meetings are sit downs with all phones on the table and batteries removed.'

'So, are there any logs or records of where they might be meeting?' More worried glances shot around the room. 'So, we're not talking on the record, run through expenses, official confidential informants then?'

'Not exactly, no.' DC Mitchell sounded nervous and the other two weren't helping him. 'Usually there's either one or the other of them. Haines and Hargreaves, I mean. They don't usually both go at the same time. But as soon as Haines left, Hargreaves didn't say a word, he just got up and left. Something's up.'

'So, what are we going to do then?' DC Angel couldn't believe this. It was like an old boys club. Something inside her snapped. She was fed up of all their bullshit, the furtive glances, the conversations that ended when she entered the room.

With purpose, she snatched the phone out of its cradle. She stabbed at the keyboard with more force than strictly necessary as she became aware that the three men in the room were watching her. 'Yes, this is DC Angel. I've got DCI Haines out of a meeting with the super, and let me tell you, he was not pleased! Anyway, he's given me the authority to sort this out. You need to call your desk sergeant and get him to send some bodies down. They'll be in charge of securing the scene and taking statements from anyone hanging around or walking past. I'll get in touch with the coroner and the pathologist and get them out to you. I'll be on my way too, with a detective sergeant.'

There were gaps in this long list of instructions as she listened to the uniformed officer's answers. When she hung up, the others were looking at her with awe.

Finally, DS Stonor spoke up. 'What the hell are you going to say when this gets back to Haines, not to mention the super who's meant to be in a fictitious meeting?'

'I don't know yet. If they want to make something of it, then I'll ask them where they went without phones or records, while they were on shift.' All she got back was more stares. 'Right you two,' she pointed at the two DCs, 'phone the coroner and the pathologist. Stonor and I have to go off and inspect a crime scene.' She paused for effect. 'Oh, and if Haines or Hargreaves do decide to show up, here's where we'll be. But we won't be that hard to find as we'll leave our phones switched on and take Airwaves with us!'

CHAPTER EIGHTEEN

The realisation that the case was in serious trouble dawned on DCI Haines in stages.

Once he'd left his meeting, he reinstalled the battery in his phone and there was a flurry of beeps and vibrations as messages filtered in. He saw immediately that most of them were from work and he knew something was badly wrong. He made a bad decision to ignore his messages and instead use the time to drive back into town as fast as he could. While he drove, he called up Hargreaves on his hands-free.

'It seems that they can't cope without us for an hour. That new bird, Angel, is getting in a flap. Something about a body being found. Lord knows why they can't just tell the coroner, run through protocol.'

'Where are you now? Are you on the scene?'

'I'm about five minutes away from the station now. I only just picked up the message as well.'

'What do you mean? Weren't you available? You knew I had a meeting.'

'It wasn't for long, I just popped out for half an hour or so.'

'That's not good enough, where were you?'

'On personal business.' Hargreaves voice was clipped.

'I'm your superior officer, I need to know where you were!'

'I wasn't on shift. Your name was down on the rota. You should have been contactable.'

There was a dangerous pause. 'Glen, you haven't got command of the team yet. You better watch your step. You knew full well I was meeting King and I expected you to have my back.' There was another pause. Haines decided he wasn't going to get anything out of Hargreaves right now. 'Right. Well, let's put that behind us for the moment. I'll see you in CID in ten minutes, yes? See what we can save from this mess.'

Without waiting for an answer, he stabbed the button to disconnect the phone. DCI Haines had a bad feeling. He knew he had his team well drilled to cope in his absence and something had happened to spook them. He pressed down on the accelerator, now worried. As he drove, he examined his reactions to this crisis and realised that he didn't like Hargreaves' dismissal of Angel. He thought her instincts were usually right.

As soon as he burst into the office, DCs Mitchell and Hobbs both started talking at once. He rounded on both of them, picked Mitchell and silenced Hobbs and Hargreaves, and sat down to listen.

The body of a female had been found in the woods with injuries similar to those on Mazey Taylor. A man had been jogging through the woods on his usual route when he'd spotted a pair of feet sticking out from some undergrowth. He'd investigated further to find a young woman lying motionless on her back.

'I was worried that I'd be under suspicion,' he'd said to the responding officer. 'You know, with all the Me Too stuff. And that Stanford rapist, who'd assaulted that woman who was drunk. So I jogged on to the road, it wasn't far and flagged down a car.'

He'd been joined by a no-nonsense woman in her fifties who was a nurse. Together they'd investigated and found that the woman was dead. DCI Haines knew they'd have to investigate their jogger, but he didn't seem a good fit for the killer.

Soon, he was holding a coffee, chatting quietly with DC Angel. In his mind, the doubts that had begun when he saw the messages on his phone were now forming together into something solid. They were looking down at their fresh victim.

She was young and pretty, lying on her back just off the main path through the woods. The path was a well-known shortcut. DC Angel thought about the time she'd been found and made a mental note to check if she was on her way home after work. Once they knew who she was they'd start to piece together her movements.

Her beauty was marred by the dark red mark straight across her throat. The ground around her was churned up but there weren't any drag marks – had she been killed right here? With all his experience, Haines got as close as he could without disturbing the body. His inspection revealed a large bruise on her left temple and some broken nails on both hands.

'Are you doing my job for me?' Dani Price, the pathologist had good humour as she walked up behind DCI Haines.

'Well, you took so long to get here, I thought someone ought to have a look!'

'I'll have less of your cheek.' She smiled at the DCI. 'What have you seen so far?'

'There's a bruise on her temple so she could have been struck first, then driven back off the path.' He looked down. 'There's no drag marks, so our attacker strangles her here. Not sure how she got to the ground, but that blow on the head could have knocked her off balance. She fought back, judging by her hands.'

'Well, if you ever want to change career, you could do your medical degree and I'd take you on as an apprentice.'

'Yeah. Thanks but no thanks.' The pathologist was already carrying out a preliminary examination. 'I know you hate me asking, but it could be critical in this case–'

'Time of death?' The pathologist interrupted Haines.

'Only in terms of a day, really. We're not interested in hours yet.'

The pathologist looked around with a frown. She gently picked up the victim's wrist and felt for temperature as well as the onset of rigor. 'Well, unless something properly weird is going on with freezers and staged body dumps, I'd say that our woman has been lying here substantially less than a day. Maybe even a few hours.'

Haines looked up and down the path. Sunset had been and gone and twilight was now deepening the shadows. 'This is a busy path. It might be that someone strong drove her to the end of the path, picked her up and dumped her here. But if you're saying a few hours, then that more suggests that she was killed here.'

'Yes, there isn't much disturbance to her clothing either.'

Haines had a sour expression as he nodded his curt thanks and turned around to talk to DC Angel. His doubts were now looming large in his mind. He hadn't got to where he was now by ignoring problems. He preferred to face them head on even if that meant admitting that he'd been wrong.

'What's your opinion then, Angel?' The stress made his words short and clipped.

'As to whether we can link this to Mazey Taylor?' Haines nodded. 'Well, it looks initially as if the cause of death is the same and the victim is...' she paused and frowned. 'The victim is similar in some respects to the first one. They're both women, but this one looks older and they have different hairstyles and body shapes.'

'You think she's older?' Haines frowned and tried to look past the pathologist to the victim's face.

'Not by a lot but I'd suspect that she might be early twenties or late teens. Something about her doesn't say student or sixth former. I don't know. I may be wrong, it's just a hunch.'

Haines nodded. Over the years he'd learned to rely on hunches but also to give them the correct weight within an investigation.

'Based on where she is and the likely time of death, it also looks as if she could have been coming home and was attacked and killed right here. So she might have a job. But we do have a young woman who was strangled and left where she died.'

'On the other hand,' Haines argued, 'she does look different. The area is different, this one is in the woods not in a business area. And we have our three prime suspects neatly wrapped up and on remand at the moment.'

'What's the plan then, boss?'

'Well, we'll wait for the pathologist to complete their findings and see how many similarities there really are between the two. At the same time we can really press on with identification of the body, which will lead to building up a picture of her last hours. Again, we can compare this with the Mazey Taylor killing. We give it twelve hours, then draw up what we've got and make a decision.'

'And what shall we do if it looks the same?'

'Then we'll have to investigate the two in parallel. This is not a TV serial killer who takes a trophy or leaves a signature. There's no definitive forensics from the Taylor scene so any decision to link them will be subjective, based on weight of evidence more than anything else.'

'It does look like this lets the WankyBois off the hook though?'

'Listen to me.' Haines finally let his irritation bubble over. 'Nothing will let them off the hook. They are perverts who traumatised any woman whose mobile number they could get hold of. We caught them at the beginning of what could've been a long and damaging career. I still feel that they've got some connection to this case, somehow. They were very technologically savvy. Maybe they sent out the blueprint for these killings so they'd look innocent?'

Angel didn't trust herself to argue. She'd been wading through the technical data from their computers. Considering how high tech their crimes were, the three boys were surprisingly isolated from their peers. They didn't chat much to anyone else outside their group. She took a deep breath and thought that she'd have to wait out the twelve hours and then make her representations when they had more data.

As she was down to cover the phones overnight, DC Angel diverted the phone up to the MIT room and worked on a new board next to the one for Mazey Taylor.

The victim still had her handbag and was soon identified as Stella Evans, a nineteen-year-old who worked as office assistant at a local estate agents. The day before, she'd finished work at six and picked up a few items in a corner shop on the way home. The site where the body had been found was on the most direct route from work to home.

DCI Haines stayed in the room too, working the phones, coordinating the coroner, the pathologist, and the uniforms who were all working to get as much data as fast as possible.

As well as filling in the board with her details, Angel got a flip-chart and drew up two headings – similarities and differences.

Under the first heading, she listed the facts. Both victims were local young females. Both were attacked as they returned home. Both women had been killed by compression of the windpipe, and the bodies appeared to have been left where they were killed. There was no CCTV coverage for either crime scene. There was also no sexual assault or other interference with the bodies. They both appeared to be opportunistic killings.

Under the second heading, DC Angel wrote that one victim was a sixth form student, the other had worked since leaving school at sixteen.

She stood at the board thinking for a minute. 'Boss, they were both found walking home from work, but one was in a bit of scrub land, the other was behind a row of shops. Does that count as a difference?'

'I think so,' Haines replied. 'They're quite different areas, and if we're looking at someone who waits for a victim and then leaps out at them, well they're different areas and times of day that he's waiting.'

'Yes, but it's all in Bradwick itself. He might have a range, but it's not a huge one.' She paused. 'I'll put it down, I guess.'

Other items in the differences column were that they were different in hair colour and that Stella had been in a relationship for the last eight months. Finally, she wrote that no mobile had been found at Stella's scene although she was wearing headphones.

Now the case was looking more complex, DI Hargreaves had been drafted in to give more weight and experience. He was the first to speak. 'The thing is, everything that makes these cases similar is a definite. We know who was killed and how and where. If there is a single killer responsible, then unless he's a stalker as well, he won't know if they're a student or not. He can't tell by looking if they've got a boyfriend or not. If it is just one person, then they obviously aren't choosy, just young women.'

'What about the mobile phone?' DCI Haines queried. 'She was found with headphones and worked for an estate agent. It hasn't been found anywhere.'

Hargreaves shook his head. 'When we did the press release for Mazey Taylor, to get more information on our three suspects, we said that we'd got data from the victim's mobile. If we have a single perpetrator, then he'd have read that and realised that he'd failed to destroy Mazey's phone. The safest thing for him to do in the next attack is to completely remove the mobile from the scene.'

DCI Haines nodded slowly and turned back to the board. He was undeniably the boss, the governor of this team, and no one spoke while he considered all the facts.

'Right. Lockwood, Knight, and Small are perverts and they've been caught. But at the moment they're out of the frame for these killings. We'll package them up, make sure our notes are ready for court and then dump the whole thing on the CPS and forget about it. Don't think of this as a mistake, we've got three very nasty men off the streets and that's always a win.' He stopped to take a deep breath. 'However, it does mean that we're back to square one, with a whole new enquiry. We need a full profile of both victims, paying particular attention to any overlaps. We also need to consider that we might have a killer who's picking victims at random that he doesn't know. We need to hit the streets, pick up informants. We're behind on this and we will need to run to catch up.'

PART 2

CHAPTER NINETEEN

Emma finally drove home on Saturday lunchtime having been awake for over twenty-four hours. No police officer wanted to find a body but this one was worse than most. When she turned into her road, she was disheartened to see a motorbike was parked outside the house.

Her worst fears were confirmed when she saw the lanky frame of David Marks relaxing on the sofa. He had a beer in his hand and looked completely at home. Emma shot a look at Michelle, her housemate who was obviously to blame.

Out of David's eyeline she shrugged and rolled her eyes. Obviously, she had been unable to dislodge him. Emma held one hand up to David to indicate he should wait. He didn't look like he was going anywhere soon.

She went into the kitchen and got herself a beer from the fridge. She rolled the bottle across her forehead, feeling the cold drips trickle down. She closed her eyes and tried to figure out what she should do.

One part of her wanted to completely unload everything that was going on in her head straight at David. Tell him that her case was completely screwed, had driven itself into a brick wall. It was a dead end that she'd seen coming but had been unable to stop. She hadn't said anything because she was new to the team and a woman as well so she wouldn't have been listened to. In fact she had tried to steer the team away from this disaster and been ignored.

She was exhausted and felt grimy after so long on duty, which made her less tolerant. Added to which she was due on and cranky so she didn't want to be nice to anyone. There was no way David was getting her into bed. She knew she was being irrational and moody but all she wanted was a bath, a glass of wine, and a slab of chocolate. She'd have to make do with a shower as the chances were high that she'd doze off in the bath.

She took a deep breath and decided the first problem was an easy one. She needed to remove David Marks, both from her sofa and then from her life.

She marched back into the living room. 'Right, you need to go now.'

'I just arrived. Michelle let me in. Couldn't we at least have a drink and see where things go from there?'

Emma knew exactly what he meant and needed to head that idea off at the pass. 'You can't behave like this, David. It's not on.'

'What? I thought we were an item. We haven't been communicating so I thought I'd pop over.'

'Not communicating? We had a row and then you sulked by not answering my texts. And now you just turn up and hope to pick up where you left off? You know we all work shifts, that some days the work takes over and others I can have lazy mornings. I can't just be picked up and put down without any regard for my job. It might surprise you but this is the twenty-first century and women have careers and have to work harder than men to get ahead.'

David chose to ignore most of her words and focus in on the original argument. 'But it's okay for you to just pick me up when you want a roll in the hay? That's okay is it?'

'That's not what happened. I texted and asked if you wanted to come over and you agreed. That's how grown-ups have re-lationships, they communicate and agree a time and place to meet up. They don't sulk and then turn up with no warning.' Before David had another chance to talk, she carried on. 'I can't be doing with all this. This is my house and you're leaving now.' She took his beer from him and looked at the door.

David stood up and assessed his options. Lucy had heard the raised voices and stood at the top of the stairs, arms crossed and a determined look on her face. Michelle was stood in the doorway to the kitchen, looking similarly resolute. He knew when he was beaten and muttering under his breath about 'a house full of dykes' he strode out and slammed the door.

Emma collapsed on the sofa with her beer. Michelle and Lucy collapsed into the armchairs. They glanced at each other then all collapsed into giggles as the tension dissipated.

CHAPTER TWENTY

Haines wished he could go back to his office and close his eyes for ten minutes. But he was in the first twenty-four hours of a murder enquiry and the picture was getting increasingly bleak. They had gone up a blind alley with the three suspects they had in custody for the Taylor killing and now had to start from scratch.

He knew about the golden twenty-four hours but he also knew that he was close to burning out. He had one last check to make sure that everything was proceeding. Search teams, what little CCTV there was, interviews with family and forensics were all in progress.

He made sure his mobile was charged and decided to head down to the club. Hopefully Patterson would be there on a Saturday afternoon and he could try to regain a sense of perspective.

Soon he was installed in his usual leather-lined booth in the main bar of The Bradwick. Seated opposite him was Reg Patterson.

Rather than rehash the failings in the murder case, Haines had something else on his mind.

'What do you make of Hargreaves?'

'That's an odd question, Rob. Don't tell me you've worked with him for five years and now you don't trust him?'

Haines briefly recapped the debacle on Friday night when neither of the senior officers were available.

'So?' Patterson said. 'The guy has a right to a private life. You know what Glen Hargreaves is like, don't you? Always a bit buttoned up, never really shared much with the team.'

'Yes, well, after all that fuss when he was a desk sergeant, it's hard to blame him.' Years ago, Hargreaves had been sergeant to an intake of probationer PCs. One in particular had been very slack in terms of the basics – proper uniform and starting her shift on time. Finally, he'd had to issue her with a warning, and she replied by offering him favours in return for her staying on. He turned her down straight and she went to the inspector with a trumped-up sexual harassment claim. He was suspended, investigated, and exonerated, but ever since Haines had noticed that he'd been very reserved, especially around female officers.

'Listen, Rob, you were on rota and he was off and that's all there is to it. You got caught with your pants down, so just move on. For all we know Hargreaves likes being spanked by some leather-clad dominatrix or gets his rocks off with other men. It doesn't matter at the end of the day.'

'Yeah, you're right. It's just that Billy is getting increasingly twitchy. He's got men undercover in the Latvian gang and is trying to get me info. If it all plays out then I'll have a big raid before I move up and it'll take all the pressure off Billy while he's getting used to Hargreaves.'

'And if it doesn't play out?' Patterson always had a knack for asking the awkward questions.

'Then I'll still get my promotion and most likely Billy will be finished. It'll be the end of an era. And Hargreaves will have to deal with the Latvians.'

Patterson nodded. 'That'll be messy.'

'That's why I'm throwing everything at this. I've started rounding up immigrants, paying special attention to the Latvians. You know how tribal these gangs can be. I reckon if they've got people here picking fruit or whatever, they're probably the ones actually handing out the beatings. They'll be leant on by the people back in the cities. With a bit of luck I'll disrupt their networks and buy Billy some time.'

They lapsed into a companionable silence, both sipping their drinks. 'How's the new girl shaping up?' Patterson finally asked.

'DC Emma Angel? She's as good as she looks on paper. She does martial arts in her spare time. I'd be surprised if she's over five foot three but I've seen her subdue suspects with no problems. She's sharp too.'

'It does sound too good to be true,' Patterson said gently.

'Well, she's not really a team player. She's managed to put Stonor's back up several times, and I don't think Hobbs is her greatest fan either. And she does go off on her own without telling people what she's up to.' He stopped to think for a moment. 'Trouble is she's got a degree in policing and while she's not on the official fast track, you can see that she's going up through the ranks. She's got to learn how to rub along with these folks as I can see her outranking them within five years.'

'Hargreaves has got his work cut out then!'

'Yeah. I said I'd size her up before handing over. But she's a closed book, she seems to be all about the job.'

Patterson nodded. 'Those are the ones you've got to watch out for. Everyone needs a life outside the job.'

'We can talk. Look at the two of us, sat here on a Saturday afternoon drinking and talking about work.' He left a small pause. 'How are you coping without Mary? The house seem too big yet?'

'Oh, you know. It is a big hole, you know, married for all those years. But you have to keep your routines, your discipline. I still go out for my daily run, still go to the gym. Come here for a drink. No sense in sitting around moping, staring at the walls. How about you? How's Jem and the kids.'

'Kids? Abby's in her third year at university and Charlie has a job in Bristol. Between you and me I think Jem is looking forward to my promotion more than I am.'

'Working out ways to spend the money?'

'No, drawing up a list of DIY jobs to do now that I'll have more evenings and weekends at home!'

The conversation flowed after that and eventually circled back around to the killings. Patterson held firm to his belief that if you dug around hard enough in someone's background, then you'd find a link, find a reason why they were killed.

Eventually Haines said, 'I really ought to swing by the office one more time and check that the ship's on course before heading home to see what Jem's got for dinner.'

Chapter Twenty-One

DC Angel stood on the doorstep where she'd last seen Lukas. In her head she rehearsed the questions she'd need to ask to find out where he was now. She assumed two things – that he would have moved on and that his former housemates wouldn't co-operate.

She was on her way home from the first meeting of the MIT. She knew she should be focusing on Mazey Taylor and who had killed her, but the crime figures were niggling at her. Why could she not make sense of them?

She took a deep breath to steady herself. This was what she needed to do. It was clear that she was the new girl in town. And that something decidedly odd was going on with both Haines and Hargreaves. She wasn't going to be left behind, so she had to use all of her available resources to get up to speed as fast as possible. And to do that she needed to start forming her own network of informers within the town of Bradwick. Which led her to here. She knew all the reasons why Lukas was dangerous – both her own reaction to him and what he knew about her past. But he was also her best shortcut into the underbelly of the town. Without much hope, she rapped on the door.

When it opened and Lukas stood there, she was surprised he was home. He wasn't expecting her either, and both were struck dumb.

'Lukas,' she said finally.

'Yeah, um, yeah. Not a good time, really.' He looked up and down the road nervously.

Emma sighed dramatically. 'So, how long before the dealer gets here?'

Lukas looked as if he was about to argue with her. Then he gave a half-shrug and said, 'He said thirty minutes, maybe an hour.'

'So, I'll be gone in twenty-five.' Not waiting for an answer, she pushed past him but he didn't make any effort to stop her. She tried not to notice being so near to him but couldn't avoid the physical closeness that the narrow corridor forced on them. Not for the first time she had serious misgivings about coming here. She planned to ignore plenty of evidence of drug use and other crimes.

Eventually they had negotiated the social niceties of coffee – black because there was no milk – and were sat in the lounge. As Lukas moved around the room, he had the natural grace of a rock star who was off duty. His jeans hung low on his hips and his T-shirt was too big making him look like a waif. Emma sat on a worn-out sofa while Lukas sprawled opposite in an armchair. She saw ashtrays, empty beer cans and take-away containers on the coffee table, littered among other mess that she tried hard not to study.

'So, babe, what brings you to my house?'

'Your house?' Usually she'd be irritated by being addressed as babe, but this was Lukas. He was overly affectionate with everyone he met and wasn't being patronising. He was a genuine hippy.

'Well, you know, turn of phrase. It's where I am right now. Anyway, what's up?'

She paused. This was the problem. 'I need information on the local dealers–'

'Oh no! Come on babe, you're way better than that. We're better than that. You and me, we go way back and you blunder in here like that.' He reached for a tin and started rolling a cigarette.

'No, you idiot! We have files and lists of names. We don't need you to finger who sells you a bit of gear now and again.' She paused for breath. 'Even you must've noticed that there have been attacks on people around here.' She paused. Now she was sat in front of Lukas, she couldn't exactly say what she was thinking. Scrotes, lowlifes, petty criminals, the scum of the estates. 'Well, let's just say that our victims aren't used to being on the other side of the table, giving statements.'

'Oh that. Well, yes. It's definitely going on.' Lukas lit his cigarette without meeting her eyes.

'And...?'

'And what?' He theatrically let his arm hang over the side of his chair, smoke curling up from his fingers. Damn, he knew how to work that laid-back look.

'What do you know about it? I need something. A link, anything. A name to talk to.'

'And then what? Would you actually solve it? Would the police be bothered or would they just think it's a good thing, dealers bumping off other dealers?' He paused to consider his next words. 'You know what is was like growing up. Us and them. Only now you're them.'

'I'm not them. That's the whole point. I want to do the job properly. No bias, not make any assumptions. Investigate when a dealer gets a beating as much as if it was a middle-class wage slave.'

'Even when the victim doesn't want your lot involved?'

'What do you mean?' Emma wasn't comfortable with how far she was being drawn into his world, reminded of her past.

'You know what I mean. You grew up in that world too. It's whole, enclosed, sufficient unto itself. If someone gets a beating, we'll rely on our bosses to sort it out.' He paused again, taking a slow drag on his cigarette. 'Listen, people will want drugs, so other people will sell them drugs. There might be beatings and turf wars and what have you but when the dust settles, we'll be back where we started.'

'Never had you down as a philosopher!'

'Ah well. I like to keep surprising you.'

Emma frowned for a moment. Something was niggling at her. 'So, it is a turf war then?'

'Jesus! You really haven't even got that far then? Yeah, it's turf. Everyone who's had a beating has been dealing for the biggest local gang.'

'Are you sure about that? The victims all have fairly thin records. Occasional cautions for possession or going equipped. But not serious amounts of drugs or possession with intent to supply.'

Lukas shut his eyes and appeared to be meditating. But he was thinking hard. 'Babe, you have no idea what goes on down here. Are you sure you want to go down this road?'

'What do you mean, Lukas?' She wasn't used to him being serious and it unnerved her.

'How are things at work? Are you part of the team, or do you have a strange feeling that there's something you're not being told?'

Emma thought about Hargreaves and Haines and their mysterious disappearances. It was clear that most of the constables and sergeants knew what was going on, and that she wasn't being told.

'You see! I thought so!' Lukas was gleeful. 'You ain't in on it are you? You'd have said otherwise. I can read you like a fucking book!'

'Yes, you're right,' Emma conceded finally. 'But I'm getting a bit fed up with always being outside of the big secret.'

Lukas took a deep breath. Then he fished out his phone. 'This ain't no quick thing. Let me put my friend off 'til tomorrow and then we can talk without interruption.'

There was a pause as he quickly sorted out his evening. When he was done, he put his phone down and said, 'Listen, babe, I hate to bring it up, but I'm a bit low on the old cash. Is there anything you could do?'

'I could sign you up as a confidential informant. We have a fund to pay for information.' Lukas nodded and didn't say anything. 'Shall I get a takeaway in? Indian?' She already had her phone out, and he nodded enthusiastically.

'Right then. So these guys who are getting beaten are actually drug dealers who mysteriously we've never been able to catch. Do you know who's doing the beating?'

'Kids. Teenagers. Funny accents, foreigners. Turn up on the train, kick the shit out of someone, bugger off back to where they came from. Home in time for tea!'

'Where do they come from, do you think?'

'Cities. Don't matter if it's Bristol or Birmingham or London. You can always get there and back in a day.'

Emma rolled her eyes. County lines – the practice of exporting inner city drug problems to provincial towns. She'd have to look into it when she got back as usually the city gangs fought each other, not the locals.

There was a noise as someone moved around upstairs. Both of them tried to ignore it but Emma noticed that Lukas looked nervous.

Lukas snapped his fingers and pointed at her. 'Did you know that you're the ninja cop? They're still talking about the short blonde who had Robbie over the bonnet of an unmarked car. You're legendary.' Lukas was obviously proud by association. 'Does this mean I get some kind of protection? Like Robbie? You had him bang to rights and he walked with a caution.'

She had to consider her reply carefully. She still hadn't figured out the lie of the land, except to know that arresting this Robbie had ruffled some feathers. 'You mean to say, that's why none of those people who were beaten have serious drug records?' Lukas nodded, watching the truth dawn on Emma. 'They're all signed up?'

'Well, maybe not all officially on the record. Listen, you're not like the old guys, are you? You know, they've been filth their whole lives, always are, always will. More than that, most of them have been in the town forever too.'

Emma shut her eyes and rubbed them. She was struggling to get her head around what Lukas was saying. 'There's no way that we have the resources to sign up every drug dealer in Bradwick as a confidential informant. And that's not what's happening anyway as our crime stats are good. We're not letting people off, we're nicking a good number of dealers, getting product off the streets.'

'Have you ever heard of King Kabs?'

'Obviously, they're one of the main companies in Bradwick. Most people have their number so they can get home after a night out. But that's not what you mean, is it?'

'Word is that if you work for them, then you're insured. And I don't mean driving a cab. In return, they hand over the details of their rivals. It's the perfect system, they have no competition and your lot get plenty of arrests.'

'That's quite a big accusation there.' Emma was stalling for time. Her mind whirled through the whole lexicon of Professional Standards and bent coppers and how she felt about it. 'Do you know who might be doing this? Here?'

'Well, some people in the... in your crew.'

'In my team?' She leaned forward.

'Yeah. People I've seen you with. Or people that I then see working with them. We pretty much know what CID looks like. I reckon they've all got their hand out, one way or another.'

Emma frowned. 'What do you mean, hand out. I thought it was just information flowing to and fro.'

'I'm from out of town, so every now and again I run into a dealer I've met before. You know at festivals and what have you. Here and there. Apparently, there's a gap between what you get nicked with and what turns up on the charge sheet at court.'

'Skimming? These are very serious allegations, Lukas. I suppose none of it's provable?'

'Course not. It stands to reason though don't it. Whoever gets nicked ain't gonna stand up in court and say "excuse me your honour, I had another kilo of gear that's got lost" now are they?' He paused and realised that Emma was still confused. 'The gear goes back to King Kabs and the missing money must be hidden away somewhere, probably in the back pockets of your colleagues.'

'So, it was all working 'til recently. What changed? Why the beatings?'

'Well.' He stopped to scratch his ear and tug on the gold hoops threaded through it. 'New guys are coming in. You see we used to know what we were doing. It took me a while to be trusted when I first moved down here. But once I was in, I'd buy off someone who trusted me. He was introduced to me by a friend who'd known him since school. You know, after a year or so, he gave me stuff on tick and I'd go round my regulars and they buy it. I get enough to pay off the tick and buy the next lot. The system works. But now there all these rumours of Latvians coming. They're all about quotas and profits and selling more. And they'll be bringing underage girls over to work in the brothels, men with guns. Fancy cars and guys you've never met before. No tick, no friends. Whole different ball game.'

Just then the Indian takeaway arrived. By the time clean plates had been found and everything dished up, Emma had had a chance to think. She could see the sense in what Lukas said, but none of it was particularly provable either. But it did have the advantage that it fit all the available facts. She resolved to file it away until it came in useful.

She did like spending time with Lukas. He was easy company, and although he was on the other side of the law, they had a shared background. She had to remind herself to treat him as a little brother. Someone she could be fond of but would always have to protect as well to some extent. This level of involvement was dangerous enough – it couldn't go any further.

When they were mopping up curry sauce with naan bread, she brought the conversation back around to business. 'There's somewhere else we're stuck at the moment. What do you know about these murders? The young woman who was killed and dumped?' Lukas looked shocked and leant back from the table. 'No, not you. You're not a suspect. But you get around. Meet people. The sort who wouldn't talk to the police.'

She stopped talking and let the silence draw him out.

'It's a bad business that. I'd never, you know. I mean, I might sell a bit of blow, I could find you a stolen TV if you want, I might even give someone a slap if they deserved it.' He paused, considering his words. 'But killing a woman? What was she seventeen? Still a child really. Horrible.'

Emma sighed. If she was a few years younger or if Mazey or Stella had been a few years older, they would've been contemporaries. Even now it wasn't impossible that she'd have friends in common through Lukas and a network of families. She took a deep breath. She had to get her professional head back on and bury her feelings if she was to have any chance of catching the killer. 'Any names come to mind?'

Lukas went silent. He rolled a cigarette and only when he'd lit it and taken a drag did he talk. 'I have heard one thing. Just the weirdest thing really. You heard of a bloke called Gregory Watts?' Emma shook her head. 'A mate of mine was mouthing off about him last night. Apparently, he's a right flash git. Grew up on the Seaview Estate. That's the rough area around here, ex-council houses. But this guy, as soon as he could, put on a suit and became an estate agent. Got loads of money and moved out.' Emma was considering whether to interrupt to bring him round to the point. 'This mate of mine was getting all wound up. His younger sister was hanging around with this Gregory Watts. He was always chatting up schoolgirls. According to this friend of mine, he's knocked up three or four of the estate girls. Once they've had a couple of kids and start looking a bit old, he trades up to a younger model.'

'So, he's a paedophile?'

'Maybe. But he's dead smart. He drives them around in his car, buys stuff for the girls, takes them out for food. Then he moves 'em into his big flash house and they think they've got it made. That is until their time is up, then he boots them and moves on to the next one.' Lukas paused for a bit to consider his next words. 'Anyway, this mate of mine was trying to round up a posse to go round and sort him out. His sister says that he always picks up girls who look young but are over sixteen so the police can't do anything.'

'And how did you leave it?' Emma asked, full of concern.

'Well, it's a mug's game, innit? Some bloke who I see now and again, his sister reckons that someone is a bit dodgy and we all go round and beat him up? Nah! How do we know if she's got a beef with him about something different? Or the message has been garbled in Chinese whispers or something?' He shook his head violently. 'I mean, I'm all for justice, but you've actually got to know, haven't you? Before you go taking risks.'

'But you reckon he's worth a look?'

'Hey, you can do the research can't you? Older man likes teenage girls. He's obviously wound up some of the locals around here. Just do your own work, yeah. Make sure first.'

'Okay. I can do that. Gregory Watts, estate agent.' Emma made a note. Sometimes it seemed the universe had an inexhaustible supply of men who wanted to use women. 'I'll run him through the system, see what pops out.'

'Yeah, you can give him a look. But do your own work on it, you know. This is all second-hand to me. My friend's sister nearly got caught by him. But he picked someone else in her year. He sounds proper creepy though, worth keeping an eye on.'

'Cheers for that. And I'll do my own homework, don't worry.' There was an awkward pause. 'And for the other stuff, you know.'

'What you going to do about that?'

'Nothing for now. It was just bugging me that I was being left out. But there's not much that I can do without proof. You don't move against your whole team without being totally certain.' She paused and weighed it up. 'It'd need doing carefully or not at all. Otherwise, no one would ever talk to me again.'

'Well, you be careful, babe. I know you. Know what you're like. You've never liked anyone cheating or cutting corners. But this is the way things are around here. It's been that way for ages.'

'Until now, that is. I have a feeling that everything is about to change.'

* * *

DC Angel decided to walk home from Lukas' house. He'd given her a lot of information and if even half of it was true, then she had a lot to think about. She wasn't sure what she'd do with it or how she'd set about finding out what was true.

Outside a pub, a woman said 'excuse me' as she approached. She stopped and saw that the woman looked vaguely familiar. She had straight black hair and the kind of pretty face that suggested an Asian grandparent or two. DC Angel took a couple of steps closer and mentally upgraded the other woman from pretty to stunning.

She was expecting a request for a light or the time, but the woman was holding out a wallet as if she'd found it on the street. DC Angel looked down and saw a warrant card. Maxine Jones. The photo matched and the card looked genuine.

Not willing to be drawn into a conversation, DC Angel frowned a question at Maxine Jones. Sergeant Jones, she corrected herself.

In reply, the other woman handed over a business card. Department of Professional Standards.

In a low voice Angel said, 'This is a bit cloak and dagger, even for you lot, isn't it?'

'Well, you're a hard woman to get on her own. You go to work, eat in the police canteen, live in a house full of colleagues.'

'So? You know that much about me, you must know I'm clean.' DC Angel turned to face the other woman who she didn't trust one bit, an impression she'd had when she first saw her and that was only confirmed when she learned where she worked.

'It's not you we're interested in.' DC Angel's heart sank. Her head was still spinning from Lukas' suspicions. 'Do you fancy a drink?' She indicated the pub they were standing outside. It was one of those that had survived in the middle of a street of terraced houses. DC Angel had a feeling it wasn't a question she could say no to. She knew that once Professional Standards took an interest, they didn't give up.

Once inside, she saw why it had been chosen. It was a traditional bar, the sort of place that you'd come for a couple of drinks before moving into the town centre proper. Michelle Jones chose a table far from prying ears.

When halting pleasantries had been exchanged, and drinks bought, Michelle launched straight into her pitch.

'We're interested in your team at CID. Whispers have started reaching us that they might be less than honest. Possibly not everything they seize gets entered as evidence. As I'm sure you're aware, dealing with drug dealers means a lot of untraceable money and other items flow through your hands.' DC Angel nodded, wondering what this had to do with her. 'You're new in the team, so I don't expect them to trust you straight away. But, from what we can see, you're ambitious. You don't let opportunities slip past you. If what we're hearing is right then you must know that it won't last forever. Sooner or later, there'll be a big case or a slip up or something. We already think that things are changing in the town, we just don't know quite how. But it could go wrong at any time. When, and that is a when, not an if, that happens, you need to decide which side you are on. Because I think you'd want to still have a career.'

'Wow! You don't mess around, do you?' DC Angel shook her head.

'No. I think the direct approach is best.'

'And do you also think that if I spy on my colleagues, work for you on the quiet, then it'll be okay? People talk, you know. And these are the people I have to rely on, who need to have my back when it gets dangerous. And I just don't mean while I'm in CID, I mean if I stay in the force. I won't have a shadow hanging over me.'

'It could be managed. We think you're bright enough.'

Flattery, DC Angel thought, interesting opening gambit. 'Bright enough for what?'

'Well, you're new, you're a woman, and you're from out of the area. If we close up the case soon, within a year or two, you could play it that it was an old boys club that you were never invited to join.' There was a carefully calculated pause. 'It would also make it easier to explain your good fortune in climbing the ranks.'

Bribery and flattery, DC Angel thought. That's their angle. She leant back from the table and considered the offer. They were right about one thing, she was ambitious. But to take a job like this, she'd have to be sure of her motives.

Sure, she hated the police, had done as long she'd been old enough to understand what they were and what they did. But she'd rationalised that by joining the enemy she could maybe change them from within.

But this was different. Her original plan was to be a new kind of police officer, one who was engaged and not prejudiced. This offer was one level beyond that. She could take down a whole corrupt department.

But then she thought about her friends, the people who'd made her feel like part of the team. True there were some people – DI Hargreaves and DS Stonor for example – that she would rather not work with. But Professional Standards? Could she really put an end to that many careers?

'You haven't said no, and that's all we need at the moment,' Jones said. 'It also means that they haven't got to you first. I want you to think about everything we've just said. Give me your phone and I'll put my personal mobile in. Text me like one of your friends and I'll get the message.'

DC Angel nodded, unable to think of anything coherent to say. With deep misgivings she passed her phone over and watched as the other woman expertly entered her number.

'There is one thing we need to clear up,' DS Jones said. 'We've been through your file to see if you'd work with us. Your next of kin address is an aunt in Nottinghamshire, small village.' DC Angel nodded, wondering if Michelle could read minds. 'Yet you went to school in Nottingham itself. Must be a good twenty-five, thirty miles from your aunt's house. No address on record for your parents either.'

DC Angel noted that there wasn't a question, just an open statement of a gap in her file. The silence stretched and as it did DC Angel got more annoyed. 'You don't get to treat me like a suspect! What do you want me to be? On your side or investigated by you? Cos I won't work with people who go sneaking around digging back into my past. I take it you've already been through all my police records?' Jones nodded and Angel continued. 'So you know I have a good record. I always play it straight. But if you want me to work with you, then you've got to play me straight.'

'You still haven't answered the question.'

Angel sighed and looked up at the ceiling. There hadn't been a direct question, but she wasn't about to point that out. 'I had a big falling out with my parents when I was doing my GCSEs. Typical teenager stuff, hormones and exam stress. So, I moved in with my aunt. Sometimes if I had a late class or an early start, I stayed in Nottingham, kipping on friends' sofas, other times she gave me a lift in as she worked part-time in the city. There's no big mystery.'

Michelle Jones nodded soberly. 'I'm sorry for the intrusion. But you're going to be in a stressful situation. And we want to make sure that no one has any leverage over you.'

'You don't need to worry. Once I've figured out what it is, I always do the right thing.'

'That's what we're hoping for.' Without another word, she stood up. 'I've taken up enough of your time. You have my number. Anything you think I ought to know, drop me a text.'

CHAPTER TWENTY-TWO

The mood in the MIT was very low – they knew that they'd messed up. DC Angel was sat at her desk, reading through the case file for what felt like the twentieth time. The pathologist was as certain as she could be that both attacks were the work of one person. The only slight difference was that this time the mark across the neck was slightly sharper. This might have been due to the body being discovered sooner or the attacker might have escalated and started using a weapon.

It was always depressing how the official reports reduced such a traumatic event down to a series of technical details. Angel knew that not only had Stella Evans lost her life, but that her death would reverberate through her family and friends for years to come. She tried unsuccessfully to avoid wondering if it was all her fault. Could she have been pushier? Might she have persuaded Haines to listen to her concerns that the WankyBois were not killers?

As if summoned by her thoughts, her boss barged into the open-plan area and went straight to his office without a side-ways glance. This was her chance not to repeat the mistakes of the first investigation. She waited until Haines was settled before she went to talk to him.

'DC Angel. What's up?'

'I've got a couple of leads on the murders.' She sat down opposite him.

'Really? I thought we were at a dead end.'

DC Angel quickly brought him up to speed on both Gregory Watts and the Dark Car Man.

'How long have you know about these two leads? Are they in the system?' DCI Haines was annoyed at being out of the loop.

'Dark Car Man is. I only heard about Gregory Watts last night.' Angel immediately went on the defensive. She'd done the right thing by bringing this to Haines. 'They were both just information received. And until the weekend, the team had settled on the WankyBois as the main suspects. We were stretched thin with the multi-disciplinary operation so there didn't seem any point in chasing them.'

'The point, DC Angel, is that we're a team.' Haines emphasised the words carefully. 'Now I know that you came highly recommended – fast track application, university degree, all that – but it doesn't count for anything if you can't work with other people.' There was a resentful silence from Angel. 'You just need to keep me in the loop. Even if you're not spending a lot of time on these things, I still need to know. They need to be on the system and you need to let us know so other people can pick them up and contribute their experience too.'

'I'm sorry.' DC Angel bit her lip and tried not to add a "but" to her apology.

'Water under the bridge. What do you want to do now?'

'We can have a look at this Gregory Watts character and start to hit the CCTV on both crimes to see if any car matching the DCM turns up.'

'I thought they were in CCTV black spots?'

'The crimes were, but if the car was involved, it would have to travel there and back. The streets around each scene must have cameras and we're fairly tight on both times of death. If we get one number plate it could give us another suspect.'

'Okay, but prioritise Watts.' Haines knew he had to take charge of someone like Angel. 'Someone driving a dark coloured family car made by Ford near a crime scene at about the right time is too vague for my liking.'

DC Angel nodded and left the office. She didn't agree with her boss but kept that to herself. Someone was driving around terrorising young girls in Bradwick. Surely it was logical that he could escalate to actual violence?

Still, his words about being a team player had stung, so she spent the rest of the morning writing up what she had learned about Gregory Watts. When she'd completed that task, a thought struck her. What if Dark Car Man and Watts were the same person? They both seemed obsessed with teenage girls.

She had already checked and found that Watts wasn't on the Police National Computer. Now she went through to the DVLA system and looked him up. He was only down as owning one car – a two-year-old white Mercedes. All his previous cars were similar and none of them even vaguely resembled a dark Ford Fiesta or Focus. He was not someone who drove family hatchbacks. She sighed, realising that life was never that easy. Finding Dark Car Man would be a slog.

Armed with his name and address, she went to check the electoral roll and found that Gregory Watts was listed there as well, together with an Amanda Goode.

With no other sources to go on, she decided to hit up Google instead. Unsurprisingly, Watts had quite a large online presence. It wasn't one hundred per cent clear what he was doing, or selling for a living, but he had a website offering his services as a consultant, working with estate agents among other businesses. She looked at the photo, trying to get an idea of what he would be like in person.

He was tanned, with high cheekbones, cropped black hair, and piercing blue eyes. Conventionally he was very handsome but there was something about the photo that was disturbing. The picture was professional and he obviously knew how to pose to look his best. She mentally tagged him as someone who would be image obsessed, spending all his time down the gym.

She moved away from the photo and went through the rest of the website. He had several estate agents listed as clients, which rang alarm bells with Angel.

She flicked through the files and found that Stella Evans was a receptionist at an estate agent that Watts had worked for. Could their paths have crossed somewhere? There was a simple way to check if Lukas was right, and in the process she could prove she was a team player.

She walked over to Haines' office and stood in the doorway. 'Boss, do you still have the school secretary on speed dial?'

'Not exactly, but I can call her. What do you need?'

'I've got one Amanda Goode who seems to be living with our Gregory Watts.'

'Right, and you want to see if he's chasing schoolgirls or not?'

'As usual, sir, exactly right if not totally politically correct.'

He gave her a grin that meant he knew what he was doing. 'Yeah, okay, leave it with me. I'll see exactly how young she is.'

'This will be interesting. I've run him through DVLA and the electoral roll and he's thirty-two.'

There was nothing to say after that so DC Angel went back to her desk to plan her strategy for interviewing Watts. His online presence suggested he was confident and she knew she wouldn't be able to go in there and start throwing accusations around. On the other hand, it did look as if all the evidence was that he had an unhealthy interest in schoolgirls.

She decided to mull over that problem while tackling the other one. She grabbed an old paper street map of Bradwick and called up the computerised map of the CCTV network covering the town.

While both crimes had taken place in black spots, she found some cameras on the surrounding roads. She carefully worked out which direction a car would have to travel in in order to go past each crime scene.

Eventually she ended up with three red dots around each crime scene. Carefully, she noted down the numbers of the cameras and called them through to the CCTV control centre. Using DCI Haines' name and the MIT she extracted a promise that the video files would be sent over as soon as possible.

It was only when she put down the phone that she realised she'd asked for six thirty-minute-long videos – she had just let herself in for watching three hours of tape.

Chapter Twenty-Three

DC Angel had serious misgivings when she pulled up outside the home of Gregory Watts. She was accompanied by DS Stonor who was his usual dour self. She knew they were on very thin ice and would be relying on Watts' good humour.

His house was on the outskirts of Bradwick – not the top echelon houses that overlooked the sea, but definitely an up and coming, nice area. She noticed the Mercedes on the drive. With a movement that would become a habit, she looked up and down the road for a dark Fiesta.

'You going to do the interview or stand here gawping up and down the road?' Stonor was still frosty.

'I'm gathering intelligence,' Angel said airily. 'If he has an unregistered Fiesta it might be parked around here somewhere.'

'You think Watts is Dark Car Man?'

'He might be. He certainly has a seventeen-year-old living with him even though he's thirty-two.' She felt like needling him a bit. 'Shall we go and find out?'

Gregory Watts opened the door and when they explained who they were, frowned. 'Is everything okay?'

'Yes, Mr Watts. We just need to ask you a few questions. Do you mind if we come in?'

'Of course, always willing to help the police. Can I offer you a coffee?'

They followed him into the house, DC Angel taking in all the details. It was a lovely house, expensively decorated. And, as if he'd been created to match, Watts was perfectly turned out. Razor sharp creases in his trousers and a soft blue shirt that hung perfectly on his frame.

DC Angel had a trick to restore her confidence in situations like this. She looked for the flaw. No one was perfect – they always had something, somewhere. As they went through to the kitchen, she surreptitiously watched him. He had cut himself shaving, two tiny red lines on his jaw. Whenever it got too much, she could focus on that.

Soon they were seated around an island in a large kitchen with coffee from one of those machines with the little capsules. Gregory Watts took delight in being able to provide any variation of coffee that a visitor might ask for.

'So, you do work for estate agents?' Angel opened the questioning.

'Yes. Mainly taking photographs and writing up the descriptions. I used to work for them full time but recently I've started doing it on a freelance basis. The advantage is that I can take jobs when the agents are too busy and fill in with work for the new online agencies in between times.' He turned round to perch on the worktop. DC Angel guessed that he was aware that he was perfectly lit from the window to show off his cheekbones. 'You see, people go on these new sites like Purple Bricks and the like and they think that it's easy. But, if you get a professional like me to take the photographs, draft the description, well you can add thousands on to the price. Pays for itself really.'

'You know Hayes in town?' DC Angel was aware that she'd cut across him, but Watts was almost lecturing them so he didn't notice. 'Did you ever work with them?'

'Hayes. Of course. I have good contacts with all the local agencies.' He paused and a frown passed across his face. DC

Angel thought that he was acting. He was also talking directly to DS Stonor. 'Oh no. It's not that case I saw on the news is it? That poor girl?'

Before DC Angel could answer, they were joined in the kitchen by a woman. She was short, with long dark hair. DC Angel presumed she was the seventeen-year-old Amanda Goode, but she didn't look it. Her hair was swept back with a simple headband and she had a plain T-shirt over leggings. Angel frowned because she was sure that her loose T-shirt was hiding the bump of pregnancy. Her face was round, without make-up but still with traces of puppy fat. She was the age where you could see the adult features just starting to break through.

'Mandy! Are you all right?' Gregory Watts strode across the kitchen to stand between his visitors and the young woman.

'May I have a glass of water, please?' Even her voice was childlike.

'Well, be quick. This is the police and you shouldn't be worrying in your condition. I'll call for you when we're done.'

Stonor and Angel silently watched her get a glass of water and then depart. While Gregory Watts had his back turned, seeing Mandy out of the room, they glanced at each other. With a shake of her head, DC Angel indicated that they shouldn't reveal to Watts that they'd already investigated enough to know the name of his partner.

'Right. Sorry about that. Where were we?' His usual smile and calm, confident demeanour was switched back on.

DC Angel wanted to take control of the conversation. 'We're just trying to establish your connection with the estate agent. You said you worked with Hayes. Did you ever have any contact with Stella Evans?'

'Evans?' He looked out of the window with a theatrical gesture. 'Was she a receptionist or something? I might have spoken to her once or twice. Making appointments and the like.'

'Was that the extent of your relationship with her?'

'As far as I'm aware.' He sounded tetchy at being questioned so closely and looked to DS Stonor for support.

'Okay. Where were you last Friday evening?' Watts looked shocked so DC Angel decided to soften the blow. 'It's just routine, trying to see who was where and when.'

'Well, I'd have to get my diary. Stay here for one moment.'

Angel and Stonor found themselves stranded in his kitchen. Angel sipped her coffee and reluctantly realised that it was very good. She looked at Stonor but couldn't tell what he was thinking. Watts was a bit creepy and controlling but Stonor looked completely at ease. He ran his hand over the black marble worktop and experimentally opened a drawer. When he touched it, it slid shut with a soft-close mechanism. She didn't want to say anything in case Watts overheard from wherever he'd just gone. Was she sitting in the kitchen of a predatory paedophile? Did he restrain himself and deliberately choose sixteen-year-olds to satisfy his urges while staying within the law? A shiver ran down her spine as she contemplated how dangerous he could be.

'Here we go!' Watts breezed back into the room holding an old-fashioned diary, black with brass corners. 'If I don't write it in this diary, then it doesn't happen.' He lay it down in front of DS Stonor and stood next to him so they could both look at it. He ran a finger down the page. 'Ah. That evening I was out at a lovely house just to the north of Bradwick. On a slight rise, quarter of an acre. I was looking at the light to take some photos. It has these fabulous views, right across the estuary. You can see Wales on a clear day.' For just a second, he caught the expressions on their faces. 'Anyway, I was there for over an hour. I wanted to see what the sunset would be like for the photos. It's that kind of attention to detail that builds my business.'

'Right. That does cover the timeline.' DC Angel decided to reach a bit. 'And the owners of this house, we could check with them?'

'I'm afraid not. You can't contact them. My business is built on reputation and reputation is built on trust. If word got out that I was somehow involved, however tangentially in a murder enquiry, then no one would want me to sell their house.'

Stonor shot Angel a warning look – they were on thin ice. She picked up on it and said, 'That won't be necessary then. I think we have all we need.' She put down her coffee cup and looked at the door. Watts picked up the hint and soon they were back in their car, driving away.

'Well, that was fun.' Back in the car, Stonor was as deadpan as ever. 'I'm not entirely sure what we have learned though.'

'Well, he's creepy and very controlling. Didn't like to be challenged. And he was speaking far more to you than he was to me. Even when I was asking the questions.'

'But you can't nick someone for that. Hell, you probably couldn't even do them for harassment if that happened in an office.'

DC Angel shot him a look – it was a strange thing to say. 'What about Mandy though? We know she's seventeen, but she's clearly pregnant and looks like a schoolchild.'

'Yeah, but again there's nothing illegal there. Over the age of consent.' He paused to choose his next words carefully. 'Besides, look at it from her point of view. If she's from Bradwick High, well she might not have come from a good area. A lot of teenagers want kids, and she's got a good-looking man, lovely kitchen, all the latest gadgets, nice big house. There's every chance that it's exactly what she wants.'

DC Angel had no answer to this. She wanted to scream at Stonor that buying someone a Nespresso machine doesn't give you the right to own them like a slave. But she knew that she would sound irrational. On the surface Gavin Watts had been polite, charming, and had answered all their questions. But her gut feeling was that something was badly wrong.

She took a deep breath. 'So, to you, nothing about that interview seemed a bit off?'

'No, not really,' DS Stonor said.

'Not even when I'm asking the questions and he's answering to you? I was being cut out of the conversation.'

'But I was the ranking officer in the interview. Maybe he just picked up on our ranks when we introduced ourselves.'

'I just wish there was a way to nick him for something,' DC Angel said. She could hear the dissatisfaction in her own voice and hated it.

'We have checked, Haines says she's seventeen and will be eighteen next month.' Stonor clearly wanted to end the conversation.

'And you and I both know that Watts is thirty-two. That makes him nearly old enough to be her father? And you don't think that's weird?' DC Angel wasn't letting it go.

'Well, maybe it's a bit off. But we're police, we don't get involved in people's relationships. He's done nothing wrong.'

'And don't you ever have people you can put on a black list? Keep an eye on them until they do something wrong?' She waited nervously for the response. She had kept the request from DPS at the back of her mind, but Stonor's attitude had spurred her to finally do something about it. Stonor on his part didn't respond, but instead he turned and looked at Angel with a quizzical look. 'What's that look for?'

'See, the thing is, we as a team, well we don't really know who you are?' Stonor was hesitant. 'You're fast track, you're dropped in here with your university degree and all that. Haven't spent years on the beat, fighting your way up through the system. We thought you were all straight-laced, not likely to bend to rules.'

'You do know me. I'm DC Emma Angel, age twenty-five, moved down here three years ago.' She tried to brush the comment off as a bit of a joke.

'Yeah, everyone knows that. But all your friends are job, your housemates all work shifts. You never come to the pub, we don't know what team you support, nothing like that.' Unspoken was the further question, how far will you bend the rules?

Angel was well aware that she found it hard to trust people and knew that she was self-contained to an extent that she came across as cold and remote. She remembered her instructions from DPS however and knew she had to fight her natural tendency and get under the skin of her team. 'You know what it's like. As you said, I'm on the fast track, I never have time to do anything. And, on your side, you've never invited me down the pub with the lads.'

Stonor frowned. DC Angel guessed that he wanted to say that they don't invite girls on a lads' night out but he couldn't. 'Okay then, next Friday, the Crown, we'll all be in there. It'll be football on the big screen.'

'Thank you. I'm sure I'll cope. I can drink pints with the best of them and stand my round as well.' She paused just long enough. 'Mind you, I'd rather watch rugby – it's a proper sport.'

DC Angel died a little inside. Somehow she was supposed to be one of the lads and drink beer down the pub while still being sensitive enough to get information from teenage girls. DPS were asking her to keep a big secret and spy on her team while at the same time acting like their friends and becoming one of them.

'Hmph. We can see about that.' There was another awkward pause. 'So you want to put the squeeze on Watts then? He got under your skin that much?'

'Oh, I wouldn't say that,' DC Angel said. 'But there is something wrong there and I think we ought to have a little poke around.'

DS Stonor actually seemed animated, the first time that DC Angel had seen him relax even a little. 'We can certainly mark his card. Keep an eye on him. For a start, did you see his house and car? And that BS about consultancy? Nah, the money's coming from somewhere else and we could try to find out where.'

'That would be a start. I can dig around in his background. If nothing else it's a bit odd that we've got someone killing teenage girls and a bloke in his thirties who has a teenage girlfriend.' She paused and thought for a second. 'We've already found a link between Watts and the second victim Evans. If I can find a link between him and Taylor, then we might be onto something.'

With that, she started the car and they drove back to the station.

CHAPTER TWENTY-FOUR

For about ten seconds, Emma awoke and luxuriated in her bed. It was a day off and she didn't have to get up. Then reality crashed in on her. It wasn't quite a day off; it was a work event. Halfway between going to work and being social and worse than either.

She reviewed her options – Haines had made it clear that being on duty was the only excuse for non-attendance. And as she was new in the department, they had made sure she wasn't on rota, so she had to go. The event was a huge barbecue thrown by Haines' Aunt Bea. She had lived around Bradwick all her life and had family and connections across the whole area. Her previous occupation as a schoolteacher merely cemented her position as the spider in the middle of a web of gossip.

Emma was nervous on many levels. There was always the minefield of what to wear to the event. Her childhood had allowed her to develop her own unique style. She could tear through charity shops and find the right combination to look good. But a professional, yet casual engagement was out of her experience.

She knew she didn't want to go too short on her skirt length – she was determined to succeed in this job on her abilities and not invite a single suggestion that she had flirted and used her looks to get ahead. On the other hand if she turned up looking frumpy or in an outfit that in any way invited ridicule, she'd never hear the end of it.

In the end she chose a long flowing, slightly retro sundress. It had a swirling blue green pattern and more importantly fell to below the knee and had short sleeves – ideal whatever the day might bring. She paired it with a shawl and her favourite boots and sunglasses. She hoped she would fit in yet retain her own quirky style.

She understood why Eddie Mitchell had insisted on giving her and Osborne a lift when they arrived in the village of Highcliffe. Not only was Aunt Bea's driveway stuffed with cars, there were vehicles parked on the verge either side. If they'd done the usual trick of everyone driving one car, the entire village would have been gridlocked.

Seeing her arrive with two other police officers, Aunt Bea swooped in on her.

'You must be the new DC, Emma Angel.' She was tall, grey, and imposing. 'I told that nephew of mine, Robbie, that he should leave you in the office today. You've only just started in that department and now they've thrown you into the bear pit of one of my barbecues.' Emma warmed to her immediately. She realised that Bea kept talking, partly to steer her away from her department and also to make sure that she felt that she didn't have to say anything. She took the pack of beers that Emma had brought with her. 'I'm guessing you brought these because they're what you'd rather drink.' She put them into a cooler full of ice and water, and retrieved a bottle of the same brand, but cold. 'Here you go. Come and sit over here, with your back to the hedge so you can watch everything and decide when you want to join in.'

Soon Emma was installed at a table, and most of her team had followed her, setting up camp around a few tables with chairs.

She saw that there were three gas barbecues, with men attending to them, with a big cold box of raw meat on one side and plates of cooked meat leaving the other to a line of waiting people. Looking further around, she saw that the cottage had a long garden, leading down to what was obviously the edge of an old orchard.

Around the garden were maybe fifty or sixty people, some at the makeshift bar where several tables were covered with bottles and glasses and there were several cool boxes full of ice with bottles floating in them.

'Thank you so much,' Emma said. 'I was a little nervous but I didn't know there'd be this many people.'

'That nephew of mine! I suppose he told you that I was a schoolteacher before I retired. After educating the town for nearly forty years, I've got to know a few people.'

'Did I hear you say you were a schoolteacher?' Rob had wandered over, looking relaxed with a beer in his hand. 'She was the head teacher for years before she retired.' Emma could hear the pride in his voice.

Bea waved away his praise. 'Oh, they just did that because everyone else had a go before me. If you stay in the job long enough, they promote you.' Emma had a strong suspicion that this wasn't true.

Another woman came over to join them. She was tall and stately, with a tumble of dark hair that was just starting to grey at the temples. Emma noticed she had the confidence not to hide her age behind make-up and operations – she had crow's feet that were obviously from smiling often.

'Hi, I'm Jem,' she said, snaking her arm around Rob's waist and confirming that she was his wife. 'You must be Emma. I see Rob's chucked you in at the deep end then. Keep your eyes and ears open – anything worth knowing in the area will be discussed here! Miss Mathews is the most connected woman in Bradwick.'

'Bea! Call me Bea! Or I might reveal how long it is since you were in my classroom, Jemima,' Bea teased.

'You'll always be Miss Mathews to me,' Jem said. Emma could tell it was a running joke that had gone on for years. Jem turned to survey the garden and indicated an old man with neat grey hair and round glasses. 'There's Rob's old boss – Reg Patterson. What was he when he retired? Chief super? ACC?'

'ACC,' Rob answered. 'Some more of the old guard are here.'

'And it's not just police.' Jem leaned in as if she was sharing a secret. 'There's the editor of the local paper, taxi firm owners, politicians. Like I said, everyone's here.'

'And I must circulate,' Bea said. 'It's fairly straight forward here. The men are manning the barbecues.' Emma could see that Rob was being summoned back to his post. 'Next to them is a table with sauces, breads, salads, etc. And help yourself to drinks and don't feel you have to circulate before you're ready.'

Emma sat back with her beer. Whenever there was a quiet moment, two conversations went around her head. Lukas Mills and Michelle Jones. Having two entirely unconnected people raise similar concerns on the same day set off alarm bells in her head. Especially when those conversations only acted to confirm her suspicions.

She watched the scene in front of her. In one sense it was the ideal that everyone aspired to. Police, politicians, business owners, all living, working, and socialising in one town. Community policing at its finest.

But had it turned into something darker? Had it crossed the line between co-operation and collusion? Something triggered in her memory, something Jem had said. She saw her standing a short distance away so went over to the boss's wife.

'You said taxi firm owners earlier? Is the boss of King Kabs here?'

'Yeah, of course, Billy King, over there on the corner of the patio. That's his wife and one of his grown-up sons too.'

Emma looked where Jem indicated and saw a neat looking businessman. Smart jeans, yellow polo shirt, nothing out of the ordinary. Dark hair, side parted, just starting to thin. He was leaning back and telling a story, illustrating it by waving his beer bottle around. The woman next to him was more interesting. She was large, obviously tall, and dressed in an ethnic print dress. Her jewellery was similarly exotic, necklace, bangles, and earrings all large, silver and intricate. In keeping with everything else she had a mass of curly brown hair. She was beautiful and animated and totally focused on her husband.

Were they the drug dealers of Bradwick? Here, enjoying a beer in the sunshine?

'Why do you ask? Not still at work, are you?' Jem asked kindly.

'Oh, no. It's nothing. The name came up, and well, anyone who's ever been in a pub has seen their business cards and adverts. Just nice to put a name to a face.'

'That's what these events are for. Get people mingling.'

Later on, she watched Billy as he went over to get some more food. He stopped at Haines' barbecue and the two chatted for a minute. Ordering food or something else, Emma wondered. Just when she thought it was innocent, there was a brief moment when Haines reached out to King and she could see the two men were in sync. Even from a distance, she got the impression they were friends.

Maybe Lukas and Michelle were both right. But there was nothing she could do about it. She'd hardly go to Professional Standards and explain how Haines had given King, an innocent business owner, a burger in a suspicious manner. She shook her head and resolved to enjoy the rest of the day.

Whether or not she was going to formally investigate her team, she still had another job to do. With DS Stonor's words still fresh in her mind she decided to do her best to become a member of the team. She wasn't sure that the promised invitation to the pub would ever happen. But while she was waiting, she could meet wives and partners, fetch drinks, and generally prove that she really was a team player.

CHAPTER TWENTY-FIVE

Tuesday evening was DCI Haines regular meeting with Billy King. But in the last few weeks King had called extra meetings, mostly to berate Haines for a lack of progress. Haines was tempted to cancel on King, just to let him know who was the boss. In addition, Haines now felt he should spend more time in the station, working with the MIT, generating new leads in the hunt for the killer.

But King had been insistent. So now they were meeting at an out of the way hotel just outside Bradwick. It was an old Victorian building perched on a cliff top but the bar was in a modern flat roofed extension. It being a Tuesday evening, the place was quiet and King and Haines were undisturbed in a corner. Behind them the sun was sinking into the sea, but neither man was watching the sunset.

For once, King was in a more upbeat mood. 'It turns out I was right, you know. It was a good move to leave my men in there undercover. You'll never guess what I've got here.' He tapped his finger on a folded square of paper on the table.

'It's good that you're happier. But I don't know how much time I'll be able to devote to it. I'm running an operation to take the pressure off you and we've got a second body turned up. Thought we had it all finished up and put to bed, then another one. Put us right back to the beginning.'

'I know, I saw it on the news. Don't know what the world is coming to, or Bradwick for that matter. Shocking.' He shook his head and left enough of a pause to show respect for the dead teenagers. 'But this is good news, this is. Gives you the upper hand. Buys us at least another week. It's the good stuff.'

'Go on then,' Haines said, not really caring about the information for a moment. 'Tell us what you've got.'

'This,' he slid the piece of paper across the table, 'is a list of mobile numbers for county lines. The ones that everyone uses to get their drugs.'

'What's the point though?' Haines argued. 'Those numbers will change every week. By the time the technical boys finish with them, they'll have binned the numbers and moved on.'

'Nah, you're not getting it. This is next week's list. These numbers haven't been activated yet. They're about to be sent out to towns up and down the coast. Including Bradwick.' He paused for effect. 'It's up to you how you play it. Could nick them the minute they set foot in the town. Or monitor them and let them do the deals, then nick 'em with the gear. It's up to you.'

Haines took the piece of paper and turned it over in his fingers. What could he do with this? On any other week, he'd convene a team, get regular updates from the technical department, make it happen. But he had a murder to solve. No, he had two murders to solve. And he was already running another drugs operation.

'I can certainly hand it over to the right teams. There's a squad in Bristol that specialise in county lines, all the way up and down the patch, across several counties, tens of towns. It really depends where these numbers ping up as well, whether they're in the city or sent out around the area.'

Haines stopped when he could tell King wasn't really listening. 'So, what do you reckon then?' King asked. 'It'll buy us some time won't it? Disrupt them for a bit.'

Haines simply nodded. What he needed more than anything was a big result. Ideally when he had both the murders wrapped up. He had a nagging feeling that, unless he was careful, King would have burned one of his undercover men. But he was also unwilling to burst his good mood. 'Yeah, no, this is good. No question about it.' He left a bit of pause, then asked, 'Have you any news yet about the big deal? Where or when it could happen?'

'Ah, yes, we have got something on that. Nothing concrete but my people have been able to figure out how the structure works. Apparently, some guy called Pietr Garoza is the head of the whole outfit. With a bit of luck, he'll be down here to co-ordinate the exchange of drugs and money when they have a big meeting.'

'Do you have any idea yet why he'd come down to Bradwick? It's a bit of a risk for them, isn't it? I'd have expected him to summon the junior dealers up to the city.'

Billy King shook his head. 'Not heard anything yet. I can look into it though. You are right, if this Garoza guy is the head of a gang, then he should be calling the shots. Not leaving his turf but having people in to where his strength is. Next time we talk, I'll see if I can find out what he's up to. But I'll have to tell them to tread softly.'

'Thanks. I know it's a risk for you.'

King nodded slowly. Outside the window, the sun finally slipped below the lowering cloud and lit the horizon up with a bright band of gold. Neither man noticed it though as they finished their drinks, shook hands and left the meeting.

* * *

Haines sat back at his desk and looked at the list of phone numbers that he'd been handed. Even on a quiet week, he would have baulked at setting up an operation this big, especially when it could easily spread up and down the area, from Clevedon all the way down to Bridgewater and even out of area across to Minehead. And that didn't even count the in-land towns that would be hit.

He chose a unit in Bristol that he would need co-operation from if the big raid on the Latvians ever came off.

'Terry, I might have something for you,' Haines said before launching into an explanation of the list of numbers.

Terry sucked air in through his teeth. 'How sure are you of this Rob? Is it cast iron?'

'Yeah, it is. It's not some green CI, it's a guy I've known for years.'

'No chance he's winding you up?'

'None at all. What's the problem? This is a golden opportunity.'

'Yeah, I know that. But we're all watching the budgets, aren't we? There are a dozen phone numbers here. Each one would have to be checked, passed over to the technical teams and a warrant applied for. At the very least, we'd need to know where each phone was being used, if not what messages were being sent.'

'And then you'd be tracking them all over the place, seeing where they turn up. But the good news is that at the end of it you'll take down a dozen lines.'

'Yeah, no, that'd be good. Especially on the reports at the end of the month budget meetings.'

'Okay then. We have a deal.' There was the slightest of pauses. 'Can you do me two favours in return though. Can you make sure you keep the lines out of Bradwick and remember where the lead came from?'

'Of course. You sure you want me to remember you?'

'What do you mean?'

'Well if it all goes tits-up, then it'll be on your head.'

'I've told you; this is guaranteed.'

Haines said goodbye and hung up. He sat back and stared at the ceiling. He had gone out on a limb now. But he knew

Billy and he knew that this could be important if the promise of a big raid was ever fulfilled. He hoped he'd just banked a favour that he could call on when needed.

The other piece of information he had put into the computer before the phone call. Pietr Garoza was bigger than his own force. He was well known to the national crime agency and they were in their turn co-operating with Interpol. He was definitely wanted in his home country and was a person of interest over here. There was no definite address and the NCA were keen to locate him.

Haines had made a quick decision to keep this close to his chest. He printed out some photos to circulate around his team. But at the moment he would order his men to have a watching brief. It wouldn't be enough to locate Garoza, he wanted to have him bang to rights, on his own turf.

CHAPTER TWENTY-SIX

The next day, DC Angel had her confirmation. The videos came back so she spent some time looking through them. She went through at double speed and within ten minutes, she'd seen a dark Ford Fiesta in the area of the Taylor killing. She then fast forwarded to after the time of death and found the same car on the other side. If nothing else, the driver would be a really good witness.

However, after another thirty minutes of shuttling back and forth she was frustrated. The rear number plate lights weren't working. Was that a deliberate ploy, she wondered, or just poor maintenance? From the front, the headlights washed out the poor quality CCTV meaning she had absolutely no idea of the number plate. In the dark it was difficult to even see how many people were in the car. She thought the person behind the wheel was possibly white, but that was as far as it went.

She leaned back from the desk and rubbed her eyes. Why couldn't she have a CCTV system like they had on TV shows? The kind where you just clicked a mouse and zoomed right the way in as far as you wanted and the picture just kept getting clearer. She would then be able to get the killer's face.

Not knowing if it would do any good at all, she shuttled back and forth again until she'd selected some views that were, while not brilliant, the best she could find. She pressed the buttons to save the images and send them off to print. While the computer was working, she went to fetch herself a coffee and then settled down to go through the footage from the Evans killing.

At least it was daytime, so there weren't any problems with missing lights. The CCTV was still quite shoddy, jumping and occasionally being covered with static. She almost missed it when it happened. She was skipping through on fast-forward and the camera was covering a main road. As it was around rush hour, the cars were stacked up, stopping and starting with the change of the lights.

She was watching the junction that led up to the side road which went past the footpath where the body was found. From behind a van, a dark car emerged for a couple of frames and disappeared up the road. She checked the time stamp – the driver was in the right place and the right time to either attack Stella Evans or witness her murder.

She paused it and was amazed to see that she could get a clear shot of the number plate. The whole case seemed to be cursed, but this was the first real break they'd had so far. She sent the images to print and switched over to the DVLA site. Her heart sank just a little when she saw that it came back as a hire car company. And not some small local operation either, but a big national chain that had branches everywhere.

She decided it was time to involve DCI Haines. She knocked on his open door and settled in front of his desk. She ran through everything and then showed him the photographs, first from the Taylor scene and then from Evans.

'So, you've done it. Pull the DVLA records and we'll go round there and nick him.'

'Not quite that simple. The car comes back to a national car hire place. Registered at a central office.'

'And you need me to use my rank and local knowledge to scare up a warrant quickly so we can find out who was driving that car?' The mischief in Haines' voice was easy to hear.

'It shouldn't be a problem,' DC Angel said. 'We've established a firm timeline and that car was driving past two crime scenes at just the right time to be a very good witness if not a suspect.'

'Yep, I'll get straight onto the magistrate. For the minute though, I'll keep our powder dry on the Taylor case. I know what they're like. They're all ex lawyers. The connection to the first killing is too thin. I'll give them a simple picture – the driver of that car can help us with the enquiry into the Evans murder.'

'Thanks, boss!'

* * *

The next day, DC Angel pushed herself back from her desk. If she hadn't been in a male dominated office she would have burst into tears. Instead she'd had to make do with slamming the phone down onto the cradle.

She'd just got off a conference call with BioMed – a company that was based in the north of the county just outside Bristol. They mainly sold medical supplies across the south west. The car that Angel was interested in had been hired by them at exactly the time of the Evans murder. She had learned this thanks to providing the head office of the hire car company with a valid warrant.

BioMed had confirmed that they had sent three of their sales reps to a sales conference in a hotel outside Birmingham. This information had been painfully gleaned in a call between herself, the sales manager, the head of HR, a legal advisor, and the head of the finance department. It was hard to tell who was speaking and they frequently interrupted each other. She was trying to establish who had been driving the car at the time, while all the managers had been discussing their duty of care regarding the personal information they held.

In the end they had left it that the legal advisor would have a conference with his boss to decide if they were able to release the name of the driver or if they would have to wait for another warrant.

What she had been able to learn was that three of their sales staff had been sent on a conference to learn about new products and how to sell them. To reduce costs, they had been supplied with a hire car – saving any insurance and licence complications over business use on a personal car. Unfortunately for DC Angel, this car was supposed to have been at a posh hotel outside Birmingham for three nights and the night on which Stella Evans was murdered was right in the middle of that period.

She felt like screaming. She didn't need to know much – just who had access to the car and if they left the conference. Whether she could put them in the vicinity of the murder or not. She went over to lookout of the window – she hated waiting on other people to make decisions. She saw a number of CCTV cameras on poles, all watching car parks. A thought started forming.

All she needed to know was where that car was. She reckoned on a couple of hours to drive to Birmingham. So, a five-hour window around the time of the murder would do the trick.

She went back to her desk and phoned the finance manager. As soon as she announced who she was, his tone became wary.

'I just wondered if you could tell me where the conference was held?'

'Why do you want to know?'

'It's purely routine. We just need it for elimination purposes. We don't need any names. I know you'll have handled the expenses. If you give me the name of the hotel, then I can talk to them direct.'

'Maybe I ought to phone Mr Broughton in legal. Just run it past him.'

'Listen, I know it was a medical sales conference, I know it was in a hotel outside Birmingham and I know the dates. I could find it either on the internet or by phoning all the hotels. It's not privileged information at all. We just need you to help the police with their enquiries and speed the process up a bit.'

There was a long pause as the manager considered this. DC Angel's spirits rose when she heard a sigh and the clatter of keys at the other end of the phone. 'It's a Ramada hotel,' he said resignedly, and gave the address.

Angel finally felt that she was getting a break. She had dealt with that chain before and she knew that they were generally good at helping the police. Not wanting to lose the momentum, she immediately phoned through and asked to speak to the security manager.

Stella Evans had left work just after five and had been found at a quarter to seven. There was nothing to suggest that she'd done anything other than head straight home so they were fairly confident that she died somewhere between twenty past five and twenty to six. Factoring in the two-hour drive from Birmingham, DC Angel asked for the CCTV files covering three o'clock through to eight o'clock.

There was a sharp intake of breath on the other end of the line. 'Listen, we can do it, if it's essential.' She heard the phrase and translated it in her head to "I need a more senior rank". 'But we have a total of eight cameras covering all areas of the car park and the exits, all storing the files digitally. If we were to edit that section out.' He paused doing mental arithmetic. 'That'd be over forty hours of footage. I can't just email that through, it'd break our servers. I'd need to talk to the tech guys at head office, get them to set up a secure site, upload the files, send you out the address and password. All takes time.'

DC Angel sat back and thought. What would prove things, either one way or another? 'Okay. You say you've got eight cameras? Can you email me eight stills, all taken at five thirty on that day? Just for starters?' She thought that if they were on a conference, they'd probably drink in the hotel bar and eat in the hotel restaurant, all on expenses. There shouldn't be any reason to go out in the car at all.

'Eight stills? Sure, that'd be easy.' His voice grew distracted as he wrote and talked at the same time. 'Eighth of August, seventeen thirty, all car park cameras. I'll have that over to you as soon as I've done it.'

* * *

Two hours later she had her answer and she was not happy. She printed off a single photo and angrily circled a number plate in red marker pen. Then she grabbed the two photos from the Evans scene, together with one from the Taylor killing and pinned them all up on the incident board in a neat line.

'What's all this?' DC Ed Mitchell had wandered over and was looking at the photos.

'Well.' Angel was aware she sounded like a teacher. 'This car was seen in the vicinity of the Taylor killing, but we can't identify the plate. I suspect this is the same car, shown here and here. The timings place it both before and after the Evans murder.'

'And this one in the middle? Looks like a car park.'

'Yeah. This car was approaching the crime scene at 17:14, parked in Birmingham at 17:30 and leaving the scene at 17:43.'

'What's the driving time from Birmingham to Bradwick then?'

'I'll tell you something.' Angel was frustrated and it showed in her voice. 'It's a lot more than fifteen bloody minutes!'

'Hey, calm down. You've got something here.' Before he could explain, DCI Haines entered the open-plan area and walked over. Between them Angel and Mitchell explained what they had. Then Mitchell asked, 'What was that car doing in the car park in Birmingham anyway?'

'It's a hire car, medical sales reps attending a conference.' DC Angel sounded fed up.

'So, there's two possibilities.' Mitchell was getting into his stride now. 'Either a bunch of sales reps decided to clone a number plate, fudge their attendance at a conference so that one of them could use a hire car to commit a murder.' He paused for effect. 'Or, our main suspect drove past a hire car place, saw a car with the same make and model as his one and cloned the plate.' He tapped the photos on the board. 'What you have here is a photo of our main suspect.'

'He's right, you know.' DCI Haines was nodding. 'It'll be easy to check the conference, there'll be CCTV all over the inside of the hotel, hundreds of witnesses. If I was about to commit a crime in a car, I'd drive past several hire car lots and write down the number plates.'

'Hold on a minute though,' DC Angel said. 'There's loads of legislation around number plate machines now. How hard is it to make up fake plates without a log book?'

DCI Haines clapped her on the shoulder. 'That's your next job. We know our lad is local. He's picked two spots that aren't covered by CCTV, one of which is a well-known short cut. He got his number plate from a hire car lot on the southern edge of Bristol. Have a sniff around dodgy garages, especially the small one-man type outfits. See if any have shut down recently, maybe sold off their assets? If you get names, give me a shout and I can lean on them.'

DC Angel nodded and returned to her desk. She spent the rest of the afternoon looking for dodgy number plate machines. The trouble was that the whole trade was overseen by the DVLA through a licensing scheme and anyone found breaching the conditions would face a fine of thousands of pounds and loss of their licence.

This meant that all the official sources for buying the machines were very keen to emphasise that you needed to provide documentation. She knew from experience that the whole car industry was riddled with petty crooks. Given that their suspect was in Bradwick but happy to go up nearly as far as Bristol, she had a large area to search for number plate makers. Her heart sank when the results came back – there were literally hundreds of suppliers. It seemed that every backstreet garage, second-hand car lot and small motor factor had a machine. Any one of them could've reported a theft of a machine, or simply sold it under the counter, or made fake plates cash in hand.

However, she wasn't a member of the public and she wasn't restricted to just using search engines. She called up the police computer system and started crafting a search. She had to manually scan through and discount thefts of actual number plates, although she made a note to check with the hire car company that the killer hadn't simply stolen the plates.

What she was left with was a list of more serious car crimes. She noticed that in recent years, even these had tailed off. As HPI checks moved to phones and more of the DVLA services were online, it got harder and less profitable to change the identity of a stolen car to sell it on.

She spent a long afternoon checking cases. In every one there had been a car dealer involved in giving cars new identities. And in every case, the machine for making the plates had been seized and destroyed.

At five to five she opened the last case of the day. She had been working backwards and had now got to 2001. She thought that tomorrow she'd try a different approach – she'd gone far enough back in the past to satisfy her curiosity.

There was a number plate machine noted in the evidence, but no record of its fate. Frowning, she called up the case details and phoned through to the evidence suite.

Five minutes later, she pushed back from the desk and stared at the ceiling. The machine had been checked out of evidence after the trial and had never gone back in. In her mind, she followed through the possible trail. Had a corrupt officer sold the machine into the underworld, or had they gone on to become a killer themselves?

She realised that Michelle Jones had got into her head. She was seeing corruption everywhere now. On the other hand she had a quiet voice in her head that wouldn't be silenced. Whoever had killed Mazey and Stella had known about CCTV, DNA and number plates. They had taken effective steps to avoid all of them. That left the question, were they dealing with a very careful amateur or a law enforcement professional.

She decided, despite her dressing-down for not being a team player, to keep this to herself for the moment. Before she did anything, she needed information. So, she packed up and prepared to leave her desk like a normal Monday evening.

However, this time she went down to records and pulled the case file for a car theft ring from 2001. She would read it overnight, draw her own conclusions and then decide what to do next.

Chapter Twenty-Seven

DCI Haines always thought that newspaper offices should be like they are in the films – all bashing presses and harassed reporters rushing around clutching articles.

In practice, the Bradwick Recorder had moved to an out of town light industrial estate. He had called the editor, Angela Bathgate, out about this when they first moved. She'd shrugged and pointed to the rows of monitors and quiet workers hunched over them.

'It's the internet, isn't it? This place has amazing broadband speeds and we can get lots of articles written and uploaded as well as keep up with Twitter.'

Now, they had chosen to meet, not in the office but in a cafe that did a roaring trade on the estate. Like every other building it was bland and modern. Haines and Bathgate were both locals and even though there was nearly ten years between them, they still felt like compatriots.

Once they had coffees, they got down to business.

'So, what's the latest on these two murders? Have you got a name for this serial killer yet? Butcher of Bradwick is my favourite. Or the Seaside Strangler?' There was a glint of mischief in her voice.

'You know I want to keep it quiet. And we haven't even linked the two cases.'

'Come on, I may not be a detective like you but two women, similar age, both strangled in remote areas. If we don't report it soon, someone else will.'

'I do appreciate all that you're doing. You know how important this is.'

'You don't need to explain it to me. We're on the same page – a serial killer scare could finish this place off. Even now if you say Hungerford or Dunblane, the massacres are the first thing you think of. And, I know we've gone all digital and away from paper but one thing hasn't changed. We still need advertisers. We're doing well in promoting Bradwick as a retro holiday spot. Playing down the drug trade, the high street closures – all of that can be done.'

'Why can I sense a "but" coming?'

'Everything has changed. When you and I were growing up, print was king. My predecessors would have had stringers and they would've known who was feeding the stories back to the national press. A pint here and a bottle of whisky there and a story could've been buried.

'But now, it's all the internet and Twitter. And you have to admit that both your victims are young and pretty. And, even if we didn't report it – that doesn't matter. One relative could start a hashtag, do an end run around the local press and get picked up by a national paper.' She stopped talking and spread her hands. 'There isn't an awful lot that I can do here.'

'There must be something you can do? I hate feeling powerless, knowing that some spotty teenager with a laptop could undermine everything.'

'Well, there is something I could do,' Angela said. She took a sip of coffee, looking at Haines over the rim of her cup with a mischievous look. He knew she was pausing to wind him up so didn't react. 'I could help you manage the story.'

'What does that involve?' Despite rising through the ranks of the police force, Haines was still very resistant to management language.

'Well, when the story does break, and trust me, it will break, they're going to want an angle, something to hang the story on.' Haines nodded. 'Now without management, it could be anything – no one can tell how these things get picked up. They could give the killer a name, they could focus on how the police are failing or a sobbing relative might make the front pages. But, if you let me, I could push some aspects, release stories, suppress others. Try to make a difference.'

'I don't know why you'd need me. Isn't that your job?'

'It's a two-way street. I'd need information about the case, interviews, that kind of thing. It would give my reports a bit of credibility. Quid pro quo.'

Haines took his time to answer. He could see the wisdom of it. 'You do know that we have press officers for this kind of thing?'

'Yeah, well, that's your prerogative of course. You could as-semble a focus group, run it past the press officer, take a vote before anything is released?' There was an edge of humour to her voice – she knew she was winding him up.

'Well, no. But I can't just go giving you the details on the case without at least thinking it through, working out where we want to go with this.'

'No, I do understand. But you have to move quickly on this.' Haines nodded, so she continued. 'The last thing any of us want is a story coming out about how dangerous it is out there. How there's a maniac stalking the streets, randomly attacking women.'

'Part of the problem is that this killer is giving us nothing back. There's no real evidence left at any scene.'

'That could be an angle. Maybe try to pin it on all those TV shows? You know the ones like CSI. Are they teaching people how to be better killers? Avoid detection?'

'We don't want to go giving people ideas though.'

'No, you're probably right. Give me a day or so to think about it. If I email you, will you reply? Promptly?'

'Yes, I will.' Haines looked uncomfortable. 'I know it doesn't look like it, but I do appreciate this, what you're doing. I'll get on to your emails and get the clearance if you want any further details. Hopefully we can have this managed properly.'

'Don't worry, I'll get on top of it,' Angela assured him. And get yourself a good byline, Haines thought bitterly. But it looked like he didn't have a choice.

CHAPTER TWENTY-EIGHT

As one of the youngest and newest members of the team, DC Angel had drawn the short straw and was on social media duty. It wasn't that she didn't understand the technology, it was that diving into the world of Facebook and Twitter involved plumbing the lowest depths of mob mentality. But they were right in that she had grown up with it so had a certain natural flair for it.

She was trying different search terms and trawling through the rubbish trying to find something useful. At least, she thought, she didn't need any great skills because most people didn't keep their privacy settings up. In fact, most people wanted their posts viewed and shared.

There wasn't a huge amount of useful information though. She was focused on the teenage friends of Mazey Taylor and Stella Evans. It was surprisingly easy to make jumps and find links between them, but she knew that it was illusory.

It would be easy to find a link between the two women, but people added in friends on Facebook really easily and likewise tagged each other in posts. What appeared to be a link could be nothing more than two people who'd never met with one "friend" in common.

Flicking tabs in the browser, she finally came across something of use. 'Boss, have you got a minute? I think I've found something.'

'Yeah, what have you found?' Haines came out of his office rubbing his head. 'I'm busting my brain with crime reports so I could do with distracting.'

'There's a hashtag that's picking up momentum.' DC Angel definitely caught a flinch across his face. Despite all the training, DCI Haines still wasn't up to speed on modern technology. 'It's #protectourgirls. Apparently, they're trying to set it up so that if a woman is feeling unsafe then they can use it to summon some blokes to walk them home at night.'

Haines furrowed his brow. By now the open area office had gone quiet as they all considered this information.

Finally, DC Mitchell broke the silence. 'But this is a public hashtag, yes? So if our killer's out there on social media it might become a shopping list for him?'

'It looks that way,' DC Angel confirmed. 'At the very best, they're encouraging lone women at night to contact strangers over direct message so they can arrange to meet up.'

Heads were being shaken around the office. DCI Haines asked, 'What's the general reaction online?'

'Well, it's caused a flame war. The teenage women aren't too happy with being called girls. And the thought that they somehow need protecting has really kicked things off. There are people out there comparing it to Saudi Arabia where women can't leave without a male escort. It's getting pretty vicious out there.'

'Is there anything we need to be aware of?'

'I think it's giving focus to the usual problems of this time of year. Teenage boys being bored and needing to show off and protect their territory. Add to that the odd weather, the tourists coming in, and the fact that some of them are on school holidays. I think we need to keep a close eye on them, nothing more at the moment.'

'What about the feminist angle?' DCI Haines asked.

'I think they're just sounding off at the moment.'

'You mean we won't get hordes of hairy-legged lesbian man-haters stringing up the teenage boys of Bradwick?' Stonor sneered.

DC Angel had a sharp intake of breath that she quickly converted into a cough. She felt the comment like a punch. They were trying to catch a man who drove round at night scaring women and investigating another who got schoolgirls pregnant. And to people like Stonor it was all just a joke with stereotypes.

She forced herself to calm down and consider a response. It was the classic trap – she either waded in to defend her gender or she let it slide. If she took the first option, then she could guarantee weeks of being labelled as a feminist in crude sexist terms. But she wasn't sure if she could be the person who just sat there when the jokes were made. Could she live with herself?

'You know,' Haines paused to make sure he had the attention of the room, 'I've arrested most of the teenage boys who cause trouble round here and to be honest, they'd be doing us a fucking favour!'

The whole room exploded in laughter – his timing was perfect. When the room had quietened down, he asked, 'Is there anything else of note on the internet?'

'Well, the general news sites seem to be comparing living in the country to being in the city. Saying how people are considering leaving the city for the countryside to feel safer and then asking if it really is.'

Haines frowned, then said, 'I did have a word with the press to try to spin the coverage of the murders. We can't have Bradwick associated with these crimes. I suppose it's the best that we could hope for. It's not ideal but at least we haven't got an hour long special on Channel Five about our serial killer.'

He went back to his office and DC Angel waited a reasonable amount of time before popping in to see him without it looking too suspicious.

'You know we were talking about that car with the fake plates?'

'Yeah, our most promising lead. Any further progress on that?'

'Well there must be hundreds, if not thousands, of plate making machines out there. Every shady second-hand car dealer and small garage seems to be licensed. So I started looking to see if any were reported stolen.'

'And you wouldn't be sat here if you'd found nothing.' Haines nodded. 'Why haven't you just put it on the system and followed it up?'

'Well it's a bit delicate. For a start it's a case from nearly twenty years back. There was a second-hand car dealer, acted as a clearing house for stolen cars. Had the plate machine, printer for log books, the whole lot. Was shipping the cars out to auctions in Exeter and Bristol mainly. Does that ring any bells?'

'Well, only vaguely. It's the kind of thing that went on back then.'

'Trouble is your name's all over it. Together with Patterson and Inspector Haveland, who is now superintendent. What I'm interested in is that a Sergeant Sumner signed out the plate making machine from evidence. It's the last anyone ever heard of it.'

Haines shook his head. 'That was a bad business. Old Larry Sumner. He was getting on a bit when he joined the force and was just Sergeant Sumner for ever. Left at fifty-five, but he smoked like a chimney all the time I knew him. Don't think the poor bugger even made it to his sixtieth birthday.'

'He's dead?'

'Yeah, must be at least eight years back, probably nearer ten.' Haines was sad, but with the acceptance that came from long years in the police.

'Damn! So if he did have a number plate making machine, then that's another dead end.'

'I doubt his next of kin would've known what it was. Might've gone into the auction or the rubbish. God knows.'

'I'll keep on worrying away at it,' DC Angel said. 'See if there are any other cases where one of them went missing. Or if anyone's making up dodgy plates.'

'I'll see what I can find as well. Just make some quiet enquiries.'

DC Angel knew what his enquiries were like so she thought it best not to ask exactly what his information sources were.

'There's one other vague lead as well. Gregory Watts. I know you went out to interview him. Call Stonor in and you run me through your thoughts.'

'So, what do you two reckon? Do we have another suspect in this Gregory Watts character?'

DC Angel and DS Stonor looked at each other, aware that while they disagreed, they didn't want to start arguing in front of the boss.

'Okay, you two, I can tell you don't agree, that's fine. Stonor, what's your take on this?'

'Well, boss, we can't really put him in the frame for this.' He caught an outraged look from Angel. 'I know there's an age difference between him and his partner but that's not unusual. I mean it's not like he's in his sixties and taking up with a teenager. Yes, he did know the victim. But Stella Evans worked as a receptionist in an estate agent and she was an outgoing young woman who went out most weekends. It would be more difficult to find someone who didn't have a passing acquaintance with her.' He paused before making his final point. 'And he does have an alibi.'

DC Angel shook her head. 'He is creepy. Nearly old enough to be Amanda Goode's father, yet he's already got her pregnant at seventeen. And his alibi is very thin – he refused to give us the details of someone to corroborate where he was at the time. He just said that he was taking photos for a house sale.'

'Yes, but he has his reputation.' Stonor tried to appeal directly to his boss. 'He's a regular guy, doing well for himself. He's not your average kind of loser who usually commits these kind of crimes. He's a settled bloke who's got a nice house, partner, child on the way.'

'If you'd met him though, you'd have seen something. Controlling behaviour, he didn't like to be contradicted, and he tried to cut me out of the conversation at every turn.'

Haines held up his hands. 'Okay. Okay. I get it. You, Angel, had a bad feeling about the guy, and you have to respect your gut feelings. On the other hand, I hear you, Stonor. He sounds like a good man, certainly not someone we can harass. DC Angel, you still have contacts within the estates and schoolgirls?'

'Yeah.' DC Angel sounded resigned. 'They still know me as PC Emma.'

'Good. Have a quiet nose around. If he really does have an unhealthy interest in schoolgirls, then he'll be known. See how much you can find out about him. Don't go so far that you need a warrant but have a poke around and see what comes up.'

'Right will do, boss,' DC Angel tried to sound upbeat even though she was annoyed at both his attitude and the general mood in the office. She knew what she knew and no one was taking her seriously. After the whole debacle with the Wanky-Bois she thought that they should be more open minded. She made a snap decision to take her boss at his word. As soon as she got back to her desk, she gathered her belongings to go out and see if she could learn anything.

CHAPTER TWENTY-NINE

Emma started off at the same place she'd seen the gaggle of teenagers last. She sat down at an outside table with a McDonald's coffee and an apple pie. She knew it wasn't the healthiest food but she knew it was either this or shouting at her colleagues.

She had decided to finish her coffee and food and then go back to the office. She'd had enough time to calm down and resolve to do her job methodically and prove them wrong. But when she cast another look around, she saw a couple of girls hanging around the outside tables, nervously chatting to each other. Soon another girl sidled up and then a fourth. They were all on their phones and appeared to be muttering to each other.

She wandered over to see what was up. 'You not coming into McDonald's then?'

'No, the manager don't like us just hanging around. And we're broke at the moment.' This was Shell – as in from the seaside, not short for Michelle.

'Hey! I seen one of them programs on TV. We could be like confidential informants or something. Then you'd,' she looked pointedly at Emma, 'like, have to pay us for information and stuff.'

Emma considered this for a moment. This wasn't yet a formal part of the investigation. She wondered if she'd been sent off after Gregory Watts as a way to shut her up. On the other hand she needed to know why he evoked such a negative reaction in her. She'd been used to dealing with fakes and phonies all through her childhood so she knew when something wasn't as it seemed.

'Right, come on then. I can't make it official but I can get you a few things from McDonald's. Then we'll be allowed to sit at a table and have a chat.' She knew she had a twenty in her purse and figured that it'd be worth it for some information.

They all followed her in and clustered around the till. Emma had a strange feeling of being like a mother to a group of teenagers even though she had less than ten years on any of them. Maybe big sister, she thought.

In the end they bought a strange assortment of drinks and snacks, nothing that would comprise a meal.

When they were all seated round a table – four girls and Emma, all with snacks and drinks. Emma was overwhelmed by the essence of youth that emanated from them. Despite their closeness in years she found them strangely innocent and full of energy. She knew that this was what attracted some men and made the girls vulnerable but now she just found it a mixture of endearing and irritating.

'So, then, what's so important? What's worth a load of Maccy D?' This was Mel, with the scraped-back hair and big earrings.

Emma swallowed her mouthful of chips and made a mental note to stop eating so much crap food. 'We're making enquiries into someone called Gregory Watts. Just wondered if you'd heard of him?'

'Who is he?'

'He's this consultant estate agent, lives over in a nice suburb near Spalley Road and he has a seventeen-year-old girlfriend.' There was a pause as the girls watched her and wondered if she'd actually cross the line and make an accusation. 'I just got a bad feeling from him and wondered what his deal was.'

'What do you mean?' This was Kaisia, all blonde ringlets. She was trying to look grungy but her natural beauty still shone through.

'Well, I'm not being funny, but he's over ten years older than her, lots of money, good enough looking that he could have any woman he wants. Just seems strange he'd go for someone so young.' She left the unspoken accusation hanging in the air.

The girls all looked at each other as if there was a guilty secret that they shared. Eventually Mel received the nod from the others. She started hesitantly, biting her lip. 'This can't get back to him, yeah? Not back to Gregory?'

'There's no need to be afraid. If he's up to no good, we can protect you and stop him.' Emma was excited now. Was she about to get her hands on someone grooming schoolgirls?

'We're not afraid of him. It's just that he helps out in so many places. He's always down the youth club and there are people who reckon he helps out with funding it.'

Emma frowned. 'So, why all the strange looks? What's the secret?'

Mel took a breath to gather herself. 'Well I reckon Amanda's like the fifth–'

'Fourth?' Kaisia interrupted.

'Fourth or fifth of his girls. Not all at the same time. He picks them out when they're sixteen, they have a couple of babies, then when they start to look a bit older, he moves on to a new sixteen-year-old.'

Emma was horrified. She looked around the four faces. 'And you all know about this?'

There were nods around the table before Mel spoke again. 'We all talk, you know. Older sisters, friends of friends, cousins. But the thing is that he's not bad. He doesn't just fund the youth clubs and stuff like that. You know you hear of these baby daddies that just don't want to know? Hassled by the CSA and always in front of the court? Yeah, Gregory's nothing like that. He always has visits with each of his kids. You can see the mums on the estate – they're the ones with new buggies and decent clothes and all that. He always meets his payments, makes sure his kids are looked after.'

'His kids? How many are there?'

Mel sat back and frowned. 'I dunno. His girls usually have one or two before he moves on. So I guess there must be six or seven out there? I heard Mandy's pregnant?'

'Yes, we went round there. A couple of months to go.'

'There you are then. Another little Watts' baby soon.'

Emma sat back and frowned. The law and guidelines on situations like this were changing fast. She wasn't sure what exactly was going on except that she knew it felt wrong. 'So, how does he keep finding new girlfriends? If we've got a thirty-year-old man, how can he keep meeting teenagers? He must be grooming.'

'Yeah, but is he really?' This was Mel again. 'I mean, he won't entertain anyone who's under sixteen and he has no truck with booze or drugs. I know people who've had a relationship with him, get caught with a single spliff and he won't even answer the phone – just cuts them dead.'

'So, this is all hearsay. Do you actually know anyone?'

A girl with short dark hair spoke up quietly. 'My older sister used to hang around with him, over a year ago now. She was in the same year as Mandy Goode. A whole gang of them would go out at once and he'd buy proper food at McDonald's or Burger King, then they'd go on to the pictures, drinks and popcorn, everything paid for.'

'And the parents were happy with a man in his late twenties or early thirties taking their daughters out on a group date?' Emma could hardly believe what she was saying.

'Yeah, have you met him?' Emma nodded. 'He's a proper charmer. All the mums love him. Even the dads who can be a bit possessive, he wins them round in the end.'

Emma sighed deeply. 'Okay. So apart from the fact that he likes teenagers, this guy is a saint. This isn't really my job. What's wrong with him?'

'Yeah,' Mel said, 'you want to speak to Kelsey Teague. That was all over the estate, what, three maybe four years ago. She moved into his place, had his baby, all that.'

'What went wrong?'

'Well, he moved on, she moved out. All seemed fine and everything. Then she got a new boyfriend and it all went to shit. They were in and out of family court, social workers, all that stuff.'

Emma leaned forward. This was more like it. 'What happened after that?'

Mel shrugged, her shoulders making her earrings jingle. 'Dunno. Just vanished off the face of the earth. Her mum and family still live on the estate but they're not saying nothing. I guess she's run away from Watts.'

Back in her car, Emma reviewed what she had actually learnt. Gregory Watts was certainly creepy and overly interested in teenage girls. And the news that one woman involved with him had disappeared certainly caused alarm bells to go off. But, looked at through the objective eyes of the CPS it added up to a whole load of nothing much.

When she got back to the office, she ran a check on Kelsey Teague. She had to go through a few different spellings of her name, but in the end, she got one hit for a twenty-year-old who was arrested for drunk and disorderly about three and a half years ago. She dug around a bit and found out that at the time she was listed as being on the Seaview Estate bordering Coopers End. From what she had learned, Emma feared that it would be a dead end.

She went to the case notes and read over them really carefully. There was one name that kept on cropping up all through the notes – a social worker called Julie Walker. Following her hunch, she made a call to the council and was soon connected.

'I'm looking for a Kelsey Teague and your name came up?'

'Kelsey?' Julie sounded confused. 'Oh, that was a long time back. What's she done now?'

'Her? Nothing. I wondered what she'd be able to tell me about Gregory Watts.'

'Now that is one name that I do remember.'

'What's your initial impression of him?'

'It's more than initial – the whole case rumbled on for nearly a year. The guy's a lizard or a snake. He's beautiful, everything he does is calculated and looks brilliant on the surface. But I think he's just as dangerous as any reptile.' There was a long, telling pause. 'Are you really going after him?'

'Is there a reason I shouldn't?'

'It'll be tough. He's very clever and well embedded with the whole scene down there in Bradwick. He's a real man's man. No one in CID will lift a finger against him.'

'Well, maybe if I met with Kelsey, heard what she had to say?'

This time the pause was even longer and more charged than before. 'Leave it with me. I won't make any promises but I'll reach out. If I have any success, you'll hear from me.'

And if Kelsey won't see me, Emma thought, then I won't hear from you again.

CHAPTER THIRTY

'Angel? Thank god you're back from lunch.'

'What's up, boss?'

'I know we usually use uniform but they're really stretched at the moment. I need you to go down to the motor pool, sign out a van and come to the address I'm about to send you.'

'Sure. What's going on?'

'We're at a farm outside Sutherton. Turns out the farmer has no documentation for the immigrant farm workers, not even his gangmaster's licence. On top of that Terry's been having a snoop around the tomato greenhouses and he thinks not all the plants are tomatoes. So we're going to need to collect all the workers plus a load of evidence. We've already got some uniforms here with one van but it won't be enough.'

'Okay then. I'll be with you as soon as I can.'

As she got ready and went down the stairs, she thought about all the trite things new recruits said about life in the police force. You never know what the job will bring. That morning she had been searching social media and debriefing her boss on various suspects in her case. She'd spent lunchtime sharing a McDonald's with a group of teenage girls, gathering information. Now she was on her way out to a farm with a van.

When she got to the motor pool, she was met by a surly sergeant, who was in charge of allocation.

'DC Angel, huh?' He held her warrant card under the light, as if he thought it might be fake. 'Emma Angel from CID upstairs? Well I've not had an official requisition form in for a van.'

'It's an operational issue. We attended a scene and couldn't anticipate what we'd find.' He looked sceptical so she continued. 'I can always phone DCI Haines and ask if he has time to explain it to you.'

The dropping of the rank into the conversation seemed to have the right effect. 'No, no, won't be necessary. We're used to being flexible for operational reasons.' He reached for a clipboard and started scanning through it. Under his breath he muttered, 'A van for Emma Angel.' His finger stopped halfway down and a smile spread across his face. 'Yes, that'll do fine.' He turned and unlocked a cabinet full of keys. He selected one, checked what was written on the yellow tag and slapped them down on the desk. 'Far corner of the yard. LDV van.' With that he turned away and busied himself with paperwork in the back of his office.

Wondering if she'd imagined the weird atmosphere, DC Angel took the keys and went out into the yard. There at the far end, was an old, slightly battered LDV minibus. It was parked hard up against a wall, with very little space front and back. She looked at the route she'd have to take out. Some of the gaps looked tight for a big van like that.

'You'll be all right with that, won't you?' The sergeant had materialised behind her. 'I mean, you've done the driving course and all?' He ran his eyes up and down her body. His meaning was obvious – you're too short and weak to drive a van like that.

'It'll be fine,' DC Angel said with resolve.

The van was parked so close to the wall that she had to slide across from the passenger side. Then she found that the seat wouldn't adjust forward at all. She had to perch on the edge of the seat and twist to engage the heavy clutch.

By the time she had the van pointing towards the exit two things had happened. Her arms and shoulders were aching from the steering wheel and her entire left side from below her knee to above her hip was on fire from her repeated efforts to depress the clutch. Secondly, the desk sergeant had been joined by three other officers.

She might be the entertainment for the day, but she wasn't going to give them the satisfaction. Gingerly, with eyes on both mirrors, she edged the van forward. It might hurt, but she had a position now where she could control the clutch, so she could leave the car park at walking pace.

Once she was on the road and away from the eyes of Traffic, she could relax a little. One big advantage of driving a marked vehicle was that no one complained when she drove most of the way in third gear, even if it meant grinding painfully slowly away from roundabouts and junctions.

At the farm, she took a moment to compose herself before sliding gracefully down from the seat. The effort of rounding up farm workers and supervising the removal of cannabis plants meant that she didn't have time to worry about her aches or driving the van round.

After a couple of hours they were ready to leave. She was assigned with DC Mitchell as an escort to take the prisoners back to the station. DC Angel had an unguarded moment as she prepared to get back into the van and DC Mitchell picked up on it.

'They gave you this beast to drive? What did you do to piss them off?'

'Nothing really. This was just the last van left.' Her lie was effortless and she hoped, undetected. She had an uncomfortable moment where she actually considered patching things up with Dave Parks just to get good treatment from Traffic.

'Well do you want me to drive it back?' When he saw her look, he hastily added, 'It's not that you're a woman. If you were a short bloke I'd offer too. Unless, that is, they've fixed that seat?'

'They haven't fixed the seat yet. Thanks for the offer but I'd never hear the end of it if I let a man bring it back to the pool.'

DC Mitchell stopped to think. 'I'll run you back to the middle of Bradwick, then we'll swap over and you can drop me off at the station before going on to the pool.'

DC Angel gave this suggestion some thought. On the one hand it was tempting to let someone else drive the van back to Bradwick. The last two hours meant that her sharp pains had faded into dull aches. She didn't know what another drive would do and didn't much care to find out. But, would accepting a favour from DC Mitchell put her in his debt? Her whole life she had preferred to rely on herself and her own abilities. It didn't seem fair to involve the rest of CID in her own personal squabbles.

On the other hand, he had offered. And he knew that it would avoid getting her involved in an us vs them situation between CID and Traffic. Which in turn meant that she was becoming part of the team – they were looking out for her.

'Yeah, go on then,' she said, throwing him the keys. She decided being part of the team was worth owing someone a favour.

As good as his word, Ed Mitchell stopped on Bradwick High Street and let them swap seats. She left the van in the easiest space she could find and pretty much threw the keys back at the smirking sergeant.

CHAPTER THIRTY-ONE

The next morning, DC Angel woke up early in agony. She had taken Ibuprofen before going to sleep but it had worn off now. She took two before crawling out of bed and making it to the shower. She set it as hot as possible and when she was finished, she felt at least halfway human.

With a mixture of painkillers she managed to get into work without raising too many eyebrows. DCI Haines was holed up in his office, talking on the phone.

When she was sure her boss wasn't looking, she levered herself out of her chair. She took a moment to steady herself on the table before limping over to fetch herself some coffee.

Unseen by her, DC Mitchell saw the way she moved and frowned slightly.

In his office, her boss picked up the phone as it rang. 'Haines.'

'Rob, it's Terry. I'm repaying the favour over those numbers you sent over last week. We've got one active right in your backyard.'

Haines took down the details of where and when the phone had been located. Even better news was that the phone hadn't moved for a day. This meant that the technical teams had a precise address, presumably where a dealer was staying. He made one further phone call before going through to the open-plan office and saw his quarry. 'Mitchell. We've got a job. A live one. I'll get Laurel and Hardy and meet you in the car park in five.'

'Right you are, boss.'

DC Angel looked round with an unspoken question on her face. Haines considered the situation carefully. He gave a slight inclination of his head and moved towards the stairs. DC Angel fell in beside him trying hard not to limp.

'Right, Angel. This isn't strictly on the book. You can come along to observe, but that will be all. You will not comment and if you see something you don't like you'll just put it out of your mind.'

'Yes, boss. What's the situation?' DC Angel was excited partly from picking up on Haines' emotions and partly because she might get a chance to do something to get DPS off her back.

'We've got a cuckoo; a county line being set up in my town.' He almost growled this sentence. 'It's on Walker Avenue so it'll be some sad case who's an addict, being given a rock a day while they take over his house. It's up to us to put a stop to it and send them back where they came from.'

DC Angel didn't want to think either about where the information came from or what would happen next. By now they had reached the lower floor, where they found two officers having a break.

One was tall and thin, Laurel, and the other was short and squat, but more like a rugby player than Oliver Hardy. But they were fast friends, so in the way of the station they were nicknamed after the two legends of black and white comedy films.

Haines barked quick orders that they were to meet up in plain clothes with stab vests and plenty of equipment as soon as possible.

They travelled through the town and DC Angel wondered about the feel of the place. It was overcast and muggy weather which seemed to reflect the mood of the town. Whether it was teenagers worrying about the dead girls, or the ripples through the drug scene, or even her own misgivings about Professional Standards, there seemed to be a disturbance. And that feeling was mirrored in the oppressive weather – not too hot and not sunny, just close and overcast.

Soon all five of them, Mitchell, Haines, Angel, and Laurel and Hardy were around the corner from number thirty-seven. Cars had been parked sensibly out of sight. Laurel and Hardy went forward on their knees and crouched below the front windows of the terraced house. Angel, Mitchell, and Haines waited further back. DC Angel shifted her weight awkwardly – her leg and hip were still not right after her journey in the van yesterday. Unknown to her, Haines had been watching the way she moved, noted the painkillers she was swallowing. When this was wrapped up, he resolved to turn his detective skills on his own force to get to the bottom of the problem.

'Right, Angel.' Haines spoke in a low voice, not quite a whisper. 'You won't see this on your Methods of Entry course. Our tame drug user will be along any minute. You'll be last in. Shut and lock the door behind you.' DC Angel looked at Haines. Lock themselves in with an unknown number of dealers, possibly with weapons. 'We've all got three sets of cuffs and batons. You see someone, you cuff them. No one is point scoring over collars – if you see someone in trouble, wade in and cuff their suspect. Between us we can immobilise fifteen people, should be enough.'

Right on cue, a scruffy young man approached the house. He looked both young and old at the same time – typical drug user. He knocked on the door and everyone held their breath. There was a long pause. Angel wondered if they could see anything in the reflections from the windows opposite. Or did they have contacts in the bank of terraces on the other side of the street.

Finally, bolts were drawn and the door opened to admit the user. Like sprinters out of the blocks, the two constables stormed the door, pushing everyone back inside. This was the signal and the other three piled in as well.

With a slight misgiving Angel slammed the front door and flicked the latch so it locked. The hall was empty and dingy. There were none of the shouts that usually accompanied an operation like this.

She moved to the lounge where three people were sat on the couch, hands cuffed behind them. Laurel was manhandling another one out of the kitchen. This one was dumped onto an armchair next to his friends.

'You two,' Haines pointed at Mitchell and Angel, 'secure the upstairs.' He indicated Hardy. 'Let's have one last sweep down here, make sure we're alone.'

DCs Angel and Mitchell quickly checked the upstairs. It was a thoroughly depressing, untidy two bed terrace. In the front bedroom, they found a stick thin woman in an old iron bed. Without a word, Mitchell whipped the old eiderdown off, like a magician performing a trick. Before Angel saw what was happening, her mobile was slapped out of her hand, rattling across the floor. Mitchell had her over on her front and handcuffed before Angel had retrieved the phone.

'Text written, not sent,' she reported as she held the mobile carefully by the edges. She didn't want it to screen lock, so she pressed the back key to make sure the message didn't get out.

Soon, Haines was regarding his four captives, all lined up in the lounge. The coffee table, a survivor from the seventies, had been re-righted. It now contained piles of evidence – wraps of drugs, a pile of cash, various weapons, and a pile of mobile phones.

In a similar fashion, the occupants of the house had been sorted. Four youths sat awkwardly on the sofa and armchair with their hands cuffed behind their backs. The man who knocked on the door and the woman from the bed stood behind them, not cuffed but unsure of their status. Both were twitchy and staring at the pile of wraps hungrily.

DC Angel focused on the woman – there was something vacant about her look but it was impossible to tell if she was disabled or just stoned. She wondered if there was a social worker involved. And, more interesting, why did her DCI have a local drug user on speed dial?

'Right, you guys,' Haines said to the incomers. 'Where are you from?'

They all looked at each other before one mumbled, 'Birmingham.'

'This is what's going to happen. Three of you are going to be arrested and processed at the station. You'll be strip searched to check you've not got any more of this good stuff shoved up your arses. Then, when all that's done, you'll be off to custody and remand. But, one of you will get a one-way train ticket back home empty handed.' He turned to look at them. This last statement had produced looks of fear on all their faces. 'While your bosses are kicking the shit out of you for losing their gear and their money, pass on this message. Bradwick is off limits. They send any more of you clowns down here, this is what will happen. No money, no drugs.'

'You can't do that,' one of the boys said. He was young, possibly under age and looked Middle Eastern in appearance. 'We been arrested, we got rights.'

'Yes, we can,' Haines said flatly. 'We came here to arrest you but one legged it over the back fence.' He looked around at the other officers who nodded. 'We tried to give chase but,' he shrugged. 'three in the hand and all that. Now, when you get back home, and you explain all this to your bosses, once you feel a bit better, feel free to pass the message around your lowlife mates as well. This is what happens in this town.' Haines looked around at his officers. 'Right, I've whistled up a van, should be here now. DC Angel, take these two,' he indicated Laurel and Hardy, 'and our guests, and go wait for the van.' He pointed at one of the guys on the sofa. 'He can wait in my car; I'll give him a lift back home.'

DC Angel gave a final glance at the coffee table. The money was piled up haphazardly, different notes mixed in with each other, no way to tell how much was there. Likewise, the drugs were all mixed up. She wished she could take a few minutes to count the money, check the weight of drugs. This could have been her one chance to see what was entered into evidence and how it compared to what was seized.

Instead, she had to make do with escorting the prisoners out to where the van was waiting. Now they knew what would happen to their friend, they were quiet and compliant, afraid they might become the person being sent home empty handed.

Soon everyone was bundled up and off to their respective destinations. Laurel and Hardy took the three official suspects back to the cells. Haines and Mitchell were escorting the fourth person to the train station to send him home. Angel had elected to walk back to the station in the hope that it would loosen up her hip.

She thought over all that had happened. She hadn't seen any cash or drugs catalogued or entered into evidence, so DS Jones' suspicions remained possible but unproven. Angel had also seen a vulnerable woman freed from exploitation by some really unsavoury characters. But did Haines' plan for the town include finding a social worker and giving her some proper support.

As she walked the streets of Bradwick she was aware that it was a charmed town. Drug use and its associated violence had been low for years. The only question she had was whether it was worth the price.

CHAPTER THIRTY-TWO

Haines sat on a bench in the Winter Gardens. He was not used to relaxing and all around him people were walking with pushchairs and enjoying a lunch break. He could see a thin sliver of sea between the gates of the park and over the promenade. It was a proper hot August day and the promenade was crowded with holidaymakers eating chips or ice creams. The policeman in Haines was keeping an eye out for the pickpockets and other criminals naturally attracted to the tourist trade.

He was joined by Reg Patterson, still doing his perfect grandfather act. Despite the weather he was wearing a cardigan and Haines had to check that he wasn't wearing slippers.

'So, you're taking an interest in Gregory Watts, are you?' Patterson hardly ever said hello. Haines had asked him to look into Watts when he arranged the meeting. He nodded and Patterson kept talking. 'I've asked around, you need contacts on the estate. He's a bit after my time. I mean, I was sitting in offices with deep pile carpet and proper coffee not out working the streets. But you know what I'm like, I always know who to ask.'

'And what did you learn about the esteemed Mr Watts?'

'Well, I'd forget about him if I were you. He's the kind of public we need we need on our side. Not locking up anyway.'

'Word is that he has an unhealthy interest in schoolgirls.'

'That's as may be.' The tone of his voice was clearly saying that back in Patterson's day that was just part and parcel of being a man. 'Have there been any complaints about him?'

'Not yet, no.'

'So, none of these schoolgirls you're talking about have ever put in a formal complaint?'

Haines thought to himself that there hadn't even been an informal complaint or a whisper from the local intelligence officer, but he didn't say that. 'No,' was all he said.

'You know what I'm going to say, Rob. We are police. Our job is to keep the good people of Bradwick safe. That job does not extend as far as going into people's bedrooms and asking what they're getting up to, does it?' When Haines didn't make any comment, he continued. 'Listen, I'm not some soppy old man who doesn't understand the world. I wake up at six every morning just like I used to. After a jog, I read all the papers, cover to cover. I know about the whole Weinstein affair. It's all going too far. At this rate, if a man takes a woman to his bed, he'll need to see a birth certificate and get her to sign a bloody statement of consent!'

'You think we should go back to the seventies, sir?'

'Maybe not the seventies. But I do remember in the eighties it was a lot simpler. You knew who was guilty and who wasn't. You banged up the bad guys and the good ones were protected. Now, well, I don't envy you. It seems women can make up anything and get away with it.' There was a pause as Patterson considered this. 'So, these schoolgirls that Watts is supposedly after. What happens to them? Do they join the movement and raise their voices in protest at his actions?'

'Well, it's still early days yet. Nothing concrete has come to light.'

'You'd better be bloody careful then. Once the harpies get word that there's interest in Watts then accusations will come out of the woodwork.'

'Well he has an interest in teenage girls and someone out there keeps on murdering them so I thought it was worth a look.' Haines was desperate to steer the conversation away from his friend's outdated views.

'Nah, don't worry about him. I've heard that he might be on the list for the police and crime panel at some point in the future. He already does a lot of good work.' He paused for a second. 'Even when I retired, we were starting to feel the pinch with the budgets. There's no point tilting at windmills. I reckon you're doing the right thing going after these immigrants you know. It might cost money now, but it'll pay off in the long run.'

'Yeah, I know. It all starts with the drugs and the drugs start with the immigrants.'

'Am I repeating myself?' He laughed, a soft chuckle. 'Seriously though, it's good to hear that you're listening. You might want to check out these immigrants that you're rounding up. See if any of them have alibis for when those poor girls were attacked.'

'Yeah, I could do. To be honest, they're running us ragged. Not sure how much more budget we can throw at it?'

'Is this a favour for King?'

'Yeah. I know it needs to be done.'

'Start quizzing them about the murders then you can spread the budget around.'

'That's not a bad idea.'

CHAPTER THIRTY-THREE

Back at her desk, Angel needed something to do. Something quiet and calming after the adrenaline of the raid that morning. She decided to settle the question of Gregory Watts' guilt or innocence.

He might have refused to hand over the name of the clients who were his alibi, but there weren't that many houses being sold with a view of Wales across the estuary. She spent half an hour trawling through some of the new online only estate agents. She felt very odd, looking at these expensive houses, on cliffs overlooking the sea. She wondered who would be buying and selling them. She imagined polished retired couples who drove Mercedes and had that easy way with money that only the truly rich have.

She found what she was looking for. Recently listed, a well-proportioned six-bedroom house, standing on its own acre, with views across as far as Wales. The shots were professional and taken with the sunset in the background.

She thought about her own house in the suburbs. It was a solid, well-built thirties semi but nothing exciting. It was not spectacular like this one. "The wow factor" they called it on endless daytime TV property programs. She wondered if she would ever climb the property ladder to a house like this, with its eye-watering price tag. She'd assumed she would make her career in the police, vaguely seeing senior rank in the future.

But would that be on her own or with a family and a husband who put up with the long hours?

Putting all melancholy thoughts of her future out of her mind, she set herself to the task of registering on the website and making contact with the owners. Soon she was through the maze of online forms and on the phone with them.

'Hi, I saw your house for sale online and wondered if I could ask a few questions.' Despite rejecting her parents' lifestyle, she still loved jobs like this where she could be theatrical and pretend to be someone else.

'Of course,' the voice on the end was very enthusiastic, eager to please. She thought he sounded younger than retired.

'Oh, no I don't want to buy, sorry.' After her wistful moment earlier, she didn't want to be misunderstood. 'No, I'm selling my own house and someone recommended Gregory Watts as a photographer.' She left the question hanging.

'And you wanted a recommendation? Very wise. Can't beat word of mouth, can you? What can I say, I couldn't fault him. Nothing was too much trouble, even came round in the evening, to get the perfect light. If you've seen it on the web-site, well, you'll know how well presented it is. Once he'd taken the photos, he stayed and helped us put together the words as well.'

'That's really good to hear. I'm in a bit of a hurry to sell. Was he quick?'

'Oh yes. He took his camera away to process the photos. But he sent them through the next morning and we had it listed by the afternoon.'

DC Angel made small talk and encouraging noises, while half her attention was on clicking through the website. When she'd said her goodbyes, she found what she was looking for – the date that the house was listed. Gregory Watts was taking photos and helping a couple sell their house at the same time that Stella Evans was being killed. He certainly didn't have time to take the photos and get back in time to ambush Stella.

She supposed that she could put the technical teams onto it and check the meta information behind the pictures which would show where they were taken and when, but her gut was telling her that his alibi was solid. He was in the clear for killing teenage girls. But that didn't mean that he wasn't guilty of something.

There was nothing for it but to face the music and tell DCI Haines that another lead had come to nothing.

'Boss, you know how you told me to go and have a look at Gregory Watts?' There was an awkward pause where DC Angel considered what to say next. In the end she decided to be direct. 'I wasn't sure if that was your polite way of getting me to go away or if you really meant it?'

'I don't do polite.' Now it was Haines' turn to pause. 'Especially not with people I'm starting to respect.'

'Thank you, sir.'

'It's the truth. You've got a bad feeling about this Watts character, so what did you find?'

'He's squeaky clean. In fact, he's too clean. I think he's grooming teenagers to provide babies.'

'Grooming them like in Telford and Bradford? Drugs and mobiles? Is he the head of a gang, passing them around?' Haines was still mulling over what he'd learnt from Patterson that morning. He wasn't discounting it, but he liked to hear both sides before making his decision.

'No, nothing like that. He won't go near drink or drugs. He doesn't touch anyone under sixteen. And he definitely doesn't seem the type to share.'

'So what exactly does he do then?' Haines was thinking that the balance was swinging towards his mentor.

'He gets girls pregnant, then when he's had a couple of babies out of them, he moves them out and moves a new one in.'

'Let me ask you something. If he had a thing about redheads, say. And he got a new girlfriend every three years and some of them got pregnant, would that set your alarm bells ringing?'

'Well, no, but...'

'Listen, I get it. Sometimes you get a gut feeling and it's important to run with that. But when you do follow your nose, it has to be backed up with something solid.' He paused again, considering how much to reveal. 'I listened to your concerns and did my own digging to see what I could find out about him. He's what you might call a pillar of the community. Donates to various causes, always there at the right charity events. He keeps the youth of Bradwick on the straight and narrow. If you really want to nail him, it has to be bullet proof. But my advice would be to leave well alone.'

DC Angel said, 'Fair enough.' But she wasn't prepared to let go just yet. She would certainly keep him on her radar and wait for him to slip up. 'I haven't had much luck with the number plates either,' she said.

Haines shook his head. 'Me neither. Trouble is most car stuff is now on the computer. You can stand in an auction with a phone out and check the mileage, the MoT history, any insurance problems, the whole lot within about five minutes. Against all of that, knocking up a fake number plate isn't going to swing things one way or the other.'

'So that old case I found?'

'Yeah, that was the end of an old tradition, I think. Now people car-jack high end cars and either break them up for parts of drive them straight to the docks to sell them overseas.' He looked almost sad that the old ways of car crime had been consigned to history. 'I'm sorry to say that it looks like Dark Car Man might be a dead end as well. We can hardly interview every person in Bradwick and the surrounding area who owns a dark coloured family car.'

DC Angel shook her head. But she was forming a plan that she didn't share with Haines. She knew it was a Ford, either a Fiesta or a Focus.

She went back to her desk and started drawing up a complex search on the DVLA database. She knew she could trim it down somewhat. The likelihood was that the car was dark blue, grey or black. She set the query running and tried to put it out of her mind for the rest of the day.

When she left work that evening, DC Angel was in a black mood. She'd taken enough painkillers that her hip was now a dull throb but in return she now felt faintly sick instead. She'd got back a list of literally hundreds of possible candidates for Dark Car Man. Even if she could find a way of telling which one was the killer, it could take months to find them.

When she got to her car, that she'd parked on the street that morning, she was surprised to see Watts leaning against it nonchalantly. She took a breath, ready to tell him to get the hell off her property when he levered himself upright.

'Ah, just the person.' As ever, his mood was bright, almost cheerful, but there was a chilliness to his eyes. 'I just wanted a quick word. I know you're asking around about me. Bothering my family. I won't have you upsetting my children.'

'And I won't have you telling me how or where the police can investigate!'

'Investigate?' He held his hands out for imaginary cuffs. 'If I've done something wrong, arrest me right now.' There was a stand-off where neither person moved. 'Thought so. Now leave me alone.'

In response DC Angel just glared at him and blipped her car open. He didn't move out of the way, however, meaning she had to move close to him to open her door.

'Shame I didn't meet you ten years ago,' he breathed into her ear, so softly that no one else would've heard.

'I would've been fifteen,' Angel snapped back at him.

'Twelve years ago then.' Before she could retort he was already walking away and out of earshot. She sat in her car, slid the key into the ignition and locked the doors.

She had been close enough to smell him, to feel his presence. He had whispered so close she'd felt the breath on her ear. Now she wanted nothing more than to go home and have a long hot shower. To scrub away the essence of Gregory Watts.

CHAPTER THIRTY-FOUR

Rob Haines, Detective Chief Inspector in the Avon, Somerset and Wootenshire Police, stood on the pavement outside the Red Lion and squared his shoulders. He was on the cusp of being made up to superintendent. But now he was nervous.

He knew, that in the scheme of things he was going to put the cat among the pigeons. In the politics that governed the police departments of Bradwick, this pub was clearly Traffic territory. The car park alone would have told even the casual observer of this fact.

He took another deep breath and pushed his way into the bar. He tried and failed to ignore the way the volume of conversation dipped as he walked past.

Feigning casualness he leant on the bar. 'Pint please. Bitter.' He tapped a beer pump and waited. The barman seemed to take his time selecting a glass and drawing the pint.

'Rob! Strayed into the wrong pub, have we?' Inspector Peters, head of the Traffic Division came over to meet him. 'Why don't you join me at my table. Don't want to scare the troops.'

'Thank you, Inspector, I'd like that,' Haines replied.

'Yes, right you are, sir.' Peters had picked up the use of his rank to emphasise that Haines was senior to him and making sure that it was known.

'So, here we are then. You've come here for a drink. Off your patch.'

'That right there, you see, is the problem. My patch, your patch.' Haines stopped and waved his hand around to indicate the pub. They were being very definitely ignored. 'After all, aren't we all here for the same thing. Keep Bradwick safe. Serve and protect. All that.'

'Well, yes, there is that. But you know, it takes respect, doesn't it, on all sides.'

'I just think that maybe you needed reminding. That we're all trying to catch criminals. And if people down at the ranks of constable and sergeant, say, might have a falling out, well it shouldn't affect the day to day running of each department, should it?'

Inspector Peters sat back and sipped his pint. He reviewed what was going on his department and who appeared to be crowing and why that might be. 'Is there any particular aspect of co-operation that you were looking at?'

'Well, we are rounding up a lot of immigrants, farm workers and the like. Need vans and officers who can drive those vans.' He stopped and sipped his pint. Then, without looking at Peters he added, 'Officers who aren't limping at work.'

'Right.' Peters had another long draught of beer. 'Right.' He knew now what the hints were about. He considered the extent to which he could defend the indefensible. 'Surely you're not suggesting that as ranking officers we should be overseeing the relationships of those who work under us?'

'No! Perish the thought! Let them bed-hop, marry and divorce, raise families and whatever the hell else they want to do.' He paused to make sure that his meaning would be clear. 'As long as my officers, all my officers, are given what they need to do the job and come in every morning fit and well... ' He paused again, 'I don't give a flying fuck what they get up to out of hours!'

Inspector Peters pursed his lips. He knew now what the score was. He indicated the empty glasses, tried to mend fences. 'Another? On me this time?'

'No, no, I'd better get going. Back to my own patch.'

CHAPTER THIRTY-FIVE

DC Angel had an early start, going out to the promenade to meet Haines at the site of another dead body. This one pushed the enquiry into teenage girls into the background. The victim was male and in his forties.

They met on the promenade looking at the white scene of crimes tent. The sun had barely risen, casting long shadows out towards the sea.

'Did you know him?' DC Angel asked Haines.

DCI Haines looked shifty just for a second, then recovered his composure. 'I'm sure you've heard the phrase, known to police. Well, that was how our victim, Sean Astbury started out. He was smoking weed pretty much when he started secondary, certainly didn't see school out with a clutch of GCSEs. He graduated up from there into the local drug scene.' There was the faintest of pauses. 'We lost track of him. He started driving for Billy King as a taxi driver. Cleaned his act up. Last I heard he was a director at King Kabs.'

DC Angel looked hard at her boss. She always thought he seemed to know what was going on in his town but something felt off about all of this. How did Haines have access to a potted biography just after the victim was found and identified?

'Anyway, there's not a lot to do here so we should head back to the station. I've already requested the CCTV. At least this one was in the town centre, well covered.

Soon they were convened in a meeting room – it didn't look like this one would even need an MIT forming.

'Well, they aren't particularly bright. Not like whoever killed Mazey Taylor and Stella Evans. We've already picked them up on CCTV. They caught up with Astbury in the high street. It wasn't pretty, five on one. They kept on at him, punching; some had knives. In the end he made it as far as the promenade where he gave up the ghost. Our five suspects then went back to the station, got the last train home.'

'What were they doing here? County lines?'

'Probably.' He looked hangdog. 'If you knew what we'd done to keep Bradwick safe...' It was a completely depressing crime and thankfully relatively easy to put to bed. 'Anyway we pinged the photos over to West Midlands and they've already given us names. Really all we have to do is wait for them to come back and tell us they've made some arrests. Then we can bring them down here for interview. With all the CCTV it should just be a case of packaging it up for the CPS.'

For the rest of the afternoon, she processed the paperwork. Half of the time was spent with the phone tucked under her shoulder, talking to her counterparts in West Midlands. They were more than happy to have an excuse to get the five men arrested and handed over to someone else to prosecute.

Finally, the day was drawing to a close, so she went through to talk to Haines. 'Sir, have you got a minute?' DC Angel hovered in the doorway.

'Of course, sit down.' He gestured at a chair. 'What's on your mind?'

'Well, I've signed up a CI and from what he's said, it looks like King is involved in a lot of the drug trade around here. And now you've got a director in his company killed in a county lines operation. Is there more to this than I'm being told?'

Haines nodded. 'Your informant isn't the only one. King Kabs have that reputation.'

'And then I went back to the crime reports, looking for King's name among the known associates. Turns out even his casual drivers seem to keep their names off our records.' Even though she hadn't asked a question, she still looked at Haines as if expecting a response.

'Well, just because there's a rumour, doesn't mean there's anything behind it.'

'But you just said, sir, that everyone knows that he's involved in drugs.'

Haines leant back in his chair and looked up at the ceiling. He brought his head back down to look at Angel. 'Sometimes in this job you have to play a long game.' Her heart constricted a little, she didn't want to get into the politics. 'That mugger you arrested. You got lucky there as he was known to us, wasn't really part of a gang. But a lot of these guys, low level criminals, are run by larger gangs. They'll be sent out to get wallets, bags, even shoplift, usually in return for drugs or a space in a squat. Now, if your lad was one of those, then you'd have got much further if you'd followed him and seen who he was going to hand the bag off to. Do you see what I'm getting at?'

'So, that's what you're doing? Watching King, waiting for a big chance? Following him as it were.'

Haines thought for a moment and nodded. 'There are operational reasons why we're not pouncing straight away, even though the information is there.'

DC Angel blinked once. She knew that he was lying. She couldn't say what his tell was, but she'd picked up something. She didn't think it was a huge, outright lie, but there was something she wasn't being told. 'Ah, right then, sir. Above my pay grade then. I'll leave it alone.' She thought for a moment, needed to get out of the CID office to clear her head. 'I'm just going up to the MIT room. Check on everything, see what actions need doing.'

Without waiting for a response, she went upstairs. Fortunately everything was quiet. She could let a list of actions scroll past on the computer screen while she let her thoughts run.

What was all that bullshit about the mugger and how sometimes you have to follow them? She never wanted to be the kind of police officer who would watch a crime be committed and not do anything.

She knew this was something she'd picked up from her father. He had instilled in her the importance of honour, of doing the right thing. His hatred of the police had sprung from the eighties when they had gone to war with the unions. Since then, every failure in the papers had reinforced his opinion that the police had transformed from keepers of the peace to an enemy force. She might have joined the police to spite him but she had retained his morals.

She thought of DS Maxine Jones with her business cards and immaculate image. The sort of person her father would have no business with at all. She was someone you definitely couldn't trust. She encouraged people to lie, to inform on their colleagues. All for the greater good.

She couldn't untangle whether spying on someone who was cheating the system was honourable or not. She also couldn't figure out why it mattered so much to her. She hadn't spoken to her father in over seven years so why did she care?

Anyway, there wasn't a lot she could do now – she could hardly go to Professional Standards and say that she had a vague feeling that her boss was lying about something. That he'd put himself in situations where he might be able to steal.

She had enough of chasing her thoughts around in circles. On her way back to her desk, she saw a ridiculously long list of cars on the printer. She grabbed it and put a staple in the corner.

Sitting there, she had a thought. There were no leads on the Taylor and Evans killings. They were still collecting evidence and doing house to house, but in reality, it was stalled. She would start putting these car details through the computer, checking for previous convictions. She could do a few every day, it might take months but then the case could easily drag on that long.

CHAPTER THIRTY-SIX

Emma found Bea Matthews easily in the tea shop. The place was a bit too chintzy and over-fussy for her but getting information over tea and biscuits was part and parcel of her job.

When the niceties were over and they had settled with their drinks and food, Bea got straight down to business. 'So, I assume that this isn't a purely social call?'

Emma assessed what she knew of Aunt Bea and decided to go straight to it. 'I wondered what you knew about King Kabs?'

'Me? Why do you think I would know anything? Surely in the police you have your own sources of information?'

'They're not bringing anything up. But the rumours don't stop either.' She paused for a moment. 'And I think I saw the owner at your barbecue.'

'Billy King? Yes, he was there. I taught him, and his wife Marnie. Mind you, that doesn't make them special, as I've said, a lot in Bradwick have passed through my school.'

'And there's nothing you can tell me about them?'

Bea sighed and looked out of the window. Eventually, she spoke, pointing out of the window to emphasise her point. 'Look out there, Emma. And then, read some Sunday supplements. All those horror stories about stabbings, legal highs, county lines, new drug crazes – all of that doesn't get here. And if it does, it doesn't take a hold. And do you know why?' Emma shook her head. 'Because of things like my barbecues.

Because people who grow up here stay here. That means that all the local trades people, the business owners, the police officers, they all know each other. If it happened in London, they'd all be going on about inter-disciplinary co-operation and forming working groups.' She drew herself up and looked proud. 'But here, in Bradwick, we just get on with it.'

Emma nodded and tried to unpick what she had just been told. She knew that Bradwick was a closed shop and everyone seemed to know everyone else but she wasn't aware of how deep it went and what the implications were. 'I kind of get that but–'

'I know what you're going to say.' Bea Matthews held up a hand. 'I know I didn't really tell you anything. But it's more than I really should have. You have to understand. These people, they are your colleagues or suspects. Some might have files on your system or be witnesses in your cases.

'But to me, they are ex-pupils. I've been to their cousins' weddings, I know their children, I've even been to some of their funerals. So, I really shouldn't have said all of this anyway. You are, for all that I like you, an outsider. You've come down here really recently,' Emma bridled a bit at this, 'so it'll take a while. Maybe if you married someone local, you might start to fit in.'

Emma didn't know what to say. She could almost forgive the blatant sexism because she knew Bea was of a different generation. Slowly her irritation ebbed and she saw what she was being offered. It was clear that Bea liked her and had thrown her a line. If there wasn't outright corruption, possibly there was too much co-operation, edging into collusion.

'Thank you,' Emma said. 'I didn't really think, I just got caught up in trying to see what was going on. Of course you know all these people.'

'Just take it slow. Everything will still be here a week, a month, years from now. Some things just take a bit of time to settle in to.'

Emma just nodded and drank her tea. She was still turning over the advice in her mind. Bea had actually gone quite a long way. For a start, she hadn't said that nothing was going on. She decided to play the long game and let the conversation naturally drift into less contentious territory.

She gave her usual edited highlights of her life, moving around a lot as a child before settling with her aunt while she completed her A-levels. In return she got humorous anecdotes about Rob growing up, spending long summer holidays in Wootenshire. One summer, he had even wanted to be a detective and had trailed around with his little sister looking for crimes to solve.

Finally, she thought she might try to learn a bit more. She gently asked if Bea had ever heard of Gregory Watts.

'Ah, well now. If you've been a teacher as long as I have then you'll realise that not everyone is good. The vast majority of children you teach are lazy or hard-working, good in varying degrees, and generally try to do no harm. But once in a while one comes along who purely thinks of themselves and what they can get out of life.' She shook her head sadly.

'And that was Gregory?'

Bea nodded. 'Have you set your sights on him? I mean to investigate him, obviously.'

'I'm trying but there's not a huge amount there. He makes a living as a consultant. And he owns a range of websites that are just this side of the law.'

'You mean like pornography?'

Emma chuckled. 'Nothing so exciting. Licences for everything from driving to construction workers and bouncers.'

'How is that illegal?'

'Well, they look like the official sites, but he charges a few quid on top. He takes all your details and then passes them through to the proper government site where it all goes through. But he charges more. Every now and again someone will complain that he's copying the sites too closely.' She shrugged. 'But he just shuts them down and sets up a new one.'

'And that makes money?'

'Apparently. It's all very technical but you can pay to get further up the page on google and trick people into paying for your service.'

'And if you try to stop him?'

'Well, then he claims that he's a checking service for which he charges a fee. He's probably got a lawyer on retainer. To be honest if you had the money you could pay a teenager to do the technical stuff, and a solicitor to keep it all okay and watch the money roll in.'

Bea sighed and leant back from the table. 'It seems to me that if you have a little money put by and no morals then the opportunities are there to make it grow. I pity the poor souls who just need a certificate or licence to get a job and end up feeding his bank balance.' There was a pause as Bea sized up Emma. 'I'm glad we had this chat and I wish I could say more. I really do. Listen to me love, you hang in there. I think that you'll be really good for Rob. And for this town. It'll just take a bit of time to get embedded.'

'Thank you. I am putting roots down here. There's nowhere else I'd rather be.'

There seemed to be little else to say so Emma settled the bill and they went their separate ways. She was naturally impatient so she spent the drive home thinking over the conversation and seeing if she could find a shortcut to work out what her team were up to.

CHAPTER THIRTY-SEVEN

Billy King and Rob Haines sat either side of the table. Billy was slumped on his chair, hardly seeming to have the energy to raise his head.

'You got any info on who did Sean in?' King finally asked.

'It's fairly cut and dried,' Haines replied. 'But I think you already know. It's a message from our friends in Birmingham.'

'Yeah, you're right.' He shook his head. 'I'm not sure I've got the stomach for this any more. We're not talking about losing a runner in my gang. When I started out in this game, there were three of us from school, thick as thieves.' The irony was lost on Billy King. 'Me, Sean, and Tommy. We've been in this business since then, working our way up.

'He was one of my volunteers to see what was going on in the city. This probably comes straight from Pietr. I don't know how much he knows but now I'm expecting the next body to turn up. Maybe it would be better to pull them out now.'

'You can't do that! I need the information. I need the big bust before my promotion.' He paused to assess Billy King. 'And what are your options anyway? If you give up now, they'll just take over and wipe out everyone in your gang. If you let me do my thing then we can get them out of the picture permanently.' He paused briefly, then continued. 'If your other undercover guys keep their heads down for a day or two, they should be fine. The Birmingham gang will probably think they've caught the only turncoat. They'll now be feeling a false sense of security so it should be fine. Also they'll still need contacts down here.'

'There are other options.' King seemed unconvinced. 'They've already approached me. Made me an offer. I go from running my own organisation to being a part of theirs. Obviously, I said no – I don't want to be their bagman.' He stopped for a moment to take a drink from his glass. Haines, not for the first time, regretted meeting in a pub. 'But I could go back to them. Negotiate a deal to sell out. Hand it all over to them, in return for a lump sum.'

'Come on, Billy, you're not that stupid. You know that whatever money they offered, you'd be dead before you spent even a fraction of it. Gangs like that don't leave loose ends.'

'I didn't say I'd hang around here, did I? There's a world out there and all I've ever seen is Bradwick. With money I could sell up and live somewhere else.'

'No, I don't see it.' Haines shook his head. 'You're born and bred here. You might leave, but you'd be back. Back to where someone else was running your turf.'

'You've got your promotion, why shouldn't I have mine? Go straight somewhere else?' He sounded churlish, sunk deep in his cups.

'Still don't believe it. And you'd have to convince Marnie too.' Haines paused long enough to gauge Billy's mood. He decided to push on anyway. 'Would you really sell out to the people who killed your school friend? They are the people who are trying to take your business one way or the other.'

'What should I do? Go for vengeance?' He sighed dramatically before picking up his glass. He waved it widely before continuing. 'There's a reason that people like Pietr are running big city gangs and expanding into new territory and why I've been stuck in this town for all these years. These new guys are ruthless – and if I'm honest, I'm not sure that I've got the stomach for it.'

'You've got to do something,' Haines insisted. 'Leave your men in undercover. Now Pietr has got rid of one, he'll relax, think he's solved it. You might not have the stomach for the fight, but we do. We have the resources to finish the whole gang.'

'What about my guys? You know what it's like. It doesn't take much for a beating to go wrong. I can't afford to have another death on my hands.'

'You've been in the business a long time, my friend. Why are you getting cold feet now?'

'It's not cold feet.' The pint glass slammed down on the table. 'I'm never a coward.' He paused again. 'It's just that I'm tired. And you know, the money on the table. I could reinvent myself.'

'That never works, you know. We are what we are.'

'Look at you though. Promotion. Desk job. Leaving all of this behind.'

'I'm still police though, aren't I.' He paused to make sure that Billy King was properly listening. 'And I'll still do the right thing by Bradwick. No matter what, I'll be protecting the town.'

There was an awkward pause. Then King nodded grimly, finished his pint and stalked out of the pub.

CHAPTER THIRTY-EIGHT

Emma and Lukas sat side by side on the bench and stared out to sea. On the beach in front of them, families played, all staking out their territory with towels and handbags.

'Do you know any more about King than you've said already?'

'King? What do you want to know? Runs the biggest taxi firm in the area.'

'Lukas! You know what I mean.'

'And you said you wouldn't press me for information.' He sounded hurt. 'I thought I'd be coming to you offering information.'

'Yeah, but there was that murder the other night. Something big is going on and I need to know what.' When Lukas didn't complain, Emma continued. 'The guy who was killed was a director for King Kabs. I don't know if it was a nominal position or if he actually worked. But I am getting the impression that the company is the only game in town. If you want to deal drugs, they all go through him.'

'Aww, babe! I'm not that high up the chain. If I'm honest, I just buy a bit now and again.' He paused as if considering what to reveal. 'Occasionally a few of us might club together, you know, all chip in a bit and buy a bigger amount cheaper and split it up. But you know, that's as far as it goes.'

'What about your dealer though? He has to buy from somewhere, doesn't he?'

'I suppose, I've never asked.'

'Never? Not been interested?'

'Listen, darling, it's a whole other world. I'd only have two reasons for asking my dealer where he buys from. Firstly, I might have come into some money and be looking to move up the chain. If I know who his dealer is then I could buy from him, then cut him out of the equation.'

There was an uncomfortable pause. Finally Emma cracked. 'You said two reasons.'

'Well,' Lukas looked awkward. 'It's you lot. It's what you do. Nick us for a small amount of blow, then offer up a caution if we snitch on someone further up the chain. The bottom line is that either reason is bad news. If I go around asking questions, then I'll be a risk and folk will stop selling to me.'

Emma nodded and processed this. 'I get that. But, suppose I wasn't trying to work my way up the chain. I need to go right to the top. We're back to Billy King. Have you heard anything about him?'

'Apart from Kings Kabs, I'm guessing.'

'Yeah. Anyone who works for him seems to be charmed.'

'Like I say, it's all in compartments isn't it? Need to know, all of that. I know who to buy from. I know other people I can ask if my dealer drops out, so I can find someone else. But I'm low level. I've no idea where the stuff comes from and where the money goes.' He paused, studied Emma closely. 'It's not like a rigid structure thing with percentages passed up the chain. It's just guys who buy in bulk, split it down and make a profit.'

'Yeah, I'm sorry, I just feel a bit shut out by work. Something big is happening and I don't know what.'

'I meant what I said before, you know. You need to be careful.'

'I know. I still haven't seen any proof of skimming either cash or drugs.' She shook her head. 'But I know what you said before and I think you're right.'

'And what would you do if it was all true? If you found proof? Turn on them or look the other way?'

Emma shook her head. 'I dunno. No one knows until they're faced with the decision. I really can't see there being any situation where I'd take cash under the table though. I mean that's just the end of your career right there. I wouldn't do it.' She paused, stared at the sea. 'But I work there, you know. I'm making friends. Not sure I could throw them all under the bus.'

'Even if they are corrupt?'

Emma just shrugged. 'The problem is that corrupt cops usually do bad things. Look at all the cases where they've let killers go free because they got fixated on the wrong suspect. That's a tangible wrong. But whatever's going on, look around you. They've kept this town right.'

'To a point. The bodies are starting to stack up though, babe. And I don't see your lot making many arrests, either.'

CHAPTER THIRTY-NINE

DC Angel had been sent over to Traffic again. She had been surreptitiously working through a list of cars while Haines wasn't looking. But then Haines had sent her over to Traffic for a car. Apparently, the officers from West Midlands were on their way down for a case conference. As a courtesy, they were to be collected from the train station. She could see a useless day ahead, running senior officers around to see the crime scene. At least she'd been promised a nice lunch on expenses but she was basically the chauffeur. Although Haines tried to persuade her that she would be making good contacts, she'd rather be doing real police work.

On top of all that, she thought, she had to deal with Traffic. She still remembered the humiliation of the awful LDV van and while she hadn't heard from Dave, she assumed that he would still be annoyed. She wondered what the latest trick would be.

On the other hand, she reasoned, she still had to work with the Traffic division. So, she squared her shoulders and wished she was more than her five foot three.

With a completely straight face she slid her warrant card over the desk. The sergeant in charge of car allocations looked bored as he picked up her card and started filling in the details on a clipboard.

Then he stopped and looked at her again, with narrowed eyes. 'Good to see you again, DC Angel.'

DC Angel nodded and smiled and wondered when the trick was going to be played. She decided not to prejudge though and take him at face value until something happened. Then she would come down on the lot of them with righteous anger. She was fed up with being messed around in the name of workplace banter.

Instead of the usual handing over of the keys however, the desk sergeant fetched them off the rack and walked her over to a BMW. Last year's model, she noticed. How bad could it be?

She settled in, under the gimlet eyes of the desk sergeant. The seat slid easily forward, the clutch felt light, she slipped easily into first. She sniffed cautiously. No dead fish or three-week-old cheese sandwich under the seat. Just the aroma of the air freshener hanging from the mirror.

'All okay for you?'

'Yes, thank you. This is fine.'

She started the engine and just as she started moving, she heard the sergeant say, 'Give my regards to DCI Haines.'

She drove away with her mind whirling. It appeared to be completely genuine – the car was not only fine but in far better condition than she had any right to expect. She also decoded the final message – the sergeant hadn't said Haines or Rob Haines, he'd definitely mentioned rank.

The anger slowly built as she navigated her way through the streets of Bradwick. She was not a little girl any more and the last thing she needed was her boss wading in and sorting out her own fight. If news of that spread through the force she'd have to move areas, even change to a different force. Her whole career was a series of steps she had taken, each one designed so that people would take her seriously. Since she'd broken away from her parents to take her A-levels, she'd prided herself on being independent, solving her own problems by herself.

Now all of that could be swept away. She'd be back in the seventies where the pathetic WPC would be saved by the big burly detective.

She had enough common sense though to keep quiet and act like the dutiful DC and do everything required of her. She kept a lid on her simmering anger until the out of area officers were back on the train and the car was back in the pound.

Then she went to Haines and sat down in front of his desk. 'Boss, did you say anything to Traffic?' DC Angel's tone was dangerously neutral.

'What if I did?'

'Did I ask you to? What's between me and Dave is personal.'

'It's not personal.' DCI Haines was matching her neutral tone. Voices were not yet being raised. DC Angel raised her eyebrows, inviting him to continue. 'When it affects my team and how efficiently it's running, then it becomes work, not personal.'

'But—'

'Nope. You don't get this one. I saw you the day after you drove that LDV and you were in terrible shape. I can cope with you sitting at your desk swallowing Nurofen like Smarties, but what would've happened if we'd had a suspect that day and you had to give chase? Would you have hobbled after them?'

'I don't want what happened between me and Dave all over the force though! I won't be the next piece of office gossip.'

'Either you will or you won't.' Haines shrugged. 'The truth of it is that all stations, probably all workplaces, have banter. I've been in the force since before you were in school. I've seen it all. We all gossip. We all go out with each other, fall out, argue and make up. There has been banter, before it was even called that. Jokes, wind-ups, nicknames, all of that. And trust me, the minute a station stops doing that, it's dead. Folk stop caring, they stop being a team, they don't have each other's backs.' He paused to make sure DC Angel was still listening.

'But what happened to you was beyond all that. If you weren't a woman or if you were taller, you'd have been all right. The point is that you weren't suitable to drive that van. Hell, that van should've been into the mechanics by now. But in my book that makes giving you that vehicle bullying, and I won't have that.

'You have a lot to learn. I run a team, that means we look out for each other. And I will not tolerate one member of my team being bullied, especially when it impacts on the efficiency of the whole team.'

DC Angel felt her mood lightening a bit when she realised that it wasn't just her, Haines would react the same way with anyone under his command. 'Sir, you sound almost enlightened. Did they send you on diversity awareness training?'

'As a matter of fact, they did, as part of my promotion strategy. You know what, you can always keep on learning. I'll be honest with you, I don't know what happened between you and your boyfriend, or even if it was a boyfriend or girlfriend or long term, gender fluid life partner. It doesn't actually matter. What matters is how you were treated and that was unfair.'

'Well, I suppose I owe you some thanks then.'

CHAPTER FORTY

DC Angel kept her promise to herself. She had developed a habit of changing her routes around Bradwick, partly to keep an eye out for dark Fiestas and also to occasionally swing past the house of Gregory Watts. She didn't know what she hoped to achieve but he irritated her. He had to have a weakness somewhere, and she was determined to be the one to find it.

Sitting in her own car after spending the day running the West Midlands officers around, she had to choose what to do on the way home. She decided to take a detour and see what was going on at Gregory Watts' house.

She slowed down as she went past and saw the door open. But where she was expecting either the man himself or a pregnant teenager to come out, she was surprised to see an older woman with a heavy bag.

Making a sudden decision to see if she could salvage anything from the day, she slowed down until she was alongside at walking speed. She opened the passenger window and called across. 'That looks heavy, do you want a lift?'

'My mum always told me to never accept lifts from strangers.'

Angel glanced forward then flashed her warrant card at the woman. 'Police.'

'I figured that already,' she said with heavy sarcasm.

'Let me give you a lift. Otherwise I'll be following you all the way home.'

The woman considered her options, then nodded curtly. She settled into the passenger seat, bag under her knees. 'You can give me a lift if you want, just don't expect me to talk.'

For a minute or two they drove in silence. Then DC Angel said, 'You look a bit old for Gregory Watts. Not his type.'

'Show's what you know, I was the first. Same class at school.'

DC Angel frowned. 'What were you doing back there then?'

'Housekeeper. I don't mind, it means I can still work around the school holidays.'

'Isn't that a bit of a come down?' The woman turned to look at DC Angel, so she continued, wondering how hard to push. 'I mean, one minute you must be thinking you're going to be Mrs Watts. The next, you're paid to scrub his toilets. Gotta hurt.'

'It's not just cleaning, you know. I've learnt how Gregory wants it done, how he likes his house set up. So it made sense. I'm not just a cleaner. No, I'm more like...' she trailed off mid-sentence, aware that she'd nearly said too much.

'More like what?' Emma asked, but the woman refused to answer. They drove on in silence.

'Over here. By the railway bridge.'

DC Angel pulled up by the footbridge over the railway. This led to the Coopers End estate and she realised it meant that no one would see the woman arriving home in a strange car. Emma had one last chance. 'More like what?'

The other woman didn't move or speak. Finally she said, 'More like a big sister to the new girls. Like I said Gregory is very particular and I just smooth it over.'

Angel wondered what that meant and was about to ask what happened when things didn't go Gregory's very particular way. But before she could say anything, the door opened and the woman disappeared with her bag over her shoulder.

As she drove back to the station, DC Angel considered all she had just learnt about Gregory Watts. Everything pointed heavily towards grooming but she had nothing that was either admissible or evidence of any legal wrong doing.

As long as he kept to girls over sixteen and didn't have a job like a teacher where he was in a position of trust, it seemed he could continue unimpeded. That didn't mean that DC Angel would let the matter drop though.

CHAPTER FORTY-ONE

Emma came home from work and grabbed a beer straight from the fridge before collapsing on the sofa. While she was happy in her own space, the decision not to convert the living room into another bedroom was one of the best she'd made.

Everyone in the house worked shifts but even so the communal area meant that the housemates had somewhere to chat. Once she'd had half her beer, she realised that Lucy was sat there too, swiping through her phone.

'You look like you've had a rough day.'

'Tell me about it,' Emma said. 'I've spent the day ferrying around senior officers like a taxi driver when I'd rather be looking for a dark coloured Fiesta.'

'Dark coloured Fiesta?'

Emma quickly filled her in on what she knew about Dark Car Man.

'And you don't have the number plate?'

'No, it's been running around on false plates. And the cameras aren't good enough to give us a proper colour either.'

'No wonder your boss told you it was a dead end. How far have you got?'

'Well, I started with a list of thousands and then removed those that were SORNed and those that were from the seventies, eighties and nineties.'

'And?'

'Down to a manageable one thousand five hundred and thirty-one in Wootenshire.'

'Oh my God! That's next to useless.'

'Yeah, but I'm staying after work and just running them in batches of ten, checking to see who owns them, if they've been arrested, any previous convictions that kind of thing. You never know.'

Lucy frowned for a minute and swept her fringe out of her eyes. 'What are you doing tomorrow night?'

'More of the same.' Emma shrugged. 'Unless there's an emergency, stay late, run number plates, hope for a break. Why?'

'Well, I'm on a team that runs a car club. You know those teenagers that drive too fast, have lowered cars and loud exhausts who hang around McDonald's scaring the locals?' Emma nodded; every police officer had moved them on at some point. 'Well we've got a club where we have permission to use a factory car park. We get them down there to show off their cars. Police are there to chat to them, sometimes we get Traffic to come down.' She caught Emma's expression. 'It's all right, Dave's never shown an interest. And we get MoT testers to pop in, tell them what modifications are good and what's dangerous.'

'And they go for that?'

'Yeah. We bribe them. Two or three times a year, we do track days or factory visits, that kind of thing. But they can only go if they haven't been in trouble with the police in the previous six months.'

'Okay. Sounds very worthy. How does it help me?'

'Once you get beyond the spotty teenager thing, these guys know so much about cars. They are proper car geeks. Half of them work at dealerships or garages. Bring some photos of your mystery car, see if they can help at all.'

* * *

With no better leads, the next evening DC Angel found herself in a factory car park. It was still light but the sun was going down. There was a police van with display tables and a gazebo on one side. On the other side, close but not too close, was a collection of about half a dozen cars, parked with flagrant disregard for the parking space markings. The vehicles were all modified to some degree or another. Some were lower, with wide tyres and flared arches. There were stickers and custom paint jobs, along with extra lights and spoilers.

Doors were open and headlights on, with music playing from stereos. There was obviously a degree of compromise as the volume was audible but not at the shaking bass levels that DC Angel would've expected. The teenagers hanging around struck deliberately bored poses. The odours of Lynx aftershave mixed with exhaust and oil.

She was following Lucy as she walked through the boys, chatting quietly, and looking at their cars. Before she'd become a police officer, she'd have found this crowd intimidating with their baseball caps, sportswear and gold jewellery. Now she could see through the image to the insecurity underneath. She was checking out the teenagers – there were some on bicycles and scooters as well as passengers so there was quite a crowd. She also noticed one of the drivers was a woman. Her car was low and purposeful looking, but still with a pink fluffy interior.

DC Angel was also aware that she was attracting stares and nudges. Interestingly, she was getting most attention from a mixed group of boys and girls who were gossiping to one side. Eventually one of the boys approached Lucy. DC Angel could tell immediately there was a problem.

'What've you brought her here for?' He jerked his head to indicate DC Angel.

'This is DC Angel and she needs your help.' They all looked at her.

'I'm not bloody well helping her!' His face was set and rigid.

'Listen, we're here to build bridges. I wouldn't have thought you'd have turned up if you suddenly had a problem with the police.'

The teenager looked sullen. The group had all gone silent to watch the exchange. DC Angel decided to break the tension. 'Is it me you've got a problem with?'

'You nicked my kid brother. Banged him up on remand, opposed bail. The whole thing. No way I'm helping you.'

DC Angel looked closer at him. Large jaw and dark hair, cropped close round the back and sides. She could see the family resemblance. 'You'd be an elder brother to Ceiran Knight?'

'Yeah. Anthony.' He still stared angrily at Angel.

'Do you know why we arrested your brother?'

'They said something to do with computers. Must be copyright or something like that.'

'Right. You need to come with me. We'll have a chat in private.' Without waiting for a response, she walked off to the police van. By the time she reached it, she could sense that Anthony had followed her.

They were just behind the van, where they wouldn't be overheard but Angel could still be seen by Lucy.

'I know you've got a brother, but have you got a sister? Or a cousin or niece?'

'Sister. Why, what's it to you?'

'We arrested your brother on suspicion of being involved in making the WankyBoi videos.'

Anthony went pale. 'That's as maybe but he'd never send stuff like that to Sherri, would he?'

'But these videos get passed around, don't they?' She paused for a moment. 'You've got to understand. This is serious. We couldn't ignore it. I know it's your family.'

DC Angel could see the emotions warring on his face. He wanted to uphold his family honour, but he didn't know if he should support his brother or protect his sister. Either way, it was clear that the news wasn't as much of a surprise as it could've been. Without a word he turned on his heel and stalked back over to the group. He stopped by his car, one foot on the sill, a dark look on his face.

DC Angel followed him back over to the group, who were now watching the pair of them with undisguised curiosity.

'I'm looking for a car.' She could see the sideways glances and worried expressions. 'It's not one of your cars, nothing like that. We've got a car running around on false plates and we need to trace it. We thought as you guys know so much about cars, you might be able to help narrow it down.'

There was an awkward pause as they all looked at each other. Several glances were directed at Anthony who was still staring off into space. Eventually he noticed that everyone was waiting for him to say something. To tell them either to co-operate or not.

'Do what you want!" he shouted. 'I don't really care. I've got to go now. Talk to my parents.' With that he slid into his car seat, slammed the door and left the car park faster than was advisable considering the police presence. Lucy frowned an unspoken question at Angel but she just shook her head. Not now.

'How'd you know it's not one of us?' a tall spotty lad asked. 'Could be a mate or a cousin or something?' Other teenagers were nodding and starting to drift away. Desperate to get them to help, she moved towards a group of girls. 'It's Dark Car Man. We think he might be connected to those two women who've been killed round here. And we need your help to catch him.'

The girls looked mutinous for a moment. But there were sideways glances as they looked at each other to reach a decision. Eventually one of them, with hair in a ponytail and huge earrings broke the silence. 'Have you figured out what make it is, then?'

'We know it's a Ford. Fiesta or Focus.'

'Kev! Fords are your thing.' She turned to look at a short boy. There was a tilt of the head as she summoned him to help. Kev shuffled forward. He was slightly overweight.

'I'm still not sure. What if it's, like, someone we know?'

'Kev, what if your sister or girlfriend gets done by Dark Car Man.' There was a pause as they stared each other down. Eventually the girl won and Kev smiled, revealing a gold tooth.

'What you got then?'

'We've got these photos. We think that it's the same car in all the photos, even though the number plates change. But we're not sure. And even if we were, without knowing what the number plate really is, we can't trace it.'

'Naughty! I work at the Ford dealership. They're proper strict on the plates there. Every one has to be written in the book and only certain people can make them up. If even one blank plate goes missing, someone gets a disciplinary. You wanna look into that. He must've bought a shady machine from somewhere. eBay most likely.' He lapsed into silence as he flicked through the photos. 'First off, that's never a Focus. It's a Fiesta for sure. John, come over here and hold this still.' Another lad sloped over and pinned the first photo down on a bonnet. Kev got his phone out and held it over the photo.

'Hold on a minute!' DC Angel started to intervene. 'You can't go taking photos of those.' She wasn't a hundred per cent sure if she should even be showing the photos around but she knew she didn't want them on some teenage boy's phone.

'Nah, you're all right, it's safe. Unless you've got an old-school magnifying glass, this is the best way.' With deft moves of his fingers, he zoomed in his camera to examine the details of the photo. DC Angel checked but he wasn't clicking to take pictures.

'It's a Fiesta all right, mark seven, post facelift,' Kev announced.

'What's that mean?'

He almost rolled his eyes, then flicked through until he had a photo of the car from the front. 'See, they brought out a new Fiesta in 2008 – a complete redesign. But those ones had the narrow-slit grille with the Ford badge in the middle. Then in 2013 they did a facelift. Same car, different trim. They got this grille,' he tapped the trapezoid grille on the photo. 'They did it across the whole range, Focus, Galaxy, everything got the same grille.'

'So...'

'So, this car is definitely 2013 to 2017. That's when they brought out the new one. And it's a five-door hatchback.' He was warming to his subject now. 'When a car leaves the factory it's totally stock. But pretty soon people change the wheels or add a tow bar, or stickers. Or they have an accident and things are fixed differently.' Quiet fell over the car park as he focused his phone on each photo in turn. DC Angel noticed a couple of people behind him faking yawns and rolling their eyes. Without a word he got some glasses out and slipped them on, oblivious to the looks and nudges this caused as well. 'See here. That's a dealer sticker, and the corner's missing.'

DC Angel took the photo and squinted. There was a yellow rectangle at the bottom of the rear screen, missing one corner.

'I can't see which dealer it is, but they're a bit old fashioned, you don't see many. And with that corner missing...' He trailed off as he flicked through the photos. 'There. Look at that rear wheel arch. Soppy driver can't park. Below that the wheel trim has a bit missing, must've clipped a kerb as well.'

DC Angel looked at another photo. Just visible on the rear edge of the wheel arch was a white scratch – three faint parallel lines. 'And here,' Kev said passing her another photo. 'You see, different plates, same scratch, same sticker, same wheel trim.' He looked smug as if he'd just won an argument. 'You were right. It is the same car, just with number plates that have changed.'

'Thank you.' DC Angel's head was spinning. With this definite range of only four years, she could reduce the number of vehicles to check. And she could discount any car with a tow bar. Maybe she just needed to trim the list down as far as she could, then go and physically see each one. If it was parked outside a house, it would only take a few seconds to tick it off based on the details.

'Yes.' A thought occurred to DC Angel. 'And you're sure, whoever this is, they haven't you know, changed the wheels or tried to make it look like a different year?'

Kev took the photos back and had a quick look. 'I don't think so. Look those are standard Fiesta wheels with wheel trims. That makes it povo spec.' DC Angel frowned and held up a hand to interrupt him. 'Just means that it's the lowest trim level, short for poverty specification. Most cars nowadays come with factory fit alloys so it's quite rare to get one still on steels. That's the first thing you'd change – put some alloys on it. No, that looks like a stock mark seven point five to me.'

DC Angel nodded slowly. A plan was slowly starting to form. She had not realised the complexity of looking for the Fiesta. To her, it had just looked like any other car on the road. But to an expert it was as distinctive as if it was a classic or had a custom paint job. 'Thank you, Kev, you've been really helpful.'

'That's all right, you know.' He cast a shifty glance at the group of girls who now seemed happier with him. 'Oh, and if you do get a range of dates, add two months on.'

'Why?'

'Well, sometimes they flog off the pre-face lift cars cheap after the new ones come on stream. So they can be registered weeks or even months after their build date. Or you might get lucky and get one of the early, pre-release ones.'

'Thanks.' DC Angel was distracted, already formulating a strategy for refining her search.

'Do you think it's DCM who's killing those girls then?' Teenage girl with big earrings was back.

'It might be. It's a line of enquiry that we're following. Obviously, we don't want it spread about too much.' She paused, then asked, 'How are you coping? Has it had much impact?'

The teenager put her head on one side. 'I mean, we're always careful, you know. You have to be. But now, if I need to get home, I'll be more likely to go with a friend or get a lift, even a taxi sometimes. But there's always some girls who just don't care. And those who always bang on about #MeToo and "time's up" and think that we shouldn't be frightened off the streets.'

'You sound like you don't agree.'

'I mean they are right and all that. But there's not much point having a cause if you're attacked or killed is there?'

DC Angel nodded. She'd missed talking to the kids, getting a feeling for what was happening at a ground level. But she also had a new strategy to work out. 'Thank you. And you, Kev, that was really helpful.' She said goodbye, thanked Lucy and went home. For the first time since she'd seen Mazey's body under the bin bags, she felt a little bit of hope.

CHAPTER FORTY-TWO

On Monday morning, DC Angel was in bright and early, hopeful that she could finally make a start on reducing down the list of potential Dark Cars. However, as soon as she had sent off a revised query to the DVLA database her phone rang.

'DC Angel.'

'Hi, it's Julie Walker.' There was an awkward silence, filled by her saying, 'the social worker in the Kelsey Teague case.'

'Right, right, yes.' Angel swiftly changed her thoughts away from the DVLA and over to what she knew of Gregory Watts.

'Well, if you want to meet up with her, I've managed to arrange it.'

'Good, excellent. I could probably...' Angel was quickly trying to work out when she'd be free to go tilting at windmills.

'Thing is, it has to be today.'

DC Angel made a quick decision. 'Okay then. How long do you need?'

'Well, she's around an hour away by car. Maybe forty-five minutes if the traffic isn't too bad.'

DC Angel wanted to swear. She made quick calculations in her head, guessing when Haines would call a meeting for his officers to feed back what they'd learnt. 'Okay then,' she said nervously, 'when do I leave?'

'You'll come alone?'

'Yes, alone.' DC Angel did not want to drag anyone into her own bad decisions. She stuck her head into DCI Haines' office.

'Boss, I've got a vague lead on the Taylor and Evans killings. Are you okay if I take off for a bit? I need to be north of Bristol.'

Haines looked down at his desk and shrugged. 'To be honest, even a vague lead is stronger than anything we've got at the moment. But remember what I said earlier. Teamwork. Take notes. I want to see it on the computer by the end of the day. And mobile on, stay in touch.'

During the long drive north, up the coast and around the edge of Bristol, her misgivings grew. Finally she found a parking space on a side street in a suburb of Bristol. She met Julie and together they walked along a short footpath and came out into a large park. Julie steered Angel over to a bench where they sat down next to a mum who was watching a toddler on the play equipment.

This was Kelsey Teague – Julie Walker made the introductions then Angel asked about her history with Gregory Watts.

'Well, I'll be the first to admit that I was young and naive. I think I was the second Mrs Watts and thought I could change him.'

'Mrs Watts?'

'Figure of speech.' She waved the idea of marriage aside with a hand. 'I never married him, he's not the marrying type. Thankfully. I had enough trouble getting rid of him as it is.'

'What went wrong?'

The small girl came running over. She was, like most children, oblivious of her mother's friends. When she'd been sorted out and sent back to the climbing frame, Kelsey saw the look on Angel's face.

'Oh, no, she's not one of his. No, once we settled here, we wanted one of our own. I mean, Sean's lovely with Kyle, treats him like his own, but well you know how it is. Where were we?'

'What went wrong between you and Watts?'

'Well, I had a lovely baby, but then I grew up a bit, went to a mother and baby group. Spoke to the other mums. Started to see how screwed up he was.' She paused as if deciding what to reveal. 'He controlled everything. What to wear. Where to go. All that stuff. I didn't even have a bank account. Every Sunday night Greg and me would sit down with the accounts and he'd go through the receipts and check the budget.'

'Seriously?' Angel was proud of being independent and had been balancing the books since she was sixteen. 'What did he check for?'

'Everything, clothes, food, even knew how many nappies I went through. I must admit,' she said wistfully, 'I was in great shape. Plenty of fresh food, no booze or fags, even went to the gym. It was a ladies only place though. I can see from the look on your face that you don't approve, but I was like a princess. In great shape, fabulous clothes, going to all the right parties in his flashy car.'

Complete with a tower to be locked up in, Angel thought.

'Anyway, I went to the mother and baby group and realised how weird it was. Greg and I started arguing because I wanted to buy more grown-up clothes. I just wanted to update my look, not be as young looking. And then his eye started wandering. From what I understand, it's a pattern he goes through, even now.'

DC Angel thought about the drive north and needed to know why they were so far away from home. 'So, you got away from him? I've heard he tends to treat his exes well – child payments, visitation rights, etc.'

'Yeah, that's the reward if you play the game his way. As soon as I met Sean, the rows started.' She caught the look on Angel's face and continued. 'Between me and Sean, and Sean and Greg, and me and Greg. Sean got all macho and said we didn't need Greg's money, thought I should cut him off.

Greg for his part, didn't like Sean, thought I could do better and didn't mind telling me.' She paused to take a deep breath. 'We went out for a drink. Kyle was with my mum, all safe. Anyway, me and Sean were sniping at each other about Greg all night. Some bloke bumps into Sean on the way back from the bar; Sean's not going to back down without an apology.' She looked hard at DC Angel. 'I don't know if you've had a chance to look, but it all kicked off. Sean's a good bloke but he'd had enough of Greg pushing his buttons and me being scared about how we'd cope without the money. We all got arrested and what would've been a caution for breach of the peace went tits-up when they found gear on Sean. It was only a small bit of cannabis – less than a teenth – but he was feeling angry so he wound up the coppers too.'

DC Angel nodded sympathetically. A teenth was slang for a sixteenth of an ounce - the smallest weight you could buy. She knew all too well that with an amount that small the line between a stern talking to, a caution, and a charge was very fine and down to the discretion of the arresting officer.

'Well, once Sean was charged, then the gloves came off. We had Greg's lawyers going on about an unsuitable environment for a child, all that crap.'

Julie leaned forward. 'This is where I came in. I never liked Gregory Watts from the moment I met him. The fact that he was moving on to his third schoolgirl in under eight years set alarm bells ringing.

'Anyway, Watts just threw money at it. Had private detectives following Kelsey, hired lawyers to keep making ridiculous demands,' said Julie. That was when I pushed back with my experience, suggesting that because he was currently living with a pregnant seventeen-year-old then he wouldn't be able to cope with a small child as well.'

'How did it end?' Angel asked.

Julie took a deep breath and looked at Kelsey. She took up the conversation. 'We sat down and had a long chat, Julie and me. Between us we figured out that Greg Watts doesn't have bottomless pockets. And what was probably bothering him most was that I was around; he could see me and his kid all the time. I had a long chat with my family. Eventually I picked a date and moved up here. Before Kyle started school so I could change his name as well.'

'But you said he employed a private detective. Surely you were worried he might just follow you up here?'

'I did spend the first few years looking over my shoulder, but I think he has a short attention span. Is he still the same?'

'Pretty much,' DC Angel said. 'Every few years he gets a new sixteen-year-old and keeps her pregnant until she gets too old and moves on.'

'So I was right. He ain't going to spend the money on chasing me when he's got a new woman on the go.' She paused to study DC Angel. 'You know all about him though, don't you? What was worth you driving all the way up here for?'

'Well, I don't know if you've seen the papers or not, but two teenage girls have been killed in the last few weeks.'

'And you wanted to know if maybe Greg was behind it?' She stopped to think, staring down at the grass. 'I know Greg, or I knew him anyway. Moved in with him and everything. And I have to say that I honestly can't see it. Look at me – I'm a thorn in his side, I got away and he can't control me. And he hasn't even sent a private detective after me. The only reason someone like Greg would kill is that the victim escaped from his control.'

Angel shook her head. 'We only found a tenuous connection between Watts and one victim. He certainly wasn't grooming either of them.'

'There you go then. If he's still at it after I got away, he's probably got his hands full with all his exes.' She paused. 'Or did more of the others escape?'

'No, they're all dotted all over the estate, with their hands out for money from Watts.'

'Are you going to do anything about him?'

'He is of interest to police.'

'But he's too clever? He was always smart when I knew him. Working out the angles.'

'He'll slip up. They always do.'

'Well, he's possessive, that's his weakness. He has to be in control. His family is probably the only way to get to him.'

The conversation petered out after that. DC Angel couldn't help but feel that she'd been cheated. She'd spent a whole morning chasing this lead and had come away with the same answer she always got – Watts was innocent of the murders.

As she drove back south, she wondered what she had achieved. She knew more about Watts, that was sure. But she didn't know if anything she'd learnt was going to be of use.

CHAPTER FORTY-THREE

DC Angel was driving south down the M5 when the phone rang. She stabbed at the phone on the dashboard and managed to get it onto hands free mode without causing an accident.

'Angel? Where are you now?'

'I'm heading south down the M5 just outside Bristol. Should be back soon enough.'

'Well can you make it sooner?' Haines asked. 'While you've been gone, our killer has struck again. And this time he left the girl alive.'

'Give me five minutes to get off the road, and we'll sort it. I'd rather take a few notes,' she said. 'Here's the exit already. I'll call you back in a moment.' Soon she was parked up in a lay-by on a main road. 'What do you need me to do, boss?'

'Can you go straight to Bradwick Hospital? You've spent the most time looking over the victims' details so you'll be the first to spot any connections.'

'Will do, boss. I'll give you a ring when I've seen the victim.'

'She's called Carla Jones. We've a uniform down there guarding her. I'll just check with him which ward she's been put on and text it to you.'

Before she rejoined the motorway, DC Angel reached into the glove box for a well-worn map of the area and her list of Dark Cars. She quickly scanned through the list and the map and decided that she could loop through a residential area.

Hopefully it'd only add two or three minutes onto her journey, but she might be able to tick another car off the list.

DC Angel parked up in the hospital car park. She'd crossed one entry off her list – she hadn't even had to stop; she'd just rolled past the driveway and seen that the car didn't match the photo.

She strode into the main building. Since she'd started working for the police, she'd noticed a complete change both in her attitude and that of the staff who worked there. She was now on the inside – they were all on the same side.

She was excited at the prospect of interviewing someone who'd actually seen the killer. This was the best news they'd had since the first body had been found in a grim yard behind a row of shops.

DC Angel made her way with familiarity through the corridors of the hospital. Somehow, someone had found a bed for the woman, in a side room where a policeman could sit outside in the corridor. She showed her warrant card to the burly looking PC who was working his way through a book of puzzles.

She saw the long dark hair of their victim spread out over the pillow, framing her pale face. Under her chin, a long straight bruise cut straight across her neck. DC Angel angled her head and saw a small round point bruise on the woman's temple. She was attached to monitors and had an oxygen tube under her nose. A nurse appeared silently.

'Poor thing. She hasn't stirred since she was brought in. It's that small bruise on her temple, it's a nasty head injury. The neck looks worse but the airway is open and it should heal nicely.'

'Thanks, any idea when she'll wake?'

'She's been given sedatives to help her sleep for the moment. The doctors are about to do their rounds, after that we'll find out when you'll be able to interview her.'

'Fine, thanks.'

With nothing else to do, DC Angel went out to the corridor to phone through to DCI Haines. They had a short conversation where Angel was ordered to find and conduct a more in-depth interview with the primary witness after the initial one at the scene.

After a few minutes in the car with her mobile she found out that their witness, one Barbara Weathers, was behind the bar at the yacht club.

Bradwick and District Yacht Club was a complete time-warp. DC Angel had no idea if it was members only or not so she fingered her warrant card in her pocket as she walked in. The bar was a large square room with windows around three sides, presumably so members could look out at the sea and judge the conditions. The decor was straight out of the seventies – wood panelling, photographs, oars and other boat memorabilia. It even had a huge wooden board with all the past presidents written in gold, going back to 1837. There were a few fruit machines dotted about but they were all turned off at the plug.

There were only a few people in the entire place and they were all scattered around the room sitting at tables. Behind the deserted bar was DC Angel's quarry – Mrs Barbara Weathers. She looked like a formidable matron, all bosom and carefully starched curls.

When introductions had been made, she launched straight into her story. 'I was out first thing this morning, walking Maltravers, my Labrador, when he suddenly bounded off. Well, I thought he'd just caught scent of a squirrel or something. Then I heard the barking and a man shouting. Next thing I knew there was an awful howl, and it all went quiet. I can tell you, I hurried over there as soon as I could.'

'And what did you find?'

'Well, that poor woman, unconscious on the ground. And Maltravers too, he was walking round in circles, shaking his head. I think that brute must have hit him with whatever he was attacking that girl with.'

This was what DC Angel was here for. 'Did you see the man who attacked them?'

'No, not a hair. Well, there might have been a shadow further on, you know across the heath. Just disappearing into the trees by the road. But I wasn't really looking, you know.'

'That's understandable. What happened next?' DC Angel was already making notes.

'Well, you must know all of that. I told the nice officer at the scene. I stayed with Maltravers and that woman and used my mobile to call for help.'

Angel knew full well that Mrs Weathers would have been interviewed immediately after the event and she would read that account back at the station. But it was important to cover the ground at least twice so she gently led her over the story, hoping that she'd pick up something new.

When it was over, Mrs Weathers asked cautiously, 'How is that poor girl? Was it the same as the other two?'

Angel wanted to sigh and rest her head on the bar. But she maintained her professional demeanour. She knew that Haines' attempts to keep the story from the press were ultimately doomed. But he knew it was a futile effort too, he merely sought both to delay the story reaching the press and to minimise its impact when it got there. She saw a chance to see how it was going. 'What makes you think that it might be linked to other cases?'

'Oh, don't you come like that with me! I know the local rag hasn't made much of a fuss about it but I'm the barmaid here. I get all the gossip, usually from at least two different directions. Two young girls get strangled within a couple of weeks and the whole town is bound to be talking about it. When I saw that girl with the mark across her throat... well was she the third victim?'

'We don't know yet.' Angel saw the look on Barbara's face and quickly carried on. 'No, seriously we don't. I'm not hiding anything from you. We need to examine all the evidence, including your statement and then have a case conference. Compare all three cases and see what conclusions we can draw.'

'Well, you don't need to worry about me. Mum's the word.' Barbara sounded sincere but DC Angel had her doubts. She was a barmaid after all and was obviously the centre of the gossip. 'That Inspector Hayes, he's nice, isn't he?'

'You mean DCI Haines? He's my boss.' Angel had a lot of respect for Haines, but she didn't think of him as nice. Tough, shrewd, and fair maybe, but not nice.

'That's it! Haines. He got my Maltravers moved to the vet that has the account for the police dogs. Everything he needs will be paid for. I won't have to spend anything.'

'That is nice.' DC Angel also thought that if the dog had any evidence like fibres in its teeth, then they would be the best vets to recover it. But it was a good decision in terms of PR too, she had to acknowledge. 'And your dog is a bit of hero too.'

'Well, who knows what would have happened to that poor woman if Maltravers hadn't bounded to the rescue?'

DC Angel could only nod as she had a very good idea what would have happened.

PART 3

CHAPTER FORTY-FOUR

The next day, the call came through from the hospital that they were all clear to interview Carla Jones, who had now been positively confirmed as victim number three.

She was sitting up in hospital, looking rather bored.

'Hi. I'm Detective Constable Angel and I'd like to know what you can remember about the attack.'

'I wrote it down,' she said in a hoarse whisper. 'Bored.' She brandished an A4 pad.

'Does it hurt to talk?' DC Angel asked and was rewarded with a nod. She took the pad and started reading the close, neat handwriting.

'I have to warn you, that I can't remember being attacked. The consultant said that it's to do with the memories being interrupted before they were formed or moved from short to long term. Whatever the reason, I don't remember a lot.

'I remember the normal things I did in the morning before I went to work. Waking up, shower, breakfast, all of that. When I left the house, I put the new Foo Fighters album Concrete and Gold on my phone, put my headphones in and set out for work. I definitely remember listening to Run and thinking about the video and then it's a blank.'

DC Angel stopped reading and got her phone out. Run was the second track and less than seven minutes of the whole album. They'd worked out a rough timeline, and she was attacked between fifteen and twenty minutes into her usual thirty-minute walk to work. She went back to the pad, aware that Carla Jones was watching her closely.

'It's so odd and frustrating. When people said that they don't have any memory of being drunk, I never used to believe them. I didn't think it was really a thing. But, now, here I am. Two songs, then nothing.

'I know that I was attacked. But all I remember is waking up here in the middle of the night. It was all dark, but noisy with the beeps and the nurses moving around checking everyone. I tried to ask the nurse what was going on. I could hardly make any noise. Luckily the nurse explained who I was and why I was in hospital.

'After that snapshots keep popping into my head. Lying on the ground, I could feel the grass on my neck, see the light through the trees. There was this ring of faces around me. Some woman who looked like an aunt, and a dog, and a policeman. I remember hearing barking and a yelp. I was in the ambulance, it was rocking to and fro, people were trying to help me.

'I know what you want to know, but I didn't see who attacked me, I'm sorry, that's all a big blank.'

DC Angel looked up from the pages to the woman who wrote them. She wondered what would be left after this attack. Would Carla suffer from PTSD? One attack that took less than thirty seconds could easily carry on for months and years. She looked again at the pale face, dark hair, and bruised neck and a wave of sympathy washed over her.

She tried to frame her questions in yes or no format to save the woman's voice. 'Can you remember any detail at all about your attacker?'

Carla shook her head.

'And this is all you can remember?'

A nod of the head.

'Do the doctors think any more memories will come back?'

Carla shrugged.

'Listen, this isn't an official statement. But could you just write at the bottom that this is a true account of what you can remember and sign it. Then I'll take it and enter it into evidence.' Carla nodded, took the pad back, wrote on the bottom then returned it to DC Angel. 'I'll leave you be now, to get some rest. Do you know if your voice will get better?'

'With rest,' she croaked and nodded.

CHAPTER FORTY-FIVE

When DC Angel got back to the office, a full meeting of the MIT was called, before she had a chance to debrief Haines on her interview with Carla Jones.

'Right, we've got plenty of points of correlation between the attack on Carla Jones and the first two murders. It's enough for us to consider that she is the third victim, even though she's a survivor. On that point, Angel, did we get anywhere on the interview?'

'Sorry, boss. With the combination of the blow to the head and the oxygen deprivation she has no memory of the event. I have got this statement.' She held up the pages of A4 then read them out to the assembled officers. 'As you can see, it confirms what we know and nothing more. She was on her way to work, got attacked, and was saved by Barbara Weathers and her dog.'

'Damn!' Haines said. 'We're going to have to get right on top of this, straight away. With three attacks we have a very small window to close this out before the chief super pulls it out from us with a review and passes it over to another team.

'With all of this in mind, we're terminating the multi-agency immigration checks and putting all our manpower into solving the murders.'

'What about...?' DI Hargreaves stopped to consider what to say next. He looked carefully around the room. 'What about the original reasons for launching the operation in the first place?'

DCI Haines took a deep breath. 'Well, we're near to resolving that problem. I have information received that there'll be a big meeting coming up very soon. The new dealers who are trying to get established in town are going to have a resupply and that's when we'll strike. Once we get the precise time and date then we can launch the raid and clear that whole problem out of the way. There isn't much we can do in terms of planning until we know the details. Hopefully we'll have caught the killer before we get all the details of the big drug raid. That's where we will be putting all our resources – making sure this killer is caught quickly. But, as soon as we know about the raid, we'll have to switch regardless of how we are on the murder investigation. We have to be flexible on this one.'

There were nods and mutters around the room. Everyone could see that there was plenty of overtime and hard work ahead. Haines carried on talking. 'Right. We have three attacks to deal with. Let's go back to the beginning and work all these cases hard. All three victims were on foot, so let's get good, solid timelines for each one. Likewise we need to work their social networks, look for common points of intersection. Our killer is picking these women out for some reason. We need to find that common thread and follow it until it leads to our man.'

There was some grumbling as people went away to their assigned tasks. 'Bloody poxy, that's what it is.' Inspector Hargreaves was waiting in line at the coffee machine, making the most of his audience. 'It's not like we dropped the ball on the first two killings is it? We've been over the CCTV, fingertip search, house to house, and full forensics. This might be one of those cases that comes up on Crimewatch in twenty years' time.'

'If you don't feel up to it, Glen, you could always put in for retirement.' Haines was walking past and couldn't resist a dig.

'No, boss, just a bit of banter, that's all.'

'Right, you listen. We've got three cases now. When we went over Mazey Taylor we were thinking of a single case. Now we can compare all that data to the other two, find a link.'

DC Angel found herself nodding. Most of the Taylor case was compromised because they were trying to catch the WankyBois. Finally, she agreed with Haines – they needed to start again and find the link between the victims.

'Right you are, boss,' DI Hargreaves said. But DC Angel looked at his eyes and saw something else. He was straining at the leash, counting down the days until he would no longer have to answer to Haines on a day to day basis. She didn't judge him harshly for it – she knew how frustrating it must be to be the pretender to the throne.

She took her coffee back to her desk. She wanted to go through the CCTV to see if DCM had made an appearance at the latest crime scene too. Once again, she went through her battered atlas – the crime scene was a big patch of green in the middle of a nest of streets. She sighed and reached for the computer. With a bit of zooming in and out she found out where the footpaths joined actual roads. She flicked over to the CCTV system.

She groaned. It was residential area very sparsely covered by cameras. She traced it back. There were main roads but they were quite a way from the scene. If the car did turn up there then it would be circumstantial at best.

She decided that she would call for the CCTV. She knew in her heart that Dark Car Man was behind this, and the more photos she got, the better. All of them were two junctions away from the crime scene so they probably wouldn't be used in court.

After some deliberation she just entered it on the system as part of the general enquiries around the area. Her information about Dark Car Man had been knocked back by Haines at least twice. She felt protective of her own private investigation and didn't want it up on the system only to be shot down again.

Chapter Forty-Six

Even though they had a third attack, DCI Haines still kept his meeting with Billy King as he had done every Tuesday evening. He knew he should be in the station, but Billy sounded excited. So, he slipped out and went back to the wine bar where they'd met before. As before there were two bodyguards, one in the car outside, one at the bar.

'I've got the nod,' Billy King said before Haines had taken the first sip of his beer. 'This is kosher. The big guys are going to meet somewhere around Bradwick. You're going to get everything. They're going to have a big sale, cash, drugs, and top-level dealers all in one place.'

'I'm still nervous though. Did you get an answer to our original question? Why here?' Haines asked. 'I love this town, but I am realistic. There must be hundreds of towns around this size within striking distance of Birmingham, all just as good for this kind of thing.'

'That's the thing. It not the town they want, really, or even the users here. There are punters everywhere, every town, up and down the country.'

'What do they want with Bradwick then?' Haines was getting annoyed with his rambling around the subject. Billy King fell silent and chewed his lower lip. Haines decided to wait him out.

'You see, it's tricky.' King's good mood had evaporated. 'They, the gangs in the cities, have spotted a potential, an opportunity. It might still be viable. That's what the meeting is for. It's a test.'

There was a telling pause. Was King really going to hold out, Haines wondered? 'What?' Haines asked, unable to keep the disbelief out of his voice. 'We've known each other for over twenty years. You're a drug dealing gangster and I run the local CID. I think we're kind of past keeping secrets from each other.' Haines allowed a short pause, before carrying on. 'Unless of course, you want to end our relationship.'

'No, of course I don't. It's just that, you know...'

'These people have already killed Sean.' Haines was emphatic. 'And you know they won't stop. The people we've arrested and charged so far are only foot soldiers. You can't seriously be considering working with the people who sent them.'

'No, no, you are right. This is my town and my people.' He took a deep breath. 'Harbours. That's what the city gangs are after. North of Bradwick there's a whole network of tiny creeks and abandoned shipyards. Apparently, they've been out and had a look at them. They might be out of use but some of the quays are still good and some of the channels could be deep enough to get boats in and out. Boats from the continent.'

'And you seriously thought that you might step up to be an importer? Is that why you didn't want to tell me?' There was both humour and an edge of danger in Haines' words.

'No, not really. It's just, you know, with Sean gone.' He stopped to consider his words. 'It's this town and this summer. It's just gone on and on, not properly sunny, but still not cold. We're still hot and sticky but we never see the sun. And now these girls are being killed, on top of all the beatings and revenge killings that have been bothering me.' He shook his head. 'I dunno, it's like everything's changing. Maybe it's time for me to change as well. It's not something you can carry on doing for ever.'

'But isn't that what we are doing? If we stick together now, we can send these chancers back to Birmingham. And if anyone else comes along, we can do the same thing again.'

'Stick together? It's fine for you to say that but it's my people who are being beaten out there. It's my friends who are dying!'

DCI Haines took a deep breath. 'I know that. I do know that. Believe me I don't want our town to be seen as a drug riddled, violent crime hot spot.' He paused and chose to be a bit more open with Billy King. 'Also, it'll be bad for me. I need to catch whoever's killing these girls. In fact I should be in the station right now, running the team. And I need to get a big score against these dealers from the cities as well. I'm moving up, away from the operational side of things. This is my last chance to make a difference.'

'And you think I shouldn't make the same move?' King sounded a bit truculent.

'I think,' Haines said carefully, 'that you should move on and change. But I will not have my town become a gateway between Europe and the big cities of the UK. There are other directions. You could retire. Your record isn't that bad. You could do something else?'

'No, not really. This is what I know and what I do. Anyway, I'm not going anywhere until all this is sorted out. I've just lost one of my main guys, I need to move things up and change people around. If I retired now – hell if I even disappeared for a weekend – then it would all fall apart. This town would become a battleground between the different gangs from the cities.' He stopped to think for a moment. 'No, you're right. We need to keep doing what we're doing. And you need to get Pietr off the scene for good.

'The current plan is to bring a boat in. There's an industrial estate up north of here called Brookbank. It's pretty much on its last legs commercially, hardly any tenants. Pietr has leased one of the warehouses for six months and they want a test run to see if they can land a boat and unload the product right there. The warehouse would become a distribution centre. It might be abandoned but it's not far to the M5 and from there to the rest of the country.'

'Jesus! That's dangerous that is. Once large amounts of drugs start arriving right on the edge of town, it wouldn't take long to spill over into Bradwick itself.'

'Yeah. You'd get the serious dealers setting up here, stronger drugs being sold cheaper. Wouldn't be long before the brothels and the gang fights followed. We wouldn't recognise the place in five years.'

Haines nodded in agreement. 'What's the plan then?'

'Well the plan is for Friday night. I think the main players will start to arrive from five thirty in the evening, a couple of hours before it gets dark. The boat's expected around six and then they'll have to transfer to the warehouse, split it up, weigh up packages and sell direct to the major dealers.'

Haines did some quick calculations. So we'll have to be observing from five onward. Wait for the boat to be unloaded, and as many dealers as we can catch.'

'I reckon, give or take, the first guys will be leaving about six thirty, maybe seven. I doubt it'll be that much of a party – these guys are all business.'

'Right, so, I've got a murder enquiry to run and now a major operation to plan in three days. Are these timings certain?'

'Yeah, my man is right on the inside, handling the Bradwick end of things.'

'Well, all that remains is to say thank you. Hopefully by the weekend everything will be sorted.'

Haines walked briskly back to the station, only stopping to grab a sandwich and a drink. He thought he'd got away unnoticed but within minutes of arriving back, Glen Hargreaves slipped into his office.

'Did you get it then? Did Billy come across with the goods?'

'Yes. It'll be the Brookbank Industrial Estate, north of here, Friday evening. We've got the lot.' Haines caught an odd look on his colleague's face and for a moment wondered if he should have told him. Then he caught himself. Glen Hargreaves was his inspector, his second-in-command. If he was going to launch a huge operation, of course Glen should know. Why did he feel uneasy then?

'Will King be there?' Hargreaves asked.

'Billy King? No. I bloody well hope not. It'll be a huge job. Armed response, entry teams, uniform, even the Border Force for the boat. Last thing we want is civilians standing around watching and getting in the way!'

'Might do him good,' Hargreaves said, almost to himself.

'Why?' Haines now focused on Hargreaves.

'Well, for a start it would show him that we can follow through. That when it counts, we're not some small provincial force but we can mount big operations.' He paused, but only for a second. 'Also, it might do him good to see what happens to drug dealers round here if they don't co-operate.'

'No. You can't treat Billy King like that. When all this blows over and we catch the killer, the three of us will have a sit down. But he likes to be treated gently. No throwing threats around. If you don't remember anything else, remember that he's as much a threat to us by now as we are to him.' There was another pause, more loaded this time. 'Okay?'

'Yes, boss,' Hargreaves answered. It was dawning on Haines that his friend and colleague, Glen Hargreaves, couldn't wait to get rid of him and run the show on his own. Well, let him, he thought savagely. Let him see how difficult it can be keeping all the bloody balls in the air.

CHAPTER FORTY-SEVEN

Angel came in early on Wednesday morning and was immediately called into a meeting with Haines.

'I've finally got intelligence on the big raid and it looks like we're all set for Friday evening. What we need to do now is wrap up these murder cases as well.'

Angel couldn't help thinking that they'd been plugging away for weeks without a result and now her boss wanted a result in two days.

'How did you get on with your daytrip to Bristol?' Haines asked.

'I was trying to pin something on Gregory Watts. I went there to meet one of his exes.'

'And...?'

'And nothing we can action. I'll have to conclude that you were right about him. He's a grade A creep. You definitely wouldn't want him sniffing around anyone you cared about. But he does have all his bases covered. If one of his women came forward, we could take a shot at coercive control.'

'Is that likely?'

'Not really,' DC Angel shook her head. 'They'd need to be strong as anything. The lawyers he could afford, any complainant would end up doubting their own name. It'd be a tough one.' DC Angel paused. She didn't want to talk about her hunt for Dark Car Man.

'There's something else, isn't there?'

'You remember that I said about the Dark Car Man and how that dark Fiesta drives past every crime scene?'

'Yes, I know. But we can't get enough manpower to hunt down every single Fiesta owner in Bradwick. Not to mention the data protection problem.'

'Well, we might not have to do that. I met with more of the teenagers of Bradwick. Turns out they know more about cars than you might expect. One of them works for the local Ford dealership.'

'Turners?'

'Yeah. Turns out not all Fiestas are the same. I should be able to trim down the list.' She hoped that Haines wouldn't spot the white lie.

'Without number plates?'

'Yes, we can approximate to the year and trim level and work from there.'

Haines pushed back from his desk and thought. Eventually he reached his decision. 'This feels like a time-sink. You could put so much effort in with no promise of anything back. What if this guy is just unlucky? Just happens to be wrong place at the wrong time? Any decent brief will dismiss it as circumstantial.'

DC Angel opened her mouth to argue, then saw the look on her boss's face. There would be no arguing. She had been stupid to expect him to listen to her ideas. She closed her mouth and straight away resolved to continue her own private quest.

'Anyway, Angel, wish me luck. I've got to go see the boss, sort out this drug raid.'

'Okay, boss. I'm going to head out for a couple of hours. Hang around McDonald's and see if I can get any more information out of the youth of Bradwick.'

DCI Haines was used to running his own department and so was uncomfortable going to see the boss to get approval to do his job. However, he knew it was necessary.

'So, Rob. I've got your request for operational support here. Came in this morning.' Chief Superintendent Cornish picked up a form as if to prove his point. 'It does appear to be lacking in a little detail, on some key points.'

Haines frowned. 'I stayed late last night to make sure that I filled everything in. How many arrests are expected, and that we'll need firearms support, uniforms to handle the bodies, custody suites on standby. It's all in there.'

'Ah. Yes. That's not the problem.' Cornish, Gold Commander for the area was a short, slightly overweight man whose features were rather bulbous. He always reminded Haines of a frog in a suit. 'No, the problem is in the quality of the information. For an operation of this scale, we really need some independent corroboration. We need to meet with your source.'

Haines sat back in his chair and thought quickly. He didn't want to see Billy King and his boss in the same room. He didn't trust his informant that far. 'That's not really going to be possible. It took a lot of risk to get this information, the guy is right out on a limb already. I can vouch for him one hundred percent.'

Haveland sucked his teeth. 'I'm not sure I can authorise this level of operation, the expense, and exposure of the force to negative publicity if everything should go wrong.'

'Okay. Okay. I can see that. But look, I've been given this name, Pietr Garoza. Family from Latvia. I've run his name past all the relevant authorities. If you look at the request, I've added comments from the national gangs unit, including their report on Garoza which contains information from Interpol.'

'You can spare me reading another report. Give me the edited highlights.'

'Well he was known to them. Definitely a major player. Runs one of the more serious outfits in Birmingham. Proper nasty piece of work. Even better than that, he has connections to a company that, in the last month, took out a long lease on a warehouse on the Brookbank Industrial Estate.'

'Brookbank? I can't place it.'

'Not surprised. It's an old place, used to be a shipyard and then the Victorians ran a spur of railway out there and it became an industrial site. Then Beeching shut down the branch line and the roads weren't quite good enough for the lorries that replaced trains in the sixties and the place kind of went downhill. There's not a lot of anything there now.'

'I see. It really does make your wonder what a gangster from the city wants with it?'

'Word is that they're having a trial run to see if they can still get boats in and out. It's still got overgrown docks and all the fittings.'

'Word that you can't verify.'

The two men sat across the desk and stared at each other.

'Listen. David. Sir. You can check and make sure that all the info is right. The name is right and the location is right. It all checks out.'

'So, we have outside corroboration that a drug lord has definitely leased a warehouse in a quiet estate just outside Bradwick.' Haines nodded slowly, watching Cornish closely. There was something in those piggy eyes that he didn't trust. He realised that his life would now be political battles like this. Cornish continued. 'But you said he had a long lease, so this meeting could happen any time in the next few months. What you want is for me to take the exact time and date of the meeting entirely on trust? Is that it?'

'Yes.' Haines decided to give him as little ammunition as possible.

'Trust is the thing though, isn't it? It's no secret that your promotion wasn't unanimous. There have always been rumours.' Haines leant forward to speak, but Cornish held up his hand. 'No, I know, we're not here to review your promotion. And I am aware that you have an exemplary record, your crime stats are very impressive. It's no doubt that Bradwick is safe on your watch.'

The two men paused and studied each other. Haines was determined not to be drawn into an argument. Cornish steepled his fingers and waited to see if his words had found their mark. When Haines hadn't risen to the bait, he continued. 'Timing is the problem. We can't really have all these officers sent out there and then find nothing there. We'd tip our hand to Garoza, and his gang too. And, if this goes wrong, then this won't just create ripples in our part of the force. You've got support from headquarters in Bristol, and you want to involve tactical support too. More than that, you've requested Border Force to attend as well.'

'We have to do that,' Haines explained. 'We're dealing with foreign nationals and they also have the expertise to immobilise and search a boat. They're essential to the operation.'

'And you're sure about this. About the boat?'

'Yes, sir. It's a complete dry-run. They'll bring a boat in from the continent, unload the drugs and then distribute them.'

'We could just hand all this off to Border Force. Stop them before they even land.'

Haines wanted to slam his hand on the desk and start shouting. But he knew it would achieve nothing. Very patiently he explained, 'If we did that then all we'd have would be Garoza waiting at the warehouse and being very pissed off that his delivery didn't arrive. And he's a major player with expensive lawyers and no outstanding warrants. We know where they're going to dock. We wait for them to land the product and move it to the warehouse. Then we can get Garoza and his top dealers actually in possession of the drugs and the money. Border Force will be there to impound and search the boat. And we get to share the glory, not just give it away to another agency.'

'If you're right about the timing. Otherwise we'd be the guys who let a boat full of drugs slip past while blowing our budget on raiding an empty warehouse.' There was a pause, broken by Cornish. 'How about this for a solution?' It sounded as if he'd just thought of it, but Haines was certain that he'd planned this before the meeting started. 'I'll approve this operation now and you can get on with the planning, briefing all the different departments, getting everything in place.' Haines waited for the hammer to fall. 'But, if there is any hiccup, if your principals don't show, then we'll have a thorough review of the whole situation. Your reputation, those rumours, where you got this information from, the whole shooting match.'

And my promotion, Haines wanted to ask. But he didn't, because he knew that was what was at stake. But he had gone this far with Billy King and wasn't about to quit now. He knew what the Cornishes of this world were like. All hot air and fury. The only way to beat them was to front them out. Show no weakness.

'I'm confident in my information,' Haines said levelly. 'You approve the operation, we'll catch the bad guys, and I'll get my promotion.' He got up to leave.

'We'll see.' Chief Superintendent Cornish paused and Haines waited in the doorway. 'Don't lose sight of the murders either, Rob. You need a good result on that as well.'

DCI Haines just shook his head and left the office.

* * *

Haines sat down opposite the burly man who was the tactical leader of the armed response teams.

'In short, we've got information on a team who might be moving in. One Pietr Garoza wants to swap Latvia for England. He's our principal target so you might want to read up on him, know what you're up against. Anyway we've run him through the system and although he's using several front companies, we've traced him to the Brookbank Industrial Estate.'

'Where the hell is that?'

'Out to the north of Bradwick. One of the old Victorian harbours. I say industrial estate, but it's run down and mostly derelict. There are few business hanging on but since the growth of Royal Portbury and Avonmouth, it's been pretty much dead.'

'And he's renting there?'

'Yeah, a big warehouse, plenty of space.'

'We'll go up there and have a look around, make a plan.'

'You can do that? We don't want to tip them off. This is good intelligence that we don't want wasted.'

Instead of answering, he pulled out The Field Guide to British Birds and slid it across the desk. 'This is our secret weapon. Me and my second in command get our anoraks, sandwiches and thermos flask then we can go out to wherever we want with this book. Go on, flick through it.' Haines did what he was told and saw that it was well thumbed and had dates and locations written in biro. 'Attention to detail, that's the key. But with this we can wander where we like, use binoculars, make notes and no one even thinks twice.'

Chapter Forty-Eight

Instead of looking for teenagers, DC Angel got a tattered printout from her glove box. This paperwork was her holy grail. It was the reduced list of Ford Fiestas in Bradwick and the immediate surrounding areas. She knew that Haines didn't rate her Dark Car Man theory so she planned to present him with a fait accompli. She would see if she could get eyes on every car on this list. If, or hopefully when, she saw the suspect Fiesta, then she could announce her breakthrough to the MIT. With their full resources she was sure that they could turn a name and address into a conviction.

She plotted a route and set the sat nav for the first target. She edged slowly down the residential street on the Seaview Estate – one of the poorer areas of Bradwick, houses and bungalows thrown up in the fifties when the town was in its heyday as a holiday town. They were cheap and cheerful in their day and were now a bit cheap and rundown if the owners didn't look after them.

With one eye on the sat nav, she drove slowly, looking for the suspect car. She saw it parked in a driveway, ahead on the left. It had the familiar outline that had haunted her dreams since she watched the CCTV from the first killing.

As she got closer, however, she knew she was out of luck. No sticker at all in the back window, just a collection of stick men representing the family members. Worse than that, the wheels were alloys – it was the wrong spec. She sped up and resolved to tick this one off the list next time she stopped.

The next three cars weren't present at their owners' addresses. She had a brainwave that would also let her do what she'd said she would. She started driving around the huge car park of the out of town retail centre, checking for cars.

When she'd ticked one more car off her list, she parked up next to a burger van and bought a takeaway coffee. Sat in her car, she closed her eyes for a second. Was Haines right? Was she barking up the wrong tree? First Gregory Watts was not guilty and now she was beginning to wonder about Dark Car Man.

She sipped her coffee and came to the same conclusion she always had. During office hours she'd be the dutiful officer, following leads and updating the computer. Out of hours, she'd continue her quest for the Dark Car Man and to find evidence against Watts.

In her heart, not her head, she knew that there were two dangerous men in Bradwick. Two men who believed they had a right to own, to control, to terrify women whenever they felt like it. As a woman, DC Angel couldn't let that lie and as a police officer she had the tools to put a stop to it.

She drove back to the station, choosing her route to collect one more car on the way. For the rest of the day, she put actions into the computer, chased up scientific reports and read through the door-to-door results. She left early to go to her self-defence class.

* * *

The lesson ended with some improvised weapon work. She wandered over to the stack of rubber weapons they were training with. As usual the trainer had brought some real weapons along.

Emma's eye fell on a side handle baton. It wasn't something often used in British police forces so she picked it up and turned it over. Holding it in her hands sparked an idea. 'Can I borrow you a moment?'

The trainer came over. 'Sure, what's up?'

'Just stand there for a moment, I want to try something.' She held the long end of the baton with the side arm sticking out. She gently swung it so the short end made contact with her trainer's temple. 'Now you go down.'

'For sure, if you put force behind it, I'd go down like a sack of potatoes. If you hit me hard enough there with that weapon, it might even be fatal.' He lowered himself to the mat. Emma slid her hand up the baton and gripped the short arm in her fist, with the long handle running down her forearm. Now she straddled him and placed her arm, reinforced by the shaft of the baton, across his windpipe.

'Wow! Are they teaching the police how to kill people now?'

'No, but we have to figure out how they're killed.' She released him and stood up, holding out a hand to help him up from the mat.

'You know there's another option.' He reached for the baton which she handed over. He held it near the junction with the long bar running down his arm. 'Much more subtle. If you were walking past someone, you could even put it up your sleeve even though that might be awkward.' He reached his hand up to her face and tapped her on the temple. 'One tap and down.' Obediently Emma collapsed to the floor. 'And then you just spin it around like before and boom!' He then laid his arm across her throat.

Next morning, she brought the borrowed baton into work. 'I think I've figured out how the girls were killed. Ed, can I borrow you for a minute?' There were cheers and mutters from the rest of the CID.

'Wait a minute, we think this is a man killing women. Should it be me attacking you?'

'Yeah, but I think I can explain all the wounds. Don't worry, I'll be gentle!' She smiled. 'Where these are used, the police are trained to use these for defence – disarming people with knives, restraining drunken idiots, that kind of thing. But, one sharp tap on the side of the head here,' she tapped DC Mitchell with the stick, 'would bring someone down. Then, when they're on the floor, you just have it along the side of the arm and strangle them.'

There were nods around the room. 'That explains it. And it'd be really quick too. One blow to the head and then you're strangling them. Nice work.' Haines was nodding as he spoke. 'It fits all the injuries. That blow to the temple could kill – it would certainly stun. It's very organised and calculating as well. No blood everywhere like a stabbing, no gunshots. Quick, quiet and efficient.'

'But,' Ed Mitchell said, 'they'd have to be prepared. It's not like he's just finding a rock to bash their head in with.'

'That's true. But it's going to leave very little forensic trace.' Haines had taken the baton from DC Angel. 'Nice smooth surface, you could tuck it inside a coat or up a sleeve.'

Once all the excitement had died down, Angel added a note to the board to say that they were now looking for a side handle baton. After that, DC Angel stayed true to her day job. She now had two areas to focus on – both collating the information on the attacks and now planning the big raid for tomorrow evening.

CHAPTER FORTY-NINE

DC Angel was exhausted. She'd put in the hours checking the data on the three attacks, while still doing the basic administration of co-ordinating the many teams who'd need to come together for the operation tomorrow. Nothing was said, but everyone knew that it would be a matter of days before the chief super brought in someone from outside to check the investigation into the two murders and then take over. If that happened, the whole team would feel like schoolchildren who had failed a test and had to be helped out by the teacher. It would be an awful way to start a new era with DI Hargreaves in charge.

She should have gone straight home, sunk a couple of beers, had a bath and been ready to go back to it in the morning. However, as had been her habit, she pulled a familiar tatty sheaf of paper out of her glove box. When she was feeling down, she wondered if the killer had touched up the scratches and removed the sticker. Then she realised that she couldn't think like that. This was their last throw of the dice.

She scanned down the list to the next one that hadn't been crossed off yet and tapped in the address to the sat nav. Her eyebrows raised – a nice area, just off Spalley Road. Still, she'd either do all of them, or none at all. She relaxed when it added less than ten minutes to her journey time.

When she got close to the house however, she felt a flutter of apprehension. This was the best part of Bradwick, no question. On a rise above the town, the houses were positioned to give a sea view without being close to the amusement arcades and boarding houses on the front. But this did raise a problem. The roads were wide avenues and the big houses were all detached, behind walls and fences. Hardly any cars were parked on the road and several of the houses had high gates. DC Angel doubted that she'd have much chance of seeing the car unless it was on a driveway.

She drove slowly past her target before stopping at the kerb, just beyond the entrance. She'd already clocked that the lights were out and there were no cars visible. She was about to leave when she noticed that it had a large detached garage. It was visible and accessible from the road, but she knew she was stretching the definition of what was reasonable for a search without a warrant. On the other hand, they were running out of time and she had to be thorough. If she didn't check this one out, she knew she wouldn't sleep at nights if the investigation failed.

She shook her head and got out of the car. Feeling edgy, she stepped from the street onto private property. The garage had a traditional wooden door with a line of small square windows near the top. Frustratingly, she was too short to see through them. Luckily, it had one side window, and as she peered through the grime, she saw that it did contain a dark blue Fiesta. Five door, she thought, going through a mental check list. She wiped some grime away to get a view of the wheel arch and then her heart skipped a beat. There were the white scratches – three parallel white lines, in the just the right place.

One out of three.

She went up on tiptoe and tried to see down to the wheel. Fishing out her phone she switched the torch on to look at the wheel trim. It was cracked in just the right place.

Two out of three.

She had spent so long going over the photographs that she knew she was looking at the same car. But she owed it to herself and the investigation to be sure. She walked around to the front of the garage, trying to make sense of it all. A car connected to the killings in the most expensive area of Bradwick?

No matter how she stretched, she was unable to see through the front windows. She knew she could walk away, but without the third, corroborating piece of evidence, she wouldn't be certain. She was still holding her phone, the torch switched off, and that gave her an idea. She held her phone above her head and took a photo down through the window into the garage without being able to see the screen.

At her third attempt, she got something usable. There was a yellow dealer sticker in the rear window. More than that, it had the corner missing. In those sleepless nights going over the stills from the CCTV she had memorised this too. The corner wasn't missing straight across, it had ripped in a curve, like a ski slope. And this car had exactly the same sticker.

Three out of three.

Regardless of the number plates, this was the car that had been seen near every crime scene, just before and after every attack. This was Dark Car Man's vehicle. Was she standing in the driveway of a man who'd been terrorising and killing the women of Bradwick?

She was in a grey area with gathering the evidence so she briskly walked down the drive and back to her car. She couldn't use what she'd found tonight in any way. But she knew that when she brought it to the team tomorrow, the owner would go straight to the top of their list. Somehow, they'd find a way to make it an official part of the enquiry.

No sooner had she got back to the car than a Jaguar swept past her and into the drive. Nervously, she watched in her mirror as it parked up outside the house. She experienced momentary relief when the occupant ignored her car but went straight to the front door.

She picked up her list and tracked her finger across to see whose car she had been looking at. She frowned. M Patterson. Why did that name ring a bell? Could it be connected with Reg Patterson, her boss's mentor?

She checked her mirror but was just in time to see the front door close with no idea who'd just gone into the house.

DC Angel was now very aware of how deserted the street was. She also knew that Reg Patterson was an ex-police officer and she had just carried out an illegal search on someone possibly connected to him. And which might link him or a member of his family to a series of murders.

As much as she hated the idea, she knew she couldn't tackle this one alone. She had to do two things – first get away from the scene, and secondly ask for help. And there was only one person to ask – his protege, DCI Rob Haines.

CHAPTER FIFTY

DC Angel parked up as soon as she was able to find a space. This time, she parked in a lay-by outside a row of shops. Nice and anonymous, she thought, still worried that she might have been seen.

She phoned Haines and was relieved that he actually answered his mobile – he hadn't taken the battery out for a secret meeting. She didn't want to get into this on the phone so she simply asked to meet and promised a break in the case.

He surprised her by telling her to go to his house. With the big raid tomorrow and no breaks in the case he'd decided to take today a bit easier. When she pulled up outside his house, he came out to meet her. Initially it was odd to see him in shirt sleeves but only for a second. She was the one who had disturbed his evening. He slid into the passenger seat of her car, his bulk making her car seem small.

'Where to, boss?'

'Nowhere, yet. Tell me what you've got and I'll see if it's worth my time.'

Briefly she recapped what she'd learned from her evening with the teenagers and their cars. Then she passed him her list of cars and showed where she'd been ticking them off.

'You did all this on your own? If you knew you had this lead, why didn't you bring it to me? I could've allocated some uniforms out. We'd have got here much earlier.'

'Sorry, boss, but I did mention the Dark Car Man theory to you. I got the impression you thought it was going nowhere, so I kept at it on my own. Don't worry, none of this was on the books, I haven't claimed overtime for it.'

Haines went quiet. He couldn't have his officers running around freelancing. If nothing else, that was how things got missed and officers got into danger. On the other hand, he was sure she had mentioned something about this theory, but not how far she'd gone into it. 'Right, we'll deal with all that later,' he said. 'What I want to know is how solid is what you've got now.'

She passed over her phone, already on the photo of the back of the car. 'This one was on my list, but it was in a garage accessible from the road. I took this photo; the sticker is exactly the same. And I looked in through a side window – the wheel trim and scratches match too.'

Haines tracked his finger down the list. 'This is far more serious than I thought. That is Reg's address but this says M Patterson so that'd be his wife. But she died a while back; cancer, nasty business.' He paused momentarily. 'Are you sure about this DC Angel? I mean, like one hundred per cent, no shadow of a doubt, sure? Because we can't just go barging into a retired senior officer's house and accuse him of being a murderer. Or even worse, connect it to his wife when she hasn't even been dead for a year. He deserves more respect.'

DC Angel considered the question. 'For days now I've lived with Ford Fiestas. I've studied the CCTV photos and gone over the list to reduce it down.' She missed the scowling look from Haines as she admitted to going alone. 'I've driven past so many cars without stickers or with the wrong wheels. That one car in that garage is a three for three. I haven't seen any other car with even one feature that's a perfect match.' She paused again. 'I know I can't just barge in there. I am aware of your relationship. That's why I called you, sir.' DCI Haines shook his head so she pressed on. 'It doesn't have to be him. The car's registered in his wife's name. He might have a nephew or family friend who borrows the vehicle. He might have lost track of the keys. He might have an alibi. But it is a lead that we need to follow.'

There was an awkward pause in the car. DCI Haines looked up at his house. It was a lovely summer evening. She could feel him deciding if he should leave his family and confront his mentor, his former boss. 'All right. But I know Reg. You let me do the talking and you follow my lead.'

'Yes, boss.'

'I mean it about the talking. You keep quiet and have a good look at that car. If we get the chance.'

DC Angel knew she'd pushed her luck as far as she could and kept quiet. They drove in silence back round to what she now knew was Patterson's house. It was a large detached house set well back in manicured gardens. A large silver Jaguar was parked on the drive and there was the garage where DC Angel had seen the Fiesta.

Haines looked at the scene, then back to DC Angel. 'Visible from the road?'

'Well, you can see the garage from the road.'

'You'd better hope Patterson is in a good mood and I can get him to voluntarily open the garage.'

They knocked on the door and Reg Patterson answered. 'Rob, this is surprise. Will you come in? I could put the kettle on.'

'No, we can chat out here. It's a lovely evening.'

'So, what's up, Rob? I see there's two of you so I'm guessing this isn't a social call.' Reg Patterson appeared to be an old man, but DC Angel felt it was an act. She was sure a slight stoop had crept in when he'd seen Haines wasn't alone.

'It's a bit of both. This is DC Angel; she's just joined the department. She's been trying to track down a dark blue Fiesta that was caught on CCTV near a series of crimes. It's a bit overzealous but she's been working through a list of all the matching cars in the area.' Reg Patterson's eyebrows shot up. 'I know, I know, there's a long list. Anyway, one of the names that came up was yours. As I know you, I thought it'd be polite if I came round and asked if we could have a look?'

'Of course! Always willing to help. You'll have to bear with me though. Can't remember where the garage keys are.' He disappeared into the house, returning a minute later with the keys. He kept up a running commentary as he walked over to the garage. 'It's not even my car, it belonged to Margery, my wife. It's funny how you get to the big things like bank accounts and probate and organising the funeral, then the small ones drop through the cracks. I probably should have told the DVLA that she no longer owned it. But then I was going to sell it, never got round to that either. Here we are – what do you want to see?'

Reg Patterson swung the old-fashioned wooden doors open and revealed the very ordinary dark blue Fiesta inside. DC Angel's heart leapt. It was the car that had haunted her thoughts. Three white scratches on the wheel arch and a torn yellow car dealer sticker in the back window. She moved sideways and she knew. It was five door, the right age, sitting on steel wheels with one cracked hub cap.

In turn that meant that very possibly herself and Haines were stood on the drive with a man who'd stalked and killed the women of Bradwick. She felt slightly sick at the thought. She didn't feel in danger, not with Haines there. He'd had her back enough in the past.

She turned to DCI Haines and tried to convey her excitement with a curt nod. He merely nodded back and turned to Patterson. 'I'm sorry to have troubled you. Like I said, she is overzealous. Still, it's another one we can tick off the list.'

'Excuse me, sir,' DC Angel asked as Haines took her by the elbow. 'Does anyone else borrow that car? Nephew maybe?'

Patterson stopped for a moment and a curious expression crossed his face. DC Angel swore she saw a mixture of pride and regret mixed with something else that could have been sorrow. He shook his head. 'No, no. I don't think it's been driven since. Well, since my wife couldn't drive. I took her to the last few chemo sessions. Terrible thing.' He then turned and walked back to the house without another word.

'What did I tell you? I ask the questions!' Haines was furious.

'But you weren't asking the right ones.' They marched back to his car in silence.

When they were driving away, DC Angel said, slightly sulkily, 'It was the right car. I've spent ages looking for that Ford Fiesta and I have found it.'

'And you're sure? They've been using false plates.'

'I've been looking for a mark seven point five, dark coloured, five door Fiesta SE. That's what Patterson just happens to have in his garage.'

'Of course you didn't share this with anyone!'

'It is all on the system, it's just that no one went to look for it.'

Haines was reminded of his initial assessment of DC Angel – not a team player. However, he did trust her instinct. 'Okay. I can buy that, although it'll be hard to run it past the CPS and into court.' DC Angel pulled the car over to the kerb. Haines leant back in his seat and closed his eyes. When the silence had stretched uncomfortably, he said quietly. 'It can't be Patterson. I've known him for years.'

'Okay. You've known him for years. What's changed recently in his life?'

'Don't think I can't see through you. You're trying to establish causes and reasons for offending.' DC Angel decided to let the silence drag out. 'All right! Yes, he retired three years ago.' About when Dark Car Man started, DC Angel thought, but didn't say anything. 'And of course, you know that his wife died eight months ago following a long illness.'

'Come on, sir. If this wasn't your friend, you'd be all over this. The car matches, he's had upheaval in his life and he admitted that no one else drove his car.'

'He did say that it hadn't been driven at all.'

'My point still stands. We have CCTV of that car all over Bradwick. We've caught him out in a lie. Definite probable cause.'

'We can't get a warrant. He's an ex-ACC and most of his career was in Wootenshire. He knows every magistrate. This will spread like wildfire. This could ruin him if it's not true.'

'So, go back in there,' DC Angel said. 'Play the whole old friends angle. Ask him for alibis. Let me have a good look at the car. And try to be objective, see if you think he's lying or not. Don't forget that there might be another explanation. We need to check who has or had access to keys. All we need is one copy of the garage and car key that he's lost track of and he'd be completely in the clear. But we do need to establish the facts.'

'I don't want it to be him.' DCI Haines stared out of the windscreen. The car was parked on the promenade and he was looking at a picture postcard scene of beach and sea just before sunset. 'He was the first boss I had in CID. He taught me what I know. Everything about being a police officer that they don't teach you at Hendon.'

'I know. But really this is what we do.' DC Angel stopped and thought. She summoned up from her memory what Haines had said in the past. 'Listen, you're on the same page as Reg Patterson. Whatever he taught you, you protect this town. Only thing is that Patterson might have gone rogue. He could be a danger to this town. So you need to step up.' There was an ominous silence. DC Angel thought she'd try one more track. 'Have you noticed how tough this case is? No evidence left anywhere, no CCTV, random victims. Every single aspect is a dead end. I've been thinking for a while now that the suspect has to be someone highly trained and experienced. Like a police officer.'

'I know you're right,' Haines said eventually. 'I do. It's just that it's Patterson. Reg.'

'Come on, let's go and chat to him. We'll do it by the book. I'll take some photos of his car and then we can have someone from Traffic compare it against the CCTV footage. That'll make it independent and all above board and no personal vendetta.'

DCI Haines swore under his breath as she started the engine and pulled back onto the road. He was so close to his promotion now that he could almost touch it. His philosophy, if he'd ever had one, was always to keep on moving forward. And he knew, deep down, that DC Angel was the future and that Reg Patterson was the past. As tough as it might be, that was the truth.

Even worse, if DC Angel had figured it out then someone else could come after her and reach the same conclusion. And they might also work out that he had known and done nothing.

The world now was so interconnected and so wrapped up that some days Haines felt that no secret could stay hidden forever. And he was on his way to uncover the one that would do the most damage to himself.

CHAPTER FIFTY-ONE

They arrived back and found that Patterson's car was still in the driveway. Instinctively DC Angel parked so that there was no way Patterson's Jaguar could leave.

As they walked up to the house, DCI Haines said, 'I mean it this time. I'm in charge. You've convinced me, but you must let me handle Patterson.'

'Okay.' DC Angel tried not to sound too smug. Then she saw that the side door of the detached garage was ajar, light spilling out into the darkening evening. 'Rob, look. That wasn't open before.'

'Seems to be in plain sight to me,' DCI Haines said, changing direction towards the garage.

The door opened onto the end of the garage, with the car to the right and another door to the left. This door was also open and led through to a small workshop that had been partitioned off from the main garage.

'You take the photos you need of his car, I'll check in here,' Haines said.

DC Angel was in the middle of photographing scratches and dealer stickers when she was called through by Haines.

'What have you got?' She was still looking at the car as she walked back to the workshop. 'Oh crap. I mean, I thought. Oh.'

She stood next to Haines and looked at the desk. There was a stack of number plates and a machine that she could only assume made them. Further along was a big box of letters, numbers and blank plates. From memory she recognised at least one plate that they were trying to trace.

She felt a shiver down her spine. This had been an intellectual exercise up 'til now. A case of taking photos from the CCTV and trying to match them to a vehicle. But now she had the emotional weight descend on her. She had caught Dark Car Man and undermined Haines' mentor.

She turned to Haines and saw that he was holding a black, hard cover exercise book in his gloved hands. 'What's that?' she asked.

He snapped it shut. 'It seems to be his diary, about what he was doing here, how he became Dark Car Man.' He tucked it protectively under his arm and DC Angel didn't dare ask if she could read it.

'Look,' DC Angel said. Feeling like a visitor in a museum she pointed to a walking stick hanging on a peg. Instinctively DCI Haines moved towards it. 'No. Leave it there. It's a good surface for fingerprints and our best chance for trace DNA. We should get scenes of crime in.'

DCI Haines took a deep breath and looked around. 'I know. I just want to preserve his reputation even if this is all true. He has nieces, nephews, and cousins all over the county – some lawyers, some councillors, and even a couple in the police. We need to think very carefully about who else we get involved.'

DC Angel held her hands up. She was feeling the high of finally catching the man who'd been terrorising Bradwick for weeks. But at the same time she was still being blocked by her boss who seemed more intent on protecting his friend.

'Wait a minute,' DCI Haines said, 'I never saw him with a walking stick.' He peered closer at the stick, which was shiny black with a simple hand grip at the top.

'He didn't use a stick?'

'No, he used to boast about running miles every morning. And if I'm honest, he's probably fitter than I am.' DCI Haines shook his head slowly. 'The way he looked, you'd never question a stick if you didn't know him. The guy was a fraud and I never saw it.'

'And that stick would work just like a side handle baton.' She stopped to look around. 'Whatever is going on, we need to get other people in. This is a crime scene and needs to be secured and properly processed. The same goes for the car.' When he shot her a look, she continued. 'Listen, this is a bit too pat, too easy. If we deal with this right we can see if he was set-up or not.' She paused and looked around, frowning. 'Is Patterson organised? I mean, is he one of those guys who plans things out and has a tidy desk?'

'Yeah, he was. Always cleared his desk at the end of the day, locked up his documents.' Haines stopped talking and turned full circle, taking it all in. 'This is a display. He wouldn't leave all the doors open and the equipment all spread around.' He pulled open a steel cabinet under the workbench – it was empty. 'This was meant to delay us, but also to confirm his guilt. Patterson knew that this was the best thing to slow us down.'

'So, the big question is, where is Reg Patterson now?'

'He was always boasting about how he still runs miles every day. He could've run from here or been abducted.' DCI Haines walked out to the drive and looked around. 'We've got both cars contained here but he could've got a taxi or gone to the train station.'

DC Angel joined him and pointed up at the house which was still lit up. 'When you hear hoof beats, you don't think zebras, you think horses. Let's do the obvious first. He was here thirty minutes ago, his cars are still here, so most likely he's in there.'

Ten minutes of banging on doors and calling his phone number later, they were still outside the house. DC Angel cocked her head to one side. 'Phone his mobile again,

I thought I heard something?' While he dialled, she held open the letterbox and listened closely. 'Yep. His phone's in there. Shall we effect entry? I take it you don't want to involve anyone else yet?'

Being the house of a retired police officer, this proved harder than usual. In the end they broke and removed most of a half-glazed back door before DC Angel climbed in and found the keys, out of sight on a hook.

Cautiously they both walked through the house. No amount of training or warrant cards could remove the feeling that they were trespassing. Every now and then they called out but there was no response. Both of them felt that something was badly wrong, but neither wanted to say anything to the other.

Eventually, the trail of lit rooms led them to a closed door at the bottom of a set of cellar steps. Haines cautiously opened the door. At first all they could see was a room with the light on. It was lined with bookcases and had a thick carpet with a leather armchair – a gentleman's club in miniature.

The two police officers paused for a moment on the threshold. There were unmistakable scents in the air – gunshot, whisky, and cigars. And over it all, the all too familiar metallic tang of fresh blood.

'Is anyone there?' Haines called out but neither he nor Angel expected any response. The smell of cordite meant they were suddenly alert.

When he pushed the door open further however, Haines saw Patterson sitting in the other armchair. Half his head was missing and a service revolver lay in his lap. Next to him on a small table was an ashtray with one cigar butt, an empty crystal shot glass, and expensive bottle of whisky.

'There's your answer,' he said blankly, letting DC Angel see. 'Now we can call it in. Get the circus started.'

* * *

'Come with me.' Haines gently took DC Angel by the arm and steered her away from the house. She noticed that the diary from the garage was still tucked under his arm.

Halfway down the garden they found a couple of cheap plastic chairs and set them up watching the house. The blue lights of the vehicles parked out front made shifting patterns on the walls. The lounge was lit and without curtains so they could see the dark green figures of paramedics conferring with police officers and scenes of crime.

'He's gone.' Haines sounded bleak. 'I've known the bugger more than twenty years; dragged him through all sorts of scrapes and now he's just checked out.'

'You don't think we...' DC Angel couldn't bring herself to finish the sentence.

'Killed him? No. It's all in here.' He tapped the diary on his lap. 'I've only had a chance to have a quick scan though, read the first few pages. When he first retired, he saw a girl with headphones on while he was driving past. On impulse, he stopped to warn her, she panicked and ran.

'Despite the old fogey image, he was still sharp as a tack, Patterson. He saw that people were talking about it on Twitter. He figured that if he became a bogey man, then it would make girls walking home at night take more precautions. He thought he could scare the town into being safer.' There was a pause as he stared at the lounge doors. The green-suited paramedics were shaking their heads and packing up ready to leave. 'He was a good copper. He knew we'd catch him sooner or later. Do you think he just happened to have that revolver ready and loaded? In a soundproof office? Like you said, he left that display in the garage to slow us down, make sure he had time. Reg planned. He worked out the angles before he did anything.'

'I just don't know what to say. I'm so sorry.' All of the training in how to break the bad news hadn't prepared her for this.

Haines had not only learned of the death of his mentor and friend of twenty years, but in the same instant his image of Patterson was destroyed as well.

'I need to talk to you. I've been meaning to for days but there was never the right time.' He stopped to push his fists into his eyes. 'Reg had some very fixed ideas about this town and what we could do to protect it. He believed that drugs always were and always will be the problem. They bring other crime with them and ruin communities. But he wasn't an idealist. He wasn't working to make Bradwick some great drug free town. That would be impossible.' Haines paused again as he reached the point, the sentence after which nothing would be the same. 'Reg Patterson had a close working relationship with the major local drug dealer in this town.'

'But he was your mentor. He handed over to you.' DC Angel was unable to keep the shock out of her voice. 'So that means...'

'You're a bright officer. If I'm honest I wish I had another five years so I could hand over to you, not Hargreaves. But you play the hand you're dealt. Did you never wonder about all those meetings I had to rush off to? Billy King.'

'But why? You're a good policeman!'

'I am. I did it for this town. Reg was right, we're never getting rid of drugs. But what I have done is I've kept county lines gangs at bay. I've stopped the trafficking of underage foreign prostitutes into town. I've protected our schoolgirls from being groomed into treats for out of town gangsters. Our schoolboys won't become couriers and killers before they need to shave.

'Billy King knows the limits. He knows what he can and can't do. And in return, every single one of his dealers reports in any threat which gets passed up the line to me, to us, to the police.'

'So, you're saying that Billy King is free to sell drugs across Bradwick and is doing so with police protection?'

'No. I'm saying that I have access to the best information network of any town anywhere in England!'

There was a pause as they both digested this. Thoughts of Professional Standards crept into DC Angel's head. She was still undecided how she was going to play this, so she needed more information.

'What about the drugs and the money?' she asked. When she got a querying look, she continued. 'There are rumours that after a drug bust not everything is entered into evidence.'

Haines swore under his breath. 'Yes, we do take off some money and pass some of the product over to King. But listen, the police service has no budget. I'd rather have officers who don't do painting and decorating at weekends, who don't drive their brother-in-law's taxi, who don't have an Uber account. How much better are they going to work if their wife isn't picking up extra shifts and relying on them to do the school run? It makes better policemen.'

DC Angel was silent in the face of these enormous revelations so DCI Haines ploughed on.

'After tonight and what happened to Reg, I realised that I, we as a team, couldn't keep this secret from you. One day you would have found out. So now the ball is in your court. Go home and sleep on it. Tomorrow, we'll raid the warehouse. When we've made the arrests and the dealers are all being carted off to the cells, I'll assemble an evidence team to start bagging and tagging. If you want in, if you can see the sense in what I've said, then you volunteer to join that team and I'll see that you get your cut.'

Those last three words resonated through DC Angel. Get your cut. Could she become a corrupt officer? Receiving money from known criminals. But the alternative would be reactionary policing – spending all their time and effort arriving after crimes had been committed and mopping up the mess.

She still hadn't answered DCI Haines when he gestured at the lounge window. 'I think we're needed up there. Judging by the number of people milling around doing nothing I'd say they're pretty much done and now need to take some statements. Angel, give them a brief statement, just the facts, nothing more. We've got a big day tomorrow and it's getting late already. I'll get them to basically lock down this site. Nothing's going to happen on this case now. We can do all the paperwork and sort it out over the weekend and into Monday. Now our focus must be on the raid tomorrow. Don't come in too early tomorrow either, I need everyone on top form in the evening.'

He gave DC Angel a curt nod as his only acknowledgement of his previous conversation.

CHAPTER FIFTY-TWO

DC Angel didn't remember her drive home through the dark streets of Bradwick. Her head was turning over the events of the evening. From the hammer blow of discovering who the killer of the girls was, straight to the suicide, and then before she could draw breath, DCI Haines dropped his bombshell.

She had guessed, of course. She had been excluded from conversations in the office, voices had fallen silent one time too often when she entered a room. She had tried to put it down to being new and being the only woman on the team. But, deep down, Haines' revelation hadn't been a huge surprise – it had been a confirmation of the truth that she had been working to uncover.

When she got home, she made herself a strong coffee and sat on the sofa to think. Haines had told her to take it easy but she knew there was no point going to bed.

On the one hand, Haines was a father figure to her. He was fiercely loyal to his team, and that included her. He respected her and if she kept him onside, she would have a senior officer as a guardian angel looking after her career. In some ways he had been more supportive of her than her own father.

On the other hand, if she didn't deliver Haines and his team to Professional Standards, they would get the result eventually. They already had the CID team in their sights. It might take them a few more years and not be quite as complete, but she was sure they'd get there in the end. The rumours wouldn't go away, that much was sure. Haines might have risen high enough to be above the trouble when that happened, but Angel knew that she was far more vulnerable. In all likelihood she would still be in CID when they struck. And when they did, she was sure that PSD would single her out for special treatment as they had failed to turn her. Whether or not she was on the take, she had knowledge of the conspiracy so she'd be guilty by association.

But, did she want Haines as an enemy? She'd been to his aunt's house for a barbecue, seen the extensive network that he had built up over a professional lifetime in Bradwick. He had smoothed over trouble with Traffic. He might survive this attempt by Professional Standards or he might not. But whatever happened, he would seek vengeance.

Florence the cat sensed a weakness and came to sit on her. In her own unique way she sat half on her lap and half off, sprawled on the sofa. Emma started stroking and rubbing her head without really thinking about it. She responded by purring and kneading with her paws.

Unable to see a way through the thicket of her problems, Angel thought about her parents, her upbringing. The one thing she had never liked about her family was the justifications. Her mother was clever and quick with words. In any family discussion, both her parents were agile debaters and arguments often ran on deep into the night.

The drawback to this was that it gave rise to a sense of moral ambiguity. Any wrongdoing, any transgression could be talked out of, explained, excused. Her father had been more rigid. In his world, there was a right way and a wrong way to do things. He was left wing and would always side with the workers. Pickets, strikes, and unions were sacrosanct, the workers' fundamental rights.

One of the reasons she'd turned her back on them had been to join a more black and white world of right and wrong. That is what she'd hoped for from the police service – clear rules, ranks, and structure. However now she didn't know. Should she betray her immediate team for the greater good? Would she be a scab or a whistle-blower?

By half two in the morning, she had reached her decision. She'd known she would get to this point, the moment she understood what Haines was offering. She'd just needed the time to reconcile it with herself.

She sent a simple text, "I fancy a McDs – wanna join me". She didn't know why she was being all cloak and dagger. If Haines had any suspicion, then he wouldn't have opened up to her. She shouldn't be nervous about Professional Standards following her, as she was arranging to meet them.

Within minutes she got a text back. "Ring road 30 mins."

She parked in the car park of McDonald's. At three in the morning it seemed more empty and the street lights made the litter stand out. She crossed the car park and was amazed to see Lukas coming towards her.

'Angel! Got the munchies?' He chuckled to himself.

'No, just work, all the time.' She paused as he floated past her. He had warned her. He had told her not to let the job change her. With new resolve she went into the restaurant to do the deal.

She was sat across a table from Maxine Jones. Angel's usual calming technique was to pick any small flaw in her adversary, reassure herself that they weren't perfect either. The trouble was that, even at three in the morning under harsh fluorescent lights, DS Jones looked like a model. DC Angel squinted, detected a slightly caked bit of concealer below her left eye and relaxed slightly.

'You okay, love?' Jones asked. 'This is a bit early. Or late. Although in this job you can be up at all hours.'

'I think I've got what you need.'

'You think? How certain is this?'

'Well Haines has been planning this big operation that's going to happen tomorrow.'

'Yes, we know.' DS Jones nodded. 'We've been keeping an eye on him, and whatever he's been planning. This one has been kept well under wraps but we know the plan. It's one of the nearly dead industrial estates out to the north of town isn't it?'

'You are good.' DC Angel paused and thought. 'But we've got a couple of vans full of uniform, plus an ARV, entry teams, and Border Force so I doubt we could keep it that quiet. As long as Garoza doesn't get wind of it we should all be okay.'

An awkward silence fell between the two women. Finally, Jones continued her softly-softly approach. 'Why should we be particularly interested in tomorrow's raid?'

Angel stared out of the window, still wrestling with herself.

'Come on, DC Angel.' Jones started to let some of her exasperation show. 'You've made your decision already. Otherwise you wouldn't be here.'

Without looking at the other woman, Angel spoke. 'I've been offered a cut of the take on the night. It sounds like a big sale, so there'll be plenty of ready cash around. If I stay to bag up the evidence, then that'll be a signal that I'm in and they'll give me some of the money.'

DS Jones stared out of the window, her brow furrowed in thought. 'You have a serious choice to make.' Angel looked at her and nodded. 'If you don't take the money and we nick the rest of them, all eyes will be on you as the informant.'

DC Angel thought of her treatment at the hands of the Traffic department. The last thing she wanted was a reputation as a grass following her around. 'What's the alternative then?'

'Well, as a department, we can't advocate that you break the law. But, if you were going to join the conspiracy, then we could scoop you up with the rest of them. Your reputation would be intact.'

'And what would happen to me?'

'Well, short term, we'd put you back into uniform. As a first offence, there shouldn't be much more than a reprimand on your record. Long term we should be able to have a quiet word in some senior ears. It might put your career back a few years, but nothing serious.' There was an ominous pause. 'Like I say, the decision is yours and it's a serious one.'

DC Angel pursed her lips and picked away at her apple pie. The centre was still too hot but she could pick away at the pastry and eat small flakes. It was the devil's choice. The obvious thing to do was to take the fall and trust DS Jones that her career would rebound.

But, if Jones didn't come through then where would she be? Out in the cold, with a blot on her record and no chance of promotion. It wasn't even that she had trouble trusting people, she knew that. DC Angel also had a problem trusting life and fate. What if DS Jones moved forces, or had an accident, or left for any reason? This whole operation had the feel of something that was word of mouth; you scratch my back and I'll scratch yours. A deal that neither side would want committed to paper.

It wasn't as if she could ask anyone if Jones from Professional Standards was reliable. She'd known, as soon as she saw the choice, that she would take the hit. This is what she had signed up for – to make the force better. But also, ingrained in her DNA, was the fear of being a scab – loyalty to the workers had been drummed into her. She supposed that the best she could do was arrange things so she didn't appear to be disloyal.

Her minor infidelity would be bearable because it would remove a major corruption in the force. 'Well, I think, given what you've said–'

'Hold it right there!' Jones held up her hand. 'In my line of work knowing someone's planning to break the law is nearly as bad as advising them what to do. I really don't need to know your plans.' There was a slight pause. 'It might help you to know ours though. We've got access to the operational planning and we'll put our own cordon around and outside your exclusion zone. We'll be a bit careful to let the uniforms with the bodies through then we'll stop your lot and see who's got the cash on them. I presume they lift the cash first and then sort it out later?'

'I can't see how else they'd do it. I presume that if I bite, then I'll learn more about how the whole set-up works.'

'Well, your boss Haines is off to pastures new in a week or so. This is our last chance to catch him with his hand in the till.' There was a pause, where DC Angel considered the mixed metaphors. 'Tell me something, do you know what the scam is? How is he connected to Billy King? We've been looking for an inappropriate relationship there for years. But King insists he's the owner of a taxi firm so no matter how many times he meets Haines, we can't pin it on him. Do you know?'

Angel saw Haines in her mind's eye. The look on his face when he realised Patterson was gone. And the hollow tones when he'd explained the whole system to Angel. It seemed grubby to expose her boss's weakest moment in front of this woman. 'I think his friendship with King means that King passes quality information to Haines. That's how the crime numbers have stayed so low, how Haines was always one step ahead of the dealers.'

'Apart from King's network, of course,' Jones said darkly. 'It's the oldest trick in the book. Inform on your competition and clear the marketplace so you end up being the only seller in town. Devil's own job to prove, especially when, despite all the town knowing what Billy King is, we can't pin anything on him.'

Unspoken thoughts bubbled through DC Angel's head. Was Haines actually doing a good thing? Bradwick was a safer, cleaner town with him at the helm. Then the truth hit her. She had made her choice; the wheels were in motion. Within twenty-four hours, her boss, who had become mentor and friend would be in handcuffs. And she would have put him there.

The silence stretched a bit longer, then Angel simply nodded at Jones, pushed back from the table and left into the night.

CHAPTER FIFTY-THREE

Haines stood at the front of the lecture theatre. People were slowly filing in and chatting quietly among themselves. Like a lecturer at the beginning of a class he was being left alone to collect his thoughts.

Those thoughts were chasing each other around his head. His memory recalled random events with Patterson from the past twenty-five years. Each one was reassessed in the light of the new information. Not only was Patterson the Dark Car Man, but Haines had trouble painting him as someone who'd kill himself, take the easy way out.

When he managed to tame those thoughts, DC Angel crept in instead. This was the point, the crunch time. Not only was he going to hand over his team, the whole operation to Hargreaves, it was time to see which way she would jump. This wasn't a binary decision either – if she didn't join in with the scheme then how would she react?

His team filed in, some of them catching his eye, others like Hargreaves keeping their heads down. Was he about to take the team down? Last night, when he was hollowed out by the discovery of Patterson's body, it had seemed like a good time to bring DC Angel into the conspiracy. But when he had got home, he had stayed up half the night reliving the conversation, seeing where he had gone wrong, how he could have phrased things better. Maybe he should have edged up to it closely instead of blundering straight in and possibly blowing the whole thing.

And now he'd left it so that DC Angel could go running to Professional Standards and blow the whole lot. He stopped himself for a second. Well, she might but she'd have to make contact and he'd kept his eye on her all day. She'd had no chance to phone them and it would then take ages to arrange, by which time he'd have his promotion. He'd see what she did tonight, even though she might just be taking the cash to gather evidence.

He shook his head to clear the thoughts out of it. He had to trust his instinct – she was someone he could trust, someone he could work with. And someone who would soon be under Hargreaves' command. He had the angles covered. The worst outcome would be that she wouldn't join in at all. In that case, she wouldn't last six months before she requested a transfer to a different department. It would be messy but survivable.

* * *

DC Angel sat in the front row of the lecture theatre with the rest of her CID team. She'd watched Haines carefully before the briefing but could see nothing of the broken man from last night.

The preparation for the raid passed both agonisingly slowly for DC Angel and also sped past, accelerating her towards the point where she'd have to decide and that decision would affect her whole career.

She still had misgivings and fervently hoped that when the time came, she would find a way to divert DCI Haines before the PSD raid. She'd have to see what the situation was on the ground.

She realised with a start that she had been drifting and not paying attention to Haines. But she knew the plan. There was a large warehouse at Brookbank Industrial Estate, to the north of Bradwick. There was a large roller door so the cars could be driven in. Once inside the deals would take place away from prying eyes and the cars could then leave.

The plan was to watch the whole site. The first trigger was when the boat arrived. It was an unimpressive squat vessel, once blue, now rust stained and diesel dirty. DC Angel could see the wisdom of the drug dealers plan when a van reversed right up to the ship. It was almost impossible, even through telephoto lenses to see what was being loaded.

They were under strict instructions to wait until a decent number of the mid-level dealers had parked up inside the warehouse, then seal off the whole area and start the raid, using multiple points of entry. They wanted to move before the vehicles started leaving, otherwise they'd be into car chases. Everyone was aware that the M5 was less than half an hour away.

At the same time, Border Force would go straight for the ship and make sure the crew were detained and the ship immobilised.

DC Angel imagined that a smaller, more private briefing would be underway at Professional Standards. She looked around the room and saw that pretty much every branch of the police was in the room. Traffic were there to manage the vehicles on site – expected to be high powered SUVs like Range Rovers and Mercedes. There was going to be a heavy armed presence supporting specialist entry teams. There were uniformed officers in riot gear ready to act as the foot soldiers to subdue, arrest, and transport the criminals as they were found. And finally there was the CID team that sat at the top of the whole pyramid, overseeing the whole operation.

'Right, we have sixty minutes to get into position. Surveillance are already on site and the operation is a go.' DCI Haines clapped his hands theatrically and all the different teams made their own way to the warehouses.

Chapter Fifty-Four

Angel and Haines were sat in brooding silence in the car as he drove. She was desperate for an opening to confess her sins to him, to warn him to get away before PSD could catch him. She had also noticed that he hadn't let her out of his sight since she'd arrived at work. Makes sense, she thought. At the moment she had the information but hadn't been tainted. She was dangerous.

Haines was aware of what he had said the night before and needed to know which way she would jump. But he wanted her to reach her own decision, not be pressured by him. He would know soon enough, he thought.

They parked up on the side street of the deserted industrial estate. A hundred years ago, it would've been thriving , but now the brick buildings were abandoned and grass grew out of the concrete. The edges of the roads and car parks were softened by encroaching brambles. DC Angel looked out of the windscreen. To her right she could see the oily water of the creek but there were no boats there any more.

'Sir,' DC Angel said nervously. 'Did you read that diary we found at Patterson's house?'

'I did.'

'Why did he do it?'

Haines looked at Angel, as if to ask why she wanted to bring this up now. But he understood. Close off one case in your head to concentrate on the next. 'Like I said last night, he started when he retired. Thought he was doing good. It's hard, you know, having a lifetime in the police. He made a difference, he made decisions that were literally life and death, day in, day out for thirty or forty years. Then one day, he retired, and suddenly he was a nobody. I think all this was a way of regaining some power, some control. The more his wife got ill, the less he felt in control, the more time he spent driving around.' He took a deep breath. 'When Mazey Taylor tried to take his photo, he realised how deep in trouble he was. He didn't even have the improvised baton then, just used his arm to kill her. The diary is very confused after that. I think he was still trying to justify himself. Kill a few, to save the many. That kind of nonsense.' He shook his head. 'He knew. When you came to look at the car, he knew that you'd caught him. That's what the final piece of theatre was all about.'

'It's a sad end to a good career.'

'Well, when this raid is over, I'm going to have to figure out how to let the public know the attacks have stopped without smearing his good name.'

DC Angel bit her tongue. She wanted to say that Patterson didn't deserve to have a good name. Or to ask if the diary would ever be entered into evidence. She supposed that Haines had broken far more regulations than holding onto evidence for twenty-four hours.

She didn't get a chance to find a way to bring any of this up before a shiny black BMW X5 slid past the end of their road. They just saw it turn towards the warehouse before it disappeared. There was the faint rumble and boom of a big door opening and shutting.

'Party guests are arriving,' Haines said more to himself than anyone else. His mobile buzzed and he snatched it up. 'What the hell!' Haines looked around the estate. 'Angel, can you back the car up until we can see down that alley.' He twisted around and pointed at an alley twenty metres behind them.

Angel did what she was told, and they saw Billy King with his usual two hulking bodyguards, all watching the warehouse, with their backs to Angel and Haines.

'Hargreaves was right! The bloody idiot. This isn't a spectator sport. I need to send Billy home. Wait here, I'll be back in five.'

DC Angel watched him walk down an alley between two low buildings, one without a roof. She debated with herself very briefly, then also left her car. This could be her chance to get Haines away from the operation, steer him to safety.

She followed at a cautious distance, rolling her feet and avoiding the debris that littered the floor. But she needn't have bothered – Haines was relaxed and confident. He had nothing to fear. She tucked herself into a doorway where she could watch the two men.

DC Angel could see the warm body language – the handshake with a left-hand elbow grip. They smiled and nodded in unison. DC Angel was aware of the two bodyguards. Barely discernible in the shadows the two huge figures weren't staying at the regulation two steps behind and to either side of their boss.

She became fixated on them, wondering why they were moving around. The estate was deserted, there was no one else nearby. Because she was focusing on the bodyguards, she saw one make eye contact and nod to his companion. When the other smiled and nodded back, she knew there was trouble.

She was already jogging when she saw King go down. His own bodyguard was behind him, controlling him with one enormous arm around his neck. DC Angel couldn't see what the other arm was doing but King jerked once before going limp.

At the same time the other one produced something from a pocket and hit Haines sharply just above his right ear. He went down like the proverbial sack of potatoes, catching his head on the wall as he fell. In the horror of the moment, time appeared to slow down for DC Angel. She saw her boss lying on the floor. His attacker shifted his stance and slowly brought a heavy foot back, ready for a kick. He was like a footballer, preparing to launch the ball halfway down the pitch.

She gave up any pretence of stealth and launched into a full sprint. She couldn't let her boss take a kick like that to the head. An injury like that would be life changing and was meant to kill. The absurd unfairness of it swept over her. Haines had always, despite his failings, tried to do the right thing. He didn't deserve to die in a litter-swept alley. No one did.

Her training took over and as she got close, she planted her left foot next to Haines' hand and pivoted her whole body, landing a kick squarely on the bodyguard's left knee – the leg he was balancing on as he prepared his own kick.

She heard the knee snap as they both fell over the body of DCI Haines. As soon as she knew she'd landed on top, she flailed around with her elbow. She managed to jab at his face but without any real power.

She rolled awkwardly off both bodies and scrambled back to her feet, looking for somewhere safe to stand. She backed away so she wouldn't trip over the tumbled bodies of Haines and his attacker.

The other bodyguard turned to her and smiled. He flung Billy King away like a rag doll and waved a large knife menacingly in front of him. Its long, thin blade was slick with blood. He looked absurdly happy – he was over a foot taller than her, looked like he was twice her body weight and he had a knife.

But she had anger. Ice cold rage flushed through her. Haines had been so stupid to walk into this mess, to have been sleepwalking to this point for years. She hated all forms of deception and this double-cross was the cruellest of all.

Those bodyguards were meant to protect Billy King and now he was lying, unmoving on the floor because of what they'd done. Their betrayal. Now she faced one of them. She had a clear choice. Either she would die here in this abandoned alleyway or she could fight. She could fight to ensure that, for all their faults, Rob Haines and Billy King would get justice.

She took stock of herself. Her leg ached where she'd spun for the kick then fallen over the bodies. Her knuckles were grazed and bleeding. She ached because she'd leapt straight in without the usual warm up in the gym. And she was angry and upset. She pushed those feelings aside, leaving only the nervous flutter in her stomach that usually came before a test.

She didn't want to take her eyes off the man or the knife, but she needed to know her surroundings so she took quick glances around. Haines was roughly in the recovery position, but he wasn't moving. King had landed in a heap, with a bloody stain spreading across his chest and pooling around him. If he isn't already dead, she thought, he won't last long. She was unable to feel anything about that at the moment. The other body-guard, the one who'd attacked Haines had moved himself into a sitting position. Both hands were clamped around his ruined knee as if he could hold it together and stop the swelling. She could see that his short wooden truncheon had rolled a safe distance away.

That left only one problem – the other bodyguard. He had realised that she wasn't backing off so he advanced slowly. Using both his reach and the knife to intimidate, he made a huge sweeping arc with the knife right in front of her. Like most people, she leant away from the blade, took a step back. He swung back the other way, still advancing. Again, she stepped back, praying that he'd fall into a pattern. The third swing, the third step back. But this time, as soon as the blade was past, she leapt forward.

His wrist was so huge she had to seize it in both her hands. She wrapped his arm across his body and drove him back. However, even if he wasn't greatly skilled, he was strong. He twisted his arm in her hands and nearly lifted her from her feet. She squirmed as the blade waved around dangerously.

With his left hand he flailed around, trying to land punches on her head. She turned away but he still hit the back of her head, grabbing her hair and raking her ear. She felt her earring being ripped from her lobe.

However, she still couldn't let him break his knife hand free of her grip. She was here alone, no chance to call for help despite the officers all around her. She needed to try something new so she kicked out at his kneecap but couldn't kick hard enough. In frustration, she scraped down his shin with her work boot and drove her foot hard into his instep.

In pain, he relaxed and drew back slightly. She needed to deal with the knife before anything. Taking advantage of his momentary confusion, she grabbed his little finger and pulled and twisted it back as hard as she could. As soon as the knife clattered to the ground, she relaxed and felt like she might have a chance.

She knew from training the best way to end the fight. She was tired and scared. He was far bigger and stronger than her and still might land the killer blow. She still had grip on his right hand, so she pulled downwards and backwards. As hoped, he leant forward. She bunched her legs and drove her head straight up into his face.

Finally, she had a bit of luck. The hardest part of her forehead smashed squarely into his nose at just the right angle. She heard it crack and before she jerked her head back, his warm blood flowed into her face. She was disgusted and took a step backwards, finally releasing her enemy's hand.

He was dazed for a second so she seized her chance. She swept her cuffs out, clipped one around his wrist and immediately snapped the other around an iron ladder behind him. He sank down so he was sitting with his back to the wall, his hand just above his head.

Her urge was to give him one final kick but she knew that she mustn't stoop to their level. Cautiously she walked back, keeping both bodyguards in view. The man with the knife, who'd probably killed Billy King, was not even trying to free himself. Blood was still flowing down his face; his nose was swelling and two black eyes were developing.

The other man, the one who'd coshed Haines, still hadn't moved from where he was clutching his swollen knee. Just to be safe, she cuffed his wrists together, but he wasn't bothered.

She knew the answer already, but she still made herself check Billy King. No pulse. He was dead.

Finally, having assured herself that the area was safe, she went over to Haines. Expertly she put him properly into the recovery position, checked that he was breathing and noticed the blood seeping from his right ear.

Her world slowly cracked apart around her. She shook as the adrenaline washed through her system. Everything had changed. She had no idea now of what would happen next. King was dead and Haines was just hanging on. There's no way that the two bodyguards would have done it alone. Who had ordered it?

She sank down to the ground and sat down next to Haines. She knew her first aid but she couldn't help herself. Keeping the recovery position intact she eased DCI Haines' head into her lap.

'Shhh. It'll be okay. Help is coming.' She stroked his hair. He had a graze on his forehead from the wall and blood oozing from a cut above his right ear.

His eyelids fluttered open and he groaned.

'Headache.'

'Yes. It'll be all right.'

In the distance she heard a car engine followed by the scrape and boom of the large metal door. Another dealer arriving. Reality started to seep back in.

Slowly with shaking hands, she withdrew her radio. As the adrenaline faded, reality crept in. She was not alone. In fact she was surrounded by more emergency services than anyone else in the county. Laying Haines gently on the ground, she limped to the end of the alley to get an idea of what was going on. The whole yard was quiet and empty. It felt wrong that she'd been through hell in the alley while outside nothing had happened. She raised the radio to her mouth.

'Man down! Officer down! We need an ambulance now to alleyway just north of the target on Brookbank Industrial Estate.' Then realising the ambulance would most likely spook the dealers in the nearby warehouse, she took up the radio again. 'DCI Haines is down. The operation is a go. Go, go, go! Now!'

There was a pause when the whole world seemed quiet. She could hear the sobs of the two bodyguards, the rough breathing of Haines. She saw two figures leave a small side door on the target warehouse and move briskly towards the edge of the estate.

DC Angel recognised both of them. She'd worked with Glen Hargreaves and the man with him was Pietr Garoza. His face had been all over the office as number one target for the last week.

At first she thought Hargreaves was chasing Garoza but then she saw the body language. They were helping each other escape. Now she understood what had gone wrong with the plan. Hargreaves had no intention of taking over Haines' relationship with Billy King. Instead he had chosen to work with the Latvians.

Then the night was torn apart with the whoop of sirens and the screaming of engines. Just as Garoza and Hargreaves disappeared from sight, vehicles streamed into the yard. Orders were shouted and like a well-oiled machine, the entry teams breached the doors. There was a screech of tyres and a crunch as two vehicles collided. A team of Border Force officers leapt across to the boat before it had a chance to cast off.

At the moment, all the action was with the uniformed teams. The regular uniformed officers were waiting with the entry teams for the armed response to shout 'Clear!' They were already bringing out some people in handcuffs. She could see most of her team waiting to enter. She was just counting off the remaining members of CID when she felt a presence at her shoulder.

'What's going on then?'

She half turned and couldn't believe it when she saw the pale, ghost like figure of her boss, DCI Haines standing at her shoulder.

She was unable to answer so he carried on speaking. 'Isn't this my operation? Why are we skulking over here? Where's Hargreaves? I should be in there leading my team.'

He made to move forward and DC Angel held him back with a hand on his arm. 'Sir. Wait a minute. There's something you need to know.' As much as the conversation the previous evening, this was a watershed. She knew nothing would ever be the same afterwards. Still, she couldn't let him go without trying. 'I've heard on the grapevine that Professional Standards are looking into this operation.'

'And?' He was cross and in a hurry.

'And, if you go steaming in there you might get caught up in it all. Hang back here a minute and see what happens.'

'I'm not a coward!' He shook off her hand. 'If my team's going down, I'm going down with them.'

'No, sir. You're guaranteed a promotion. If you avoid all of this, think about how much good you can do for Bradwick, for the whole of Avon, Wootenshire and Somerset Police.'

Before he could think of a response, Hargreaves came running back into the yard from an alley to their left. He was closely chased by a burly man who expertly rugby tackled him to the floor. The two men started a desperate scramble for control. With a shock, Angel saw Hargreaves knock a police baseball cap off his assailant. Haines stood stock still, one hand over his mouth.

The rest of her team had no qualms however and ran across to help their colleague. Angel could hear the shouts as they fought. Two more people, obviously police not in uniform came to help their colleague. The CID team established a stand-off with the three intruders.

'What the bloody hell is Hargreaves playing at?' Haines was scowling now, trying to decipher the scene. He turned to look behind. 'What happened back there? Is Billy King dead? What's going on?'

'You went to meet with King.' DC Angel was aware she had to choose her words carefully. 'From what I saw, one of his bodyguards stabbed King in the back and the other coshed you over the head. I guess he'd have killed you too if I hadn't intervened.'

DCI Haines shook his head. 'King's dead? And Hargreaves is fighting the police? He was always slated to take over.' There was a pause as a cloud of confusion passed over his face. 'Take over everything. You know, what I told you last night. I did tell you, didn't I?' DC Angel nodded, dumbstruck. 'Only he never liked King. I knew he'd been up to something these past few weeks.'

While DC Angel digested this information, she marvelled at the calm with which Haines had decided that his second in command had tried to kill him. Meanwhile, in the yard, a van with unfamiliar police markings sped into sight. Uniformed officers in stab vests and batons leapt out and started trying to round up her CID team. They were shrugging off attempts to handcuff them and bristling at each other. The entry and uniformed teams stood off to one side unsure how to proceed.

While all this was unfolding, the armed guys started bringing out more handcuffed arrestees from the building. They too paused, watching the chaos unfold in front of them.

DC Angel suddenly understood what was going on. A chief superintendent, in full uniform with pip and crown on the epaulette stood on the sill of the van, with a loudhailer. Behind him, Michelle Jones climbed down and approached the melee, looking supremely calm and confident.

'I am Chief Superintendent Havelock of Devon and Cornwall Police. I am the ranking officer and taking charge of this operation. All officers not in uniform will present warrant cards to my colleague.' He indicated Michelle Jones. 'They will then be processed. Anyone not in a uniform and not presenting a card will be handcuffed and arrested. Thank you for your co-operation.'

This was too much for DCI Haines. He shook off DC Angel's hand and strode forward into the melee. He was stopped by Havelock, a large man with a walrus moustache and iron grey hair. There was a short argument where Haines tried to grab the megaphone. DC Angel heard an ambulance arrive behind her and the footsteps of an approaching paramedic.

'Chief Inspector Haines, I order you to stand down.' The words floated across the night air. Havelock wasn't exactly shouting but his voice was clear and firm. 'I know this is your turf, as you put it, but I am here by invitation of your Professional Standards Department and I have overall command.'

DC Angel turned to the paramedic who'd just arrived; a woman with a short dark bob. 'That man there, arguing with the chief super? He's sustained a head injury. Now might be a good time to carry out an assessment.'

The paramedic walked briskly away.

Meanwhile, Haines broke free and got a toe onto the bumper of the van. He levered himself up. Luckily the vehicle was an old LDV with a proper bonnet and he was able to jump up onto it. He wavered slightly and reached out for the top of the windscreen to steady himself.

'Can I have your attention?' A few faces turned to look but not many. He pressed on regardless. 'I'd just like to thank you for all your work today. And over the last few weeks, leading up to this operation.' He paused, looking at the paramedics who closed in on either side of him. 'So, um.' He reached out and a paramedic held his hand, steadying him. 'Sorry, bang on the head. Bit dizzy.' He took a deep breath. 'I'd just like to thank you all for your work today. And over the last few weeks, leading up to this operation.' He frowned again and rubbed his eyes with his free hand. He struggled to keep his grip on the bonnet and in an ungainly move he scrabbled down from the bonnet. Once back on the ground, he leant over, bent double as if he was trying to catch his breath.

The paramedics carefully guided him onto a waiting stretcher.

With this last distraction dealt with, very slowly the chaos was contained. DC Angel was treated to the sight of DI Hargreaves being roughly shoved into the back of an unmarked car in handcuffs. The rest of the team were handing over warrant cards and being led to a van.

She turned to go and winced – she'd landed heavily on her knee. With all the arrests being made and Professional Standards rounding up the police, there was no point in her being here any further. She limped a few steps down the alley towards her car.

The two men she'd fought were being seen to by paramedics, with burly policemen watching over them. DS Jones left this group of people and came towards DC Angel. 'Leaving so soon? The party's just getting started!'

'Yeah, I thought I ought to swing by the hospital. Get checked out.' DC Angel started to edge away.

'Wait here, I need to find a uniform to escort you.'

'That won't be necessary, I'll make my own way. I'll be all right.'

Jones looked around at the officers and paramedics who were in earshot. 'Oh no, I'm not letting you walk away from this. As of right now, you're suspended from duty.' Angel looked shocked. 'I should chuck you in the back of the van with the other members of your team. Just look at the situation I've got here. One senior officer going to the hospital in the back of an ambulance, one man dead, and another two seriously injured. And in the middle of it all, there's little old you, the last one standing. So you are suspended and will be given a formal interview. Is that okay or shall I break out the cuffs?'

DC Angel weighed her options. Reluctantly she handed over her warrant card. 'Fine! He can drive me home then. I'll take some painkillers and see about the hospital in the morning.' She caught Jones leaning to see past her to where the paramedics were tending to the two bodyguards. She frowned and nodded in that direction, an unspoken question for DC Angel. She answered, 'I'll tell you if you let me know what happened to Hargreaves.'

'I am the investigating officer here and your superior. You should be answering questions and that's all there is to it.' Her expression softened. 'But he was going to be your boss, and I need your co-operation. We caught DI Hargreaves leaving through a convenient gap in their cordon. He was escorting Garoza off the site to a BMW that was parked up. We found cash on Hargreaves and a brick of cocaine on Garoza. Now, what happened to you?'

DC Angel quickly relayed what had happened to DCI Haines and the unfortunate demise of King.

Michelle Jones frowned. 'Is there anything more you'd like to say about the relationship between DCI Haines and Billy King?'

'I still haven't figured it all out. Haines said that he didn't trust Hargreaves, he thought that he was up to something. He wasn't happy that Billy King turned up here to watch the operation. Apart from that I have no idea what was going on.'

DC Angel offered up a silent prayer to whatever gods were listening – please protect me while I'm lying to Professional Standards.

'Right then.' DS Jones didn't look impressed. 'Well, be at your desk at nine am. I'll have an officer waiting for you. We'll take your statement and see where we go from there. And don't contact any of your team before you've given your statement.'

She turned and left her with a plain clothes officer from Professional Standards. She chucked him the keys and headed off to her car. Leaning on the roof before she got in the passenger side, she looked down the alleyway.

Haines was on his way to hospital in an ambulance. Hargreaves was handcuffed in the back of a car on his way to a cell. She could see Billy King's body, already covered by a blanket. Scene of crimes officers had diverted from the warehouse and were already laying out yellow markers and taking photos. She supposed she'd have to bag up her clothes and bring them in tomorrow. Gregory Watts was still out there in his big house with his teenage girlfriend and fancy coffee machine. She made a mental vow that however this all shook out, she'd see him behind bars, one way or another.

'You ready?' the plain clothes PSD officer asked.

'Yeah, take me home,' she answered. Home, a shower, and bed. And no thinking what tomorrow might bring.

WOOTENSHIRE

The Retirement Party is the first novel set in the fictional county of Wootenshire which is in the UK, just south of Bristol and north of Somerset. It is the first instance of a new concept in writing - a Shared Word where many authors can write stories in different genres but all set in the same world.

Please visit www.wootenshire.co.uk for more details.

Please also note that Wootenshire and the associated logos are trademarks.